Wildest Dreams

Wildest Dreams

Janice Maynard

Morgan Leigh

LuAnn McLane

BRAVA

KENSINGTON PUBLISHING CORP.

http://www.kensingtonbooks.com

BRAVA BOOKS are published by

Kensington Publishing Corp.
850 Third Avenue
New York, NY 10022

All Kensington titles, imprints and distributed lines are available at special quantity discounts for bulk purchases for sales promotion, premiums, fund-raising, educational or institutional use.

Special book excerpts or customized printings can also be created to fit specific needs. For details, write or phone the office of the Kensington Special Sales Manager: Kensington Publishing Corp., 850 Third Avenue, New York, NY, 10022. Attn. Special Sales Department. Phone: 1-800-221-2647.

Brava and the B logo Reg. U.S. Pat. & TM Off.

ISBN 0-7582-0694-1

First Kensington Trade Paperback Printing: December, 2003
10 9 8 7 6 5 4 3 2 1

Printed in the United States of America

CONTENTS

Suite Secrets

Janice Maynard

For Caroline and Jamie . . .
An intimate marriage is one of life's greatest adventures.
Nourish and care for the love you share
and it will always keep you warm.

Chapter One

Sebastian Tennant respected innocence, but he had never been particularly aroused by it . . . at least not until today. He leaned back in his leather executive chair and steepled his fingers beneath his chin, quietly studying the woman sitting with such patent nervousness on the far side of his broad cherry desk.

She perched on the edge of one of his armchairs, her knees pressed together, her legs tucked beneath her. She wore a navy suit, unrelentingly plain, save for the unusual silver and onyx brooch at her lapel. The addition of a lacy jabot would have created an ensemble worthy of the most severe of English governesses, but instead his prim visitor had omitted a blouse, leaving the fitted jacket to stand alone.

Her skin was smooth and white, her long graceful throat the elegant prelude to truly spectacular cleavage. The little kick of lust he felt didn't surprise him. What did give him a moment's pause was the rush of curiosity he experienced. In recent years, women had become a pleasant periphery to his life, enjoyable, almost regrettably necessary, but forgotten scant moments after he slipped from their rumpled beds.

He dragged his gaze from the creamy swell of her breasts and examined her face. Lush rosy lips, high cheekbones flushed with what must certainly be her irritation at his long silence. Dark, heavily lashed cobalt eyes, and a mass of inky black hair tumbling in waves to her shoulders.

Despite the innate sensuality of her appearance, he stood by his earlier diagnosis of innocence. Her body language and the hint of anxious wariness in her eyes told an experienced man everything. She saw him as a threat, not a potential lover. A fact that amused him and at the same time challenged his masculinity.

He was accustomed to an avid hunger in the eyes of women he met. A heated desire for his money and his body. Responding to those females came as easily to him as breathing. He knew the smooth words, the practiced moves that divested them of their clothes and their attempts to trap him into matrimony. It was all a game, a game he played quite well.

His guest made a little huffing breath that drew his attention back to her chest. He lingered there for one more brief, appreciative moment and then smiled reassuringly. "So, Miss Fraser. Rebecca . . . if I may?" He raised his eyebrows in inquiry, and she nodded with apparent reluctance.

He continued, choosing his words with care. "So, Rebecca . . . you work for a travel magazine."

He smothered an involuntary smile as her lips firmed in frustration. They'd been over this ground before, and although she was too polite to tell him so, his lack of attention angered her.

But she was classy. She relaxed her expression into one of casual charm, and spoke politely. "Yes, I do. But not just any magazine. Our clientele is extremely well traveled and well heeled. They are looking for the unusual, the out of the way. I want to do an article about your special hotels."

He nodded slowly. "I'd be happy to let you interview me and talk about the Tennant hotel chain."

He watched, fascinated, as she battled down her temper at his deliberate obtuseness.

She clenched her hands around the spiral-bound note-book in her lap, her knuckles white. "There have been dozens of articles about you in dozens of magazines," she said with forced patience. "I need something much more. I want to do a story about your special hotels, the ones no one can seem to gain access to."

He picked up a Waterford tumbler and took a sip of water. He'd offered her a variety of refreshments earlier, but she had declined.

She watched him drink and then went on. "I promise to be discreet about any details you wish to omit. I can even guarantee you final approval on the article once it's done, and believe me, we don't offer that to everyone."

He actually felt a twinge of remorse for having to disap-point her. It would be sheer pleasure to give this exquisite woman everything her heart desired. But business was busi-ness.

He tamped down the unexpected guilt and smiled cajol-ingly. "You're asking for the impossible, Rebecca. The en-tire raison d' etre for my hotels is privacy, complete and total discretion. Everything about those properties is top se-cret."

She frowned. "But we could give you exposure with the right target audience."

He grinned. "We have an average occupancy rate of ninety-five percent year-round, Rebecca. We're doing fine without your magazine. We run a few small print ads in some specialty publications, and word of mouth does the rest. Our clients know that their anonymity is guaranteed, and that has to be respected. Otherwise we'd be just an-other luxury hotel."

She placed her notebook on the edge of his desk and gripped the arms of the chair, perhaps to keep from stran-gling him. "How can you possibly believe none of your guests will reveal your secrets? It doesn't make sense."

She crossed her legs, and her narrow skirt rode up on her

thighs. He moved restlessly in his seat. "Everyone who checks in signs a contract with certain stipulations. If they, in the future, divulge any information to a third party, they are barred forever from coming back—and believe me, Rebecca, none of our clients are willing to accept that. So the code of silence is not broken."

She rested her forearms on the edge of his desk and leaned forward, her movement straining the buttons of her slim jacket. He watched, fascinated, as her luscious breasts threatened to escape their confinement.

She spoke earnestly, her words ringing with sincerity. "I *need* this article, Mr. Tennant. Badly. It means a lot to me." The hint of desperation in her lovely eyes affected his resolve in spite of himself.

He smiled gently. "Why, Rebecca? Why is it so damned important?"

She caught her lower lip between her teeth and dropped her gaze to his desk. Heat settled in his groin as he imagined those perfect white teeth closing over one of his nipples. He stifled a groan.

She looked at him finally, her face somber. "Because my boss thinks I don't have the balls to get the ungettable stories. He thinks I'm too nice."

Her quiet admission sent a wave of protective tenderness washing over him. For a moment he indulged the Neanderthal impulse to demand her boss's name and go beat the idiot to a pulp.

He wanted to grant Rebecca's request, badly. But it was impossible. He couldn't do it. Perhaps there was another way to make her abandon her futile quest. He eyed her speculatively. He needed a plan that offered her what she wanted without jeopardizing his position.

Then he smiled lazily. "What if I make you a deal? A proposition, if you like?"

He watched as her wariness increased tenfold. "A deal?" she asked, her voice faint.

He nodded. "The third of my special hotels is brand-new. I was heavily involved in the design and construction phases, but my assistant hired all the staff. I haven't been there since the hotel opened. I would like to make an incognito visit to check things out, but since the property is for couples only, my presence would stand out like a sore thumb."

He paused for dramatic effect. She was watching him with the stunned fascination of a mouse about to be consumed by a large, voracious cat.

Her silence urged him on. "Why don't you accompany me to the hotel, posing as my wife?"

Every scrap of color leached from her face. She licked her lips. "Your wife?"

"Yes. We could go through the whole process of initial reservation, on-site check-in, and introduction to the amenities. I could see how things are running down there and make any necessary changes."

She sat back in her chair, the perfectly erect posture suddenly erased. She seemed dazed. "So if I agree to this . . . plan . . . you'll allow me to write an article about the hotels, with pictures?"

He frowned slightly. "I have to be honest, Rebecca. I'm not making any promises. All I can guarantee is that I'll think about it. Who knows, perhaps I'll be so grateful for your help that I'll find someway to give you what you want." His tone was deliberately suggestively.

This is it, he thought, slightly sad. *Here's where she walks out of my office.* He watched her face as she visibly struggled with his outlandish proposal.

She stood up and opened her purse, tossing a small card onto his desk. "Okay," she said tersely. "I'll do it. Call me with the details."

Rebecca leaned against the hard, polished wall of the thankfully empty elevator and willed her legs to stop shaking. She'd done it. She'd pulled it off. Well, not completely, she admitted with brutal self-honesty, but close enough to satisfy Carl. When she told him she'd be accompanying Sebastian Tennant to one of the top secret, highly private, couples-only hotels, her boss would have a coronary.

She closed her eyes, and immediately an image of Sebastian Tennant burned behind her eyelids. She trembled, and her nipples tightened against the satin lining of her jacket. Never had she felt such a visceral response to a man.

He was tall and slim-hipped, with wide shoulders that strained the beautifully hand-tailored seams of his black, pin-striped suit. His red tie, decorated with yin and yang symbols, was the only visible sartorial clue that this man would be equally dominant in the nude.

When he smiled, his whiskey brown eyes crinkled at the corners, and her heart fluttered, despite the knowledge that his slightly tousled chestnut hair and cheeky grin were weapons in his war against the fair sex.

Apparently the stories about him were all true. Even in a city like New York, a man of Sebastian's caliber was the stuff of gossip mills. Ruthless businessman. Creative entrepreneur. Legendary lover.

His prowess with the female sex was no longer a puzzle to Rebecca. Up close and personal, his personality was a force to be reckoned with. He exuded such raw, masculine energy, she felt singed by his power. Her entire body tensed in his presence, her senses on full alert, the fight or flight response in working order.

Had she followed her natural inclinations, she would have accepted his refusal gracefully and left before she fell prey to his charm. But with Carl's accusations ringing in her ears, she'd been forced to stay, helplessly unable to remove herself from danger.

Her final dramatic gesture had been just that. A last-ditch performance of bravado. For her to pose as this man's wife, in any context, was sheer stupidity. Already, she tingled as she relived their brief encounter. It had been a continual struggle to concentrate on the reasons why she was sitting in his office.

She might be a bit naive, but even she couldn't miss the look of sexual curiosity in his bold gaze. He had stared at her breasts. And she had liked it. That fact galled her, disturbed her. If she couldn't be immune to his practiced charm during a short interview, what was she setting herself up for as his companion at a secluded hotel whose sole purpose was sexual gratification?

She moaned and clenched her thighs together as a brief, shockingly vivid fantasy sent a flash of arousal through her body. He would be an incredible lover. You could see it in his eyes. He knew women. Not just their bodies, but the convoluted working of their minds.

It was dangerous for a man to have such knowledge. Dangerous for a woman not to care. Dangerous to contemplate a sexual relationship that might forever ruin her for other, less exciting men.

She debated her options. She could tell good old Carl to shove it. Get herself another job. Send Sebastian a politely worded but regretful e-mail. Call the whole thing off . . . but she wouldn't.

It was a challenge, not only professionally but personally. If she could tangle with Sebastian Tennant and emerged unscathed, she could do anything.

A special messenger delivered a small packet of information to her office the morning following her meeting with Sebastian. It was thorough and disturbing, everything from clothing suggestions to a reminder to bring her birth certificate and her Social Security card.

While those requirements puzzled her, it was the last handwritten request at the bottom of the sheet of paper that made her pulse race. Scrawled in bold black letters were the startling words, "Please wear red nail polish to match your lips . . . Sebastian."

Just what kind of weekend did he have in mind? She picked up the phone and made an appointment at her favorite nail salon. If she wanted his cooperation she would have to be agreeable. It only made sense.

Two days later the stage was set. She watched with a quiver of uneasy fatalism as a uniformed chauffeur placed her large suitcase in the trunk of a limo, and then she smiled shakily as Sebastian himself got out and took her hand to usher her into the comfy interior.

When they were settled and whisking through the traffic on the way to the airport, Sebastian leaned back in his seat and crossed an ankle over his knee, his pose completely relaxed. Rebecca straightened her spine an extra millimeter and summoned a smile. "I suppose I should get some background information from you."

He waved a negligent hand. "Plenty of time for that later. Let's just enjoy the trip."

Sebastian kept his indolent pose with difficulty. He wanted to haul her into his lap and ravish those delicious carmine lips, muss that carefully styled ebony hair. He was not accustomed to denying himself any kind of sensual pleasure, and the effort to hide his instant erection from his lovely guest taxed his ingenuity.

He shifted enough to make a fold at the front of his trousers conceal his condition. He poured himself a shot of bourbon and downed it rapidly, his heart racing and his palms damp.

For the last three days he'd done damn little work. Instead, he'd been fixated on the realization that Rebecca Fraser would be his companion at the Scimitar, his newest and most inventive hotel to date. He knew what the facility had to offer, and the possibility that he might persuade Rebecca to share those delightful experiences made him sweat.

He wasn't entirely convinced that he would try to seduce her. Some small remnant of gentlemanly behavior prodded him to a wry admission that if she was a virgin, he would leave her alone. Even if she wasn't completely untouched, he felt her innocence keenly. While some part of him was aroused by the thought of her inexperience, another more practical voice reminded him that his usual companions were aware of how the game was played.

He doubted that Rebecca knew the rules. For one thing, she was far too young, probably only twenty-six or twenty-seven. He had a good eight years on her. And light-years of living.

He turned to look at his companion and found her staring out the opposite window, her delicate features in profile. Her suit today was a vivid blue, a perfect foil for her eyes. But the detail that had snagged his attention the moment he saw her standing on the street was her fingernails. They were painted red, a bright, sassy, glossy fire-engine red.

Her hand rested loosely on her left thigh, the fingers extended. In his mind he watched as those long, slender fingers reached for *his* thigh and scraped lightly toward his scrotum, tightening his body's state of readiness as they heightened the exquisite sensation of waiting.

"Can you at least tell me which airport we'll be flying to?"

Her sudden question jerked him rudely from the enjoyable daydream. He cleared his throat, and glanced briefly at his lap to see if his condition was still masked.

"Asheville, North Carolina," he said, his voice rough. He reached for a bottle of water and unscrewed the lid, downing half the contents in one gulp. It didn't hurt anything to tell her that much. It was fairly common knowledge that one hotel was in Hawaii, another in northern Maine, and now this newest site in the remote mountains of North Carolina.

The car made a sharp turn, and he realized with no small amount of relief that they had arrived at the airport. He needed the business of the next half hour to get himself under control. Otherwise it would be a very long flight.

Rebecca was definitely surprised to find they would be flying on a commercial airline. It was almost a certainty that Sebastian owned his own private jet. When she voiced her question, he nodded, his killer smile tinged with wry self-deprecation.

"Oh yes. I have my own plane. And believe me, I would rather be using it. But the Asheville airport is not all that large, and I don't want to draw attention to myself. It would defeat the whole purpose of this clandestine visit."

By the time they checked in and were settled in first class sipping drinks and waiting for takeoff, Rebecca was in a daze. Sebastian demanded service and received it, though at no time was he anything other than perfectly charming and agreeable. He simply exuded an air of authority that impelled lesser mortals to jump to do his bidding.

On the plane, the flight attendant, a lovely Asian woman, fawned over Sebastian with cloying sweetness. Or at least that's how it appeared to Rebecca, who sat in her window seat and observed the little byplay with a jaundiced eye.

In all fairness, she couldn't blame the woman. Just sitting beside Sebastian made her heart race and her throat tighten. She wanted to find out if his mouth tasted as sinfully delicious as it looked, yearned to strip away the sophisticated veneer of clothing and see the uncivilized man beneath.

He presented a picture of suave elegance to the world, but in a personal encounter, his real nature shone through. He was a man's man, virile, tough, and with a sensual appetite that both frightened and fascinated her. Despite his efforts to the contrary, she had been well aware of his physical condition in the limo.

She wanted to believe his arousal was due to her presence personally, but her more rational self reminded her that some men found any woman a turn-on. Sebastian had been linked with many of the reigning beauties in the world. Models. Actresses. Heiresses. Although he might react to Rebecca sexually, it was undoubtedly an automatic response. He was hardly likely to find her worthy of seduction.

She couldn't decide if she was relieved or disappointed by her conclusions. Was the promise of Sebastian's erotic expertise really enough to justify the possible dangers? She wanted him. That much was painfully clear. Her dreams the past three nights had been filled with dark, disturbing images of the two of them locked in a variety of carnal embraces.

But surely such consuming hunger was the result of proximity and chemistry. Surely she wouldn't be so naive as to let herself fall prey to his charm. If he chose to offer her a sexual liaison, she would accept. But she would look at it as a learning experience. A sexual apprenticeship, so to speak.

Never could she allow her deeper feelings to become involved. It would be suicidal, and she had far too much self-respect to become the pitiful kind of woman who clung blindly to a man long after his interest had waned.

Sebastian turned to smile at her, and she choked on a sip of wine. He patted her lightly on the back, his palm burning through the layers of fabric separating them.

When she regained her breath, he reached in his pocket and produced a turquoise leather box tied with white ribbon. Instead of handing it to her, he opened it and extracted the contents. Before she could protest, he took her left hand and slipped onto her ring finger a slender platinum band, and a perfectly plain diamond solitaire of such size and clarity, she gasped. It caught the light and shimmered in a rainbow of tiny sparks.

Both of his hands were holding hers as he fitted the rings carefully in place, and then raised her fingers to his lips for a teasingly amorous kiss. He took pity on her confusion. "Merely props for our escapade, Rebecca. That's all."

She held her hand toward the sunlight and admired the exquisite jewelry. She shook her head in bemusement. "Pretty extravagant window dressing," she muttered.

He clasped her hand in his and lifted their twined fingers. His head bent, he kissed each of her knuckles. Their eyes met. She shivered.

He smiled, a tiny half smile. "When I do something, Rebecca, I like to do it right."

Their gazes and their hands clung for long, heated seconds. She hovered on the knife edge of desire, her skin hot, her breasts tight and achy. His eyes darkened, and he leaned forward, whispering her name.

The moment was shattered abruptly by the ever present flight attendant. Rebecca was appalled by her sudden urge to fling a drink in the woman's face. She resented the intrusion, and the very depth of her anger shocked her into releasing Sebastian's hand and retreating to the far corner of her seat.

She had to get a grip. This was all a game to him, a business ploy, a momentary charade. Just because he had the power to make a woman feel irresistible was no excuse for losing her head. Sexual abandon was one thing, but she would guard her heart.

Moments after takeoff, Sebastian fell asleep. He slept deeply and instantly, perhaps programmed to take advantage of the infrequent moments of down time. She studied his face, not immune to the intimacy of watching him in repose. He seemed younger, less forbiddingly male. His dark lashes rested on sculpted cheekbones.

His skin had a healthy golden glow, but he definitely wasn't the kind of man who would use a tanning bed. His sun had come the old-fashioned way, perhaps a beach on the Riviera, a secluded veranda on Mykonos, a hidden cove in Antigua.

Her heart clenched as she imagined the women who were his companions in sybaritic pleasure. Was she about to become one of them? And did all those other faceless females cry when it was over, or did they simply thank their lucky stars that the meteoric personality who was Sebastian Tennant had flashed ever so briefly through their lives?

Her gaze drifted from his face to his chest. He had loosened his tie and unbuttoned his jacket. His hands were clasped across his abdomen, and a sleek gold watch peeked out from beneath his cuff.

With a little fillip of delight, she saw that on his left hand was a wedding band that matched hers. Costume or not, knowing that as far as the world was concerned, he voluntarily wore a mark of her possession, pleased her in some odd way. As long as she reminded herself this was just a game, it couldn't hurt to enjoy the benefits.

The plane hit a pocket of air, and dropped suddenly, forcing a small cry from her lips. Sebastian roused momentarily and gave her a sleepy smile. He raised the armrest between them, and tugged her against his shoulder. In seconds he was asleep again. She rested her head on the seat back, almost touching him, but not quite.

Air travel usually made her nervous, and today was no exception. But somehow, with Sebastian by her side, she felt wrapped in a cocoon of safety, as though nothing really bad could happen while he was in control. Perhaps it was shallow, but his power was part of what drew her, not because of any kind of business clout, but the sheer unassailable confidence of a man who knew himself to be in charge and accepted that responsibility, embraced it, even.

She shifted a fraction of an inch closer to his shoulder and breathed in his scent. He smelled wonderfully male, a pleasing meld of citrus, starched cotton, and soap. They were strangers. But she didn't care. He might stonewall her about the article. She didn't care. He had known dozens of women in the Biblical sense—perhaps hundreds. She didn't care. None of those realities were important.

Her focus in life had narrowed abruptly. She wanted time with this man, time to explore his fascinating personality, time to experience the expertise of his lovemaking, time to live out a brief fantasy.

She rubbed a thumb across the back of his wrist, feeling the steady beat of his pulse. He was so alive, more alive than any man she had ever known. And his vitality called out to everything female within her. Suddenly she wanted to glory in her femininity. Wanted to explore the endless, mysterious possibilities of pleasure for a woman in the arms of such a man as Sebastian Tennant.

For the first time in her life she knew what it meant to want. To hunger. To crave something with the strength of an addiction. It was happening too fast. She knew it. She was an intelligent woman, and on most occasions a pragmatist. But there were times when common sense was a useless commodity. Her eyelids fluttered shut, and she dozed off with a smile on her lips.

Sebastian had an erection when he awoke, perhaps due to the fact that his arm was tucked firmly around the soft, lush curves of one Rebecca Fraser. His other hand was tangled firmly with hers, their joined palms resting dangerously near his throbbing groin.

He allowed himself a brief moment to savor his first experience of having her in his arms, and then he gently eased away, watching as she murmured and settled into her own seat. He released her hand and replaced the armrest.

When the captain's voice sounded over the speakers, announcing their initial descent, Rebecca roused. "What time is it?" she asked, brushing her hair away from her face.

He watched, his pulse racing, as she took out a compact and touched up her makeup. When she opened a small tube, shaped her lips in a pout, and began tracing her mouth with fresh color, his hands curled into fists. The urge to touch her was almost uncontrollable.

He inhaled. "Just before noon. We'll have lunch in the car on the way."

A second limo awaited them right outside the airport. The driver greeted Sebastian cheerfully and made short work of stowing their things and ushering them into the car.

As they pulled away from the curb, Sebastian opened his briefcase and took out the next accessory in their little venture. He held out a hand, a smile of apology on his face. "I'm sorry, but I need you to put this on, Rebecca. Please."

Chapter Two

Rebecca looked down at the object in his hand and felt the blood drain from her face. Dizziness threatened, and she blinked her eyes, her heartbeat pounding in her ears.

He was holding a blindfold, a thick, black velvet blindfold. A trickle of uneasiness slithered down her spine. What did she really know about this man? What if his sexual appetites leaned toward the perverse?

He must have recognized her momentary panic. He squeezed her hand, his smile open and reassuring. "It's merely a precaution, Rebecca. I can't let you see the route we're taking."

"But what about the driver?"

"He's been with me for a decade. His discretion is complete." He cocked his head. "Are you okay with this?"

She mutilated her bottom lip with her teeth, and nodded reluctantly. "I guess so."

He reached across the seat and drew her head down far enough to settle the mask in place. The cloth was soft and tickled a bit. It smelled of lavender. The sudden transformation from bright sunlight to inky darkness was disorienting and slightly frightening.

It was ludicrous, but she felt suddenly exposed, vulnerable. She felt his fingers tangling gently in her hair, and in that instant she wanted to curl into his arms, let him soothe her anxiety.

He spoke softly, his breath brushing her cheek. "It will only be for an hour or so, I promise. When we arrive at the hotel you can take it off."

And then she felt his lips touch her mouth. With no visual clues to give her a hint of his intentions, the butterfly kiss was shocking, devastatingly unexpected. She gasped, and then moaned when the tip of his tongue met hers in a caress so swift and gentle, it was over in an instant.

She felt him move away, and her body grieved the loss. She leaned back, squirming slightly as she tried to find a comfortable position. The seats were more than luxurious, but she felt trembly and out of sorts.

A part of her wanted to rip off the mask, but a deeper, more wicked part wanted to beg Sebastian to make love to her. The intensity of her need stunned her into an intimidated silence. In some way, the blindfold made her feel like a prisoner, even though her body was in no way restrained.

She smelled the aroma of coffee, and her stomach growled in response.

Sebastian chuckled. "I was going to ask if you're hungry, but I think I have my answer."

She heard the rustling sounds of containers and clinking silverware. Seconds later, Sebastian's fingertips grasped her chin. "Open up," he said softly.

She complied, and sank her teeth into a flaky croissant filled with chicken salad. He rubbed a dab of mayonnaise from her lip. "How is it?"

She swallowed and licked her lips. "Heavenly."

They continued in that fashion for several long minutes, finishing the sandwich and topping it off with fresh whole strawberries dipped in chocolate. As good as the food was, it made less of an impact than having Sebastian touch her repeatedly. In the guise of feeding her lunch, his hands were everywhere.

Spreading a napkin across her lap, brushing a crumb from her breast, rubbing a smudge of chocolate from her chin. With her temporary blindness, her other senses were heightened. He took her hand and wrapped her fingers around a slender stem of crystal. "Drink," he said huskily.

She lifted the glass to her lips and sipped it recklessly, sealing the bond of trust between them. The sweet, crisp bite of champagne seduced her tongue, the bubbles tickling her nose. It was the most wonderful vintage she had ever tasted, and she drained the glass in short order.

She heard Sebastian chuckle softly, and she held out her empty glass.

He steadied her hand as he refilled the flute. "Looking for a bit of Dutch courage?" he asked, his voice amused.

She shook her head slowly. "No. But I am a little afraid. I don't know what to expect."

She felt him slide closer to her on the seat, felt the warmth of his thigh pressing against hers. She sipped her drink slowly, her dizziness increasing exponentially, whether from the alcohol or from his presence.

He took the glass from her hand. The next moment, she felt his arm slip around her shoulders as he tucked her against his chest and began to play with her hair. When he spoke, the words tickled her ear, his voice low, almost a whisper. "Trust me, Rebecca. I would never allow anything or anyone to hurt you, *especially* me. Nothing will happen against your will. I swear it."

She moved uneasily, embarrassed by their closeness. "Mr. Tennant . . ." She trailed off, unable to voice her reservations. He squeezed her shoulders once and released her, and she heard the rustle as he moved to his own side of the car.

Her relief battled with disappointment. She realized her hands were clenched in her lap, and she forced herself to relax them. She needed desperately to wrench the blindfold from her eyes.

Sebastian watched the struggle that was written on her expressive face. He wanted to relieve her anxiety, but the blindfold was necessary. He sighed. "Rebecca, don't you think it will be odd if you call me Mr. Tennant?"

A tiny smile tilted the corners of her mouth, and he knew his teasing question had distracted her. She nodded. "You're right, of course."

He moved closer to her once again, unable to resist. He tucked a strand of hair behind her ear, and inhaled her delicate perfume. "But more to the point, Rebecca—you've got to stop jumping every time I touch you."

He reached for her hands and chuckled when she flinched. He twined his fingers with hers. "See what I mean?"

She frowned. "Well, I can't see anything. What do you expect?"

"True. But when the blindfold comes off, you have to be convincing as my wife. Otherwise, our little ruse will gain me nothing."

"I'll do my best."

He stroked the black velvet with his fingertips, resenting the need for it, wanting to see her incredible eyes. "In my experience," he said huskily, "practice and preparation are the keys to success."

He felt her shiver, and cupped her cheeks in his hands. "Do you mind?" It went against his nature to ask, but he'd promised her the right to refuse.

He bent his head until his lips hovered just above hers. "Rebecca?"

"Yes . . ." Her response was little more than a tiny sigh, a breath of acquiescence.

He hesitated. "Yes you mind, or yes it's okay?"

"It's okay."

He could barely hear her answer. "Say my name," he muttered.

She licked her lips. "Sebastian."

He shuddered, unbelievably affected by her whisper. "A kiss for my wife."

Rebecca heard the words in a haze of desire. He had seduced her with demoralizing speed, her cooperation a foregone conclusion. And then her capacity for rational thought melted away as she responded to his kiss. He was gentle at first, surprisingly so. She sensed the leashed power of his sexuality, and expected a more determined assault.

But his lips were coaxing, sweetly cajoling. His hands were chastely at her waist, and she was frustrated at his restraint. She pulled back, wishing she could see his face, read his intent. "I'm not inexperienced, Mr.—Sebastian." She found herself vaguely insulted by his circumspect approach.

She heard the smile in his voice. "Innocence is not limited to the uninitiated, Rebecca. You practically reek of it."

"Maybe that's something I'd like to change." She listened in stunned surprise as the challenging words left her mouth, their meaning impossible to ignore. She felt him go completely still, so silent that she could hear only her own rapid breathing. She reached desperately for a lighthearted comment to neutralize her impulsive statement, but words failed her.

When he spoke, his voice was raspy, strained. "Don't say things you don't mean, little chick. My control only goes so far."

She cried out as his hand slipped inside her jacket and captured a breast. The feel of his fingers was shocking, unbearably erotic. He handled her almost roughly, and she sensed this was some sort of a test.

He tugged at her nipple, sending fire streaking through her body. His voice was hard, implacable. "Be sure, Rebecca. Be very sure."

Her ultimate answer would have to wait, for at that moment the driver tapped on the smoked glass of the partition and announced their arrival.

Without warning, Sebastian whipped the blindfold from

her head, and met her eyes with a steady gaze. "Are you ready?"

The question held layers of meaning. She smoothed her hair with a trembling hand, and looked at him, searching for the tender lover from moments ago. The Sebastian she saw now was the ruthless businessman, the intimidating executive.

She nodded slowly, reaching for her purse. "Yes."

As he got out of the car, Rebecca lingered for a moment, relishing the return of her sight. The hotel loomed in front of them, constructed entirely of mountain stone, its facade softened by rhododendron bushes laden with white and purple blossoms. The three-story building bore a striking resemblance to a European castle, complete with crenellated battlements.

She stepped from the car almost reluctantly, feeling as though she were leaving her last safe haven. The air was markedly cooler than when they arrived at the airport, and she shivered, despite her jacket.

Sebastian approached her and took her arm, leaning down to whisper in her ear. "Remember, you're Rebecca Edison, and I'm your husband, Edward."

She nodded jerkily, and inhaled as they neared the imposing oak door. Just before they reached it, the door swung wide open, and a smiling older gentleman in a severe black suit welcomed them and ushered them to a set of attractively decorated offices. A pleasant woman took Rebecca momentarily to an adjoining room where she was asked to verify her age and the fact that she was a guest of her own free will.

When she rejoined Sebastian minutes later, he was signing a credit card slip. The hostess turned away, and Rebecca tugged on his arm. "What was that all about?" she whispered.

He looked guilty. "Sorry. I meant to warn you on the

way up. We had a nearly disastrous incident in the early days. One of the guests was a minor, and her boyfriend had neglected to tell her what kind of hotel they were checking into. Fortunately, we found out and were able to get her on a plane back home before anything happened."

The hostess returned with Sebastian's credit card, and then handed them a stylish folder of information. She smiled. "We have a five-star restaurant on the premises, as well as a more casual bistro. And room service, of course. All of our amenities are outlined in the brochure, but if you have any questions at all, be sure to ask one of our staff."

She paused. "Would you like to go straight to your room or would you prefer to view the suites first?"

Sebastian wrapped his arm around Rebecca's waist, his smile at his "wife" warmly intimate. "The tour first, right, sweetheart?"

She nodded mutely, struck dumb by the return of the charming Sebastian. Was it just an act?

The hostess consulted a planner. "Excellent. I'll have Derek show you around, and after you're finished, he'll take you to your room."

Derek turned out to be an incredibly good-looking young man with an athletic build and an easy smile. As they followed him down the hall, Sebastian whispered in her ear. "Quit drooling, Mrs. Edison. Derek's not part of the package, so don't get any ideas."

She giggled at his disgruntled expression. He had to be joking. Despite Derek's undeniable sex appeal, no man stood a chance against Sebastian Tennant. Derek's masculinity was the eye candy variety. Sebastian's sexuality went much deeper. His sophisticated veneer only barely disguised the intensity and fierceness of his male power.

Her comparison of the two men ended abruptly as they stopped at a room whose door was open. From the angle where she stood, Rebecca was unable to see inside at first.

Derek smiled at them both, his casual charm friendly and

comfortable. "The suites are unoccupied every day from one P.M. until four. That gives the guests a chance to peek at all of them and make their plans accordingly. You may sign up for any suite in four-hour blocks, but we ask that you not choose the same suite more than two times a day in order for other people to have a chance to enjoy all the rooms."

Sebastian nodded. "Sounds fair." He turned to Rebecca. "Shall we, darling?" He took her hand, and they followed Derek into a fairly large room.

Derek waved a hand with some pride. "First we have the traditional classroom."

Rebecca looked around in stunned silence. It could have been any English schoolroom from the turn of the century. On one wall hung sets of costumes, and the decor was complete in every detail, down to the very real cane resting on the teacher's desk. A pair of lacy pantaloons was draped over a horsehair settee. She swallowed convulsively, her throat dry. But elsewhere she grew embarrassingly moist.

Sebastian nodded his approval. "Very, very nice. Let's move on."

Next door, they entered an oriental opium den. Velvet and satin pillows covered the floor, and a fluffy, silk-draped bed occupied one corner. Derek grinned. "The smoking paraphernalia isn't operational, of course, but you're welcome to use your own tobacco."

Before Rebecca could assimilate all the details, they were on to the next suite, this time a stark jail cell. She wrinkled her nose. The bare concrete walls and single yellow lightbulb were not at all appealing, but the handcuffs resting on the scarred wooden tabletop gave her a moment's pause.

She heard Sebastian's tiny whistle of approval when they came to the next room. It was a strip club, complete with a small stage and pole, and a table for the patron. Again, a wide assortment of costumes was available, along with a full selection of music.

A doctor's examination room, an *Out of Africa* suite, a fake outdoor setting with the backseat of a Chevy, a real but nonfunctioning elevator, a kitchen equipped with whipped cream, chocolate syrup, and other interesting edibles, and a half dozen other rooms, each more inventive than the last. By the end of the tour, Rebecca was embarrassingly aroused, her panties damp and her body aching.

She had tried to gauge Sebastian's reaction along the way, but these were his hotels, so presumably none of this was really new to him. Derek's friendly helpfulness was so matter-of-fact, he might have been selling them kitchen appliances. The two men discussed the various "entertainment" features with such open interest, Rebecca's face was permanently red.

Finally the last suite was checked off the list, and Derek escorted them to their hotel room. Rebecca was almost afraid to look inside, but the accommodations were reassuringly conventional, albeit very luxurious. She watched as Sebastian tipped the young man generously, closed the door, and turned to face her.

A small grin tilted the corners of his mouth. "So what do you think?"

Her mouth opened and shut several times before she was finally able to answer. She shook her head in disbelief. "I think if I put pictures with an article, our magazine will be relegated to the porn shelf."

He burst out laughing, and crossed the room toward her, loosening his tie in the process. He tipped up her chin with one finger and studied her face, his eyes unreadable. "Now do you see why privacy is so important?"

She nodded. "Of course. For some people, this kind of recreation could mean the tabloids, or worse."

His lips twitched. "Speaking of tabloids. I should warn you that one of our guests this week is more than a little famous."

He mentioned a name and her jaw dropped. "You're kidding. Who did he bring with him?"

He shook his head in mock disappointment. "Now, Rebecca, you know I can't tell you that. Maybe you'll bump into them at dinner."

She wrinkled her nose. "Beast." She looked at her watch. "Do I have time for a shower and a nap before we eat?"

He smiled wickedly. "At the Scimitar you get to call the shots. It's all about your pleasure."

She glanced at the bed involuntarily. It was an extra large king, big enough for a family of six.

He shrugged ruefully. "I would offer to do the gentlemanly thing and leave you alone for awhile, but that would hardly be suitable behavior for a man who just arrived for a weekend of passion with his wife."

Suddenly the platinum bands on her left hand burned her fingers. Had she made a bargain with the devil? She avoided looking at him, feeling awkward and unsophisticated. It was one thing to neck in the backseat of a limo and quite another to contemplate sharing a bed with a dangerous man she barely knew, not to mention partaking in the other activities the hotel had to offer.

She opened her suitcase and extracted a pair of slacks and a sweater, along with her robe. Minutes later she locked the bathroom door and turned on the water in the shower. Only then was she able to breathe normally. What had she gotten herself into?

Sebastian turned on the TV, muted the sound, and flipped channels restlessly. Touring the suites with Rebecca had been an exercise in torture, no pun intended. Seeing her flushed cheeks and dilated eyes and knowing she was as aroused as he was made him crazy. The depth of his own excitement made him just the slightest bit uneasy.

He was accustomed to the demands of his body, and he satisfied them as necessary, but something about being with Rebecca was different. He had the inexplicable urge to protect her from herself. Her challenging statement in the car had come close to sending him over the edge, but at the same time he was conflicted. She didn't need a man like him. What she needed was a good story for her magazine.

If he had any kind of honor at all, he would protect her from himself and from her own daredevil impulses, and send her on her way. But he had a sinking feeling he was losing the battle with his common sense.

The special suites at the hotels had been his idea from start to finish. He knew the design of each, and was well acquainted with their props and "toys." Intellectually, he knew their purpose was to enhance loveplay, to stimulate passion. But until today, with Rebecca wide-eyed by his side, he had never personally experienced the heart-pounding, dry-mouthed, driving urge to possess a woman in any one of the titillating, sexually intense scenarios he had created.

He shut off the TV with a muttered curse, and stared moodily at the bathroom door. The faint scent of almond and vanilla reached him where he lay. To hell with appearances. He had to get out of this room.

When Rebecca stepped warily out of the bathroom, Sebastian was gone. So much for keeping up the charade of a devoted husband. She flipped back the elegant, striped satin comforter and curled up beneath it, sighing as the decadent bed welcomed her. She hadn't slept much since meeting Sebastian, and she was exhausted.

When he unlocked the door an hour later and entered quietly, he found her fast asleep, her beautiful hair tumbled across the pillow. He saw, to his amusement, that she was fully dressed, but if she thought her "armor" was enough to deflect his interest, she was doomed to disappointment.

He stretched out beside her, careful not to wake the sleeping beauty. He closed his eyes and savored the sensation of complete peace. Warmth flooded over him, and he recognized it as happiness. He was content as a rule, challenged by his work and entertained by friends and associates. But happiness—this ephemeral feeling too difficult to describe was the elusive butterfly, landing for a moment on his shoulder, but sure to flit away before too long.

It didn't take a genius to connect it to Rebecca's presence. But the question was . . . why? Was she simply a novelty? Or was some deeper force at work? His eyelids drifted shut, and he fell asleep, unaware that he smiled in his sleep.

When Rebecca resurfaced to the land of the living, shadows of dusk filled the room. That was her first thought. Her second was that a man's arm held her tightly, looped beneath her breasts. Sebastian had "spooned" her, her bottom pressed firmly in the cradle of his thighs, her buttocks cradling his erection. She turned stealthily onto her back and sucked in a shocked breath when she saw that he was wide awake, his dark eyes assessing her with devastating, focused sensuality.

She managed a weak smile. "Sorry for sleeping so long."

He nuzzled her nose with his, then moved on to nibble her collarbone, his words muffled. "You obviously needed it, and the selfish part of me wants you well rested."

Her face flamed at his blatant statement of intent. She licked her lips, and then moaned as he pushed up her sweater and tugged aside a lacy bra cup to lick her nipple. "Sebastian!" Her shocked cry was one-part protest, and three-parts sheer pleasure.

He pulled back slowly, and propped one hand under his head, regarding her somberly. "Tell me the truth, Rebecca. Are you a virgin?"

"No," she said quietly. No need to admit just how limited her experience was.

"Good." He smiled faintly, and she felt a measure of relief. At some level she had wondered if Sebastian's unlikely interest in her was because he thought she was untouched.

He traced her eyebrows and her nose with a gentle fingertip, his expression hard to read. Finally he spoke again. "And one more question . . . if I tell you there won't be a magazine story, will you leave?"

His eyes were focused on her face, and for one instant she saw hesitancy, perhaps even vulnerability.

She frowned. "What do you mean?"

He sighed. "I can't let you write the story. I tried to tell you that, but you were so determined. My little proposition was to scare you off, so you'd abandon the idea. But you didn't, and I find I can't lie to you even by omission."

"I see." What he was saying was no real surprise, but the unspoken message beneath it took her off guard. She didn't know how to respond.

He took her long silence as a refusal, and his face closed, his eyes once again dark and inscrutable. "I thought as much," he said gruffly. "Get your things together and we'll head back to the airport. I'll tell them you're sick."

He started to rise, and she caught his arm, flooded with tenderness for this unusual, fascinating man. He looked at her warily. "What?"

She smiled, strangely near tears. "I don't give a damn about the story, Sebastian. And I don't want to leave." It was terrifying to lay it all on the line, but his response was swift and gratifying.

He lowered himself to the bed, covering her body with his and then rolling until she lay on top of him, his hands tangling in her hair as he ravaged her mouth. Her legs straddled his hips, and she rubbed her aching mound against the hard ridge beneath his trousers. He stripped her sweater away with impressive efficiency. "God, I love your breasts," he muttered, sucking one and then the other deeply into his mouth until she whimpered for mercy.

She reached between them to struggle with his zipper, hissing in frustration when it defied her efforts. Sebastian chuckled hoarsely and lent a hand, managing to free his cock only to curse in stunned disbelief when the phone shrilled near his ear. Only one person knew where he was, and the call could only be an emergency.

He rolled away from Rebecca and snatched up the receiver, unable even to look at her as he tried to focus on the voice at the other end.

Rebecca felt unaccountably rejected, even dirty. Sebastian's conversation was clearly serious, and after an initial terse exchange, he lapsed into French for the remainder of the minutes he was on the line. She slipped out of bed and changed from her slacks and sweater into a robe, unsure of their dinner plans.

When Sebastian finally hung up and turned to face her, his pants were fastened. He rubbed a hand over his face and met her gaze with a shrug of apology. "It was one of the hotels in Asia. A fire."

"Is anyone dead?"

"No, thank God . . . but hundreds of injuries."

"Do you have to leave?"

He walked around the bed and stood facing her, his hands jammed in his pockets. He tilted his head to one side and stared at her until a blush heated her cheeks. He took the lapels of her robe in each hand and tugged gently, until her breasts were pressed against his chest. He kissed the top of her head. "I cannot think of a single thing that could make me leave this hotel before Monday morning, not a damned thing."

He folded her into his arms and she felt the steady beat of his heart. The passion between them still simmered beneath the surface, but it was layered over with tenderness, a far more fragile and dangerous commodity. She rested her cheek over the comforting thump, thump of his heart and yearned for something she couldn't even describe.

He just held her there for long minutes, as the room grew

even darker. Finally he released her with a sigh. "Why don't you get dolled up, Ms. Wife, and I'll treat you to dinner."

She laughed, falling just a little bit in love with him. "I did bring along a rather smashing dress."

He nodded approvingly. "Good. I'll give you ten minutes to get into it. I'm starving."

She turned toward the closet, but he snagged her arm and dragged her back for one more kiss. When she was limp and tingling from head to toe, he grinned smugly. "And after dinner, Rebecca . . ."

"Yes?"

"We'll sign up for the suites we want to try out. Ladies first."

Chapter Three

Rebecca stared at her image in the bathroom mirror. Since meeting Sebastian Tennant, her face seemed to have a permanent rosy hue, either from embarrassment or excitement, or both. She could blame her heightened color on the steamy bathroom heat, but it would be a lie.

She pulled her long, wavy hair into a loose knot on top of her head and secured it with two antique ivory hairpins. Her dress was fire-engine red silk, bought just twenty-four hours ago to match the nail polish requested by Sebastian. The dress was cut low at the front and back, ruling out any bra, and she had brushed a tiny amount of glitter-filled lotion across her cleavage.

Spaghetti straps, dangerously fragile, supported the bodice. The fabric was thin, but lined with a contrasting cream silk underslip. Her legs were bare, and high-heeled black sandals, barely more than a single strap and a sole, completed her ensemble. It was by far the sexiest outfit she had ever had the courage to wear, but worthy of the new woman she was determined to be.

She opened the door the tiniest of cracks, and peeked out. Sebastian lounged on the bed, one arm tucked behind his head as he watched a news program. He was fully dressed in a severe black tux that made him even more compellingly masculine. Pierce Brosnan as Bond might have seemed effeminate beside Sebastian Tennant.

She giggled softly at her comparison and apologized silently to Brosnan. It wasn't his fault. With Sebastian in the room, she couldn't even think of any other man.

She took a deep breath, summoned a careless smile, and sauntered into the bedroom. Sebastian looked up, and she expected him to whistle or compliment her dress. He did neither. He got to his feet slowly, straightened his bow tie, and walked toward her. She felt a ridiculous instinct to flee.

He paused, just inches away, their bodies not touching. Her heart pounded wildly in her chest. The look in his eyes sent a wave of heat washing over her. He was a predator, and she the prey. She trembled as he reached out a hand to stroke the curve of her breast. She closed her eyes and her head fell forward. Her knees went weak, threatening to collapse beneath her.

"Rebecca." His voice was harsh, uneven.

She looked at him, compelled by the note of command in his voice.

He raised his hand from her breast to her collarbone, stroking the satiny skin and toying with the simple gold chain she wore. "You look like a dream," he said quietly. "A really beautiful dream."

And she believed him. Despite the models, and the actresses, and the wealthy society women, she knew he meant what he was saying. She could see it in his eyes.

Her stomach growled suddenly with an appalling lack of timing. Sebastian gave a shout of laughter, and the moment of intimacy was shattered. He hugged her and pushed her toward the door. "Get your purse, woman. I can see that I'm going to have to feed you on a regular basis."

The dining room was fairly full when they arrived, but a clever designer had positioned the tables in alcoves and behind greenery so that the illusion of privacy was preserved.

The famous guest, an Academy Award-winning actor, ended up sitting only a couple of tables away. Rebecca scarcely gave him a glance.

Dining with Sebastian was an experience to be savored. The wine he chose to accompany their dinner was deliciously crisp and fruity. The veal chops and asparagus were perfectly prepared, the fresh mango sorbet a mouthwatering dessert. But the menu barely registered. She ate automatically, her attention focused on her companion.

He was funny, and at times dryly sarcastic. They discussed movies and books. They shared childhood memories. He avoided any mention of his love life, and she didn't press. She knew he had a wealth of experience. She hoped to benefit from it, but she would just as soon not hear the details.

When their waiter brought the check for Sebastian's signature, Rebecca's pulse accelerated. He looked up and caught her watching him. "What's wrong?"

She nibbled her lower lip, a habit she abhorred. "Nothing."

His smile was affectionate. "Liar." He leaned across the table and lowered his voice. "We have to sign up for a suite so we don't blow my cover. But we can take books and read to each other, or play gin rummy, if you'd rather."

She giggled at the image of Sebastian Tennant playing cards in one of those fantasy rooms. Strip poker maybe. She took his hand and felt his fingers tighten around hers. "It's okay, Sebastian. Let's go sign up."

He looked uncertain for a moment. "I wasn't kidding about you choosing."

"I wouldn't know where to begin."

"Are you sure?" he asked in all seriousness. "Wasn't there one scenario at least that pushed your buttons?"

"Probably all but one or two," she admitted quietly, uncomfortable with discussing her private fantasies.

"Well, then . . ." There was an unspoken challenge in his tone of voice.

She met his gaze bravely. "Okay. I'll pick." She wrinkled her nose. "Do I have to go to the office?"

He shook his head. "We don't want to cramp anyone's style. Everything can be done from the phone in your room. If you can't remember all the choices, there's a description in the folder they gave us."

He paused as they left the restaurant. "Would you like to take a walk before we go back to the room?" He almost laughed at the transparent look of relief on her face.

"That sounds great."

He took her hand and led her out a side door, pausing to wrap his jacket around her. Without asking permission, he pulled the pins from her hair and fluffed it over her shoulders. He lifted a handful of silky curls and buried his face in them, breathing in the scent that was distinctly Rebecca.

He sensed her inner conflict, and he was determined not to give her any reason to be afraid of him. He smoothed her hair back into place and linked his palm with hers, leading her down a shallow flagstone terrace. In front of them, the mountain fell away, leading the eye to the distant lights in the valley below. The wind ruffled the tops of the trees, and a nearly full moon illuminated their path.

They paused at a bench, and by unspoken consent sat down. She looked up at him in concern. "Are you cold?"

He ran a hand through his hair and looked at her ruefully. "When I'm with you, angel, cold is the last thing I am."

She tucked her head bashfully, and he was reminded once again how young she was. Was he taking advantage of her? The thought troubled him.

She laid a tentative hand on his thigh, and his whole body went rock hard. He cleared his throat. "Beautiful out here, isn't it?"

She ignored his inane remark and began stroking his leg, straying perilously near his raging erection. She spoke in such a low voice he had to bend to hear her words.

"What if I pick something you don't like?"

The uncertainty and vulnerability in her voice stirred every one of his protective instincts. "Believe me, sweetheart. You can't go wrong. I've got a hell of a good imagination, and I'll be or do whatever turns you on."

She tilted her head to look up at him and the moonlight silvered her beautiful features. She had reapplied lip gloss after dinner, and the shiny curve of her mouth beckoned him.

He forced himself to concentrate on what she was saying, and then practically swallowed his tongue in shock. "Say that again," he muttered.

She shrugged and one bare shoulder slipped from his jacket. "I said that I'll probably be too nervous in one of those fancy rooms. Maybe we should start right here."

He reached to loosen his tie, and found that it was already in his pocket. "It's a bit public, don't you think?"

She closed her fingers around his cock and he groaned. She squeezed gently. "Do you really care?"

"Hell no." He forced out the words, struggling not to embarrass himself. God, she was incredible. Her tentative, almost naive explorations aroused him faster and hotter than the most experienced woman he'd ever bedded.

She lowered his zipper an inch and stopped. "Can I sit on your lap? That way I'll be able to see if anyone is coming."

He was beyond speech. He nodded jerkily and helped her release his aching penis. When the cold air hit his skin, he never even noticed. What they were about to do was hardly a novelty to him. He'd carried out far more outlandish sexual exploits as a teenager. But Rebecca's ingenuous pleasure and excitement ratcheted up his lust, making the need to possess her a piercing physical pain.

She stood up and put her arms in the sleeves of his coat. Then she put her hands on the edges of her skirt and shimmied it to the tops of her thighs. When he realized she wasn't wearing any underwear, his breath lodged in his throat. "You're going to freeze," he stuttered.

Her smile was 110 percent female siren. "I'm counting on you to keep me warm, Mr. Edison."

She stepped closer until her legs were on either side of his. He held his breath, wanting to speed things along but not about to interrupt a woman with a mission. He scooted forward on the bench and held her waist. With excruciating slowness, she lowered herself onto his throbbing cock.

It was a tight fit, and she wriggled her hips to take the last aching inch. He couldn't help himself, he groaned out loud at the feel of her hot, wet body taking him in, and then dropped his head to her breasts in silent, helpless amusement as she shushed him.

He leaned back, and it was her turn to cry out as he went even deeper. He gave her a moment to adjust to his size and then he started to move, pulling almost completely out before thrusting firmly to the hilt.

She was shaking, either from cold or passion, or both. He was perilously close to losing control, and it scared the shit out of him. Sebastian Tennant had been known on occasion to maintain an erection for more than an hour, driving his partner to multiple orgasms before allowing himself to climax. Now, he strained to hold back until she came, mentally listing the states and capitals, damned if he was going to let an ingenue break his legendary control. And then in a split second, she shattered in his arms.

He closed his eyes against a red haze of sensation and exploded, his hoarse shout ringing in the night air. Her inner muscles clenched him tightly, milking every last drop of his ejaculation almost painfully.

When each of them could breathe again, he realized that his hands stroking her bare butt were sliding over some serious gooseflesh. He lifted her reluctantly and handed her a handkerchief.

She turned away from him, her body language eloquent as she tidied herself.

He stood up and was amazed when his head swam. Hell, if it didn't sound pathetically overdramatic, he'd wonder if someone put something in his dinner wine.

She stuffed the square of white cloth in the pocket of the jacket she wore and wrapped her arms tightly around herself, still facing away.

Any tenderness he'd felt for her inexperience was obliterated by an inexplicable anger. How dare she try to win him over with such an unoriginal ploy? Sebastian Tennant was a connoisseur of the erotic arts. And little Rebecca Fraser was way out of her league.

She turned around and looked at him, her expression unreadable, despite the moonlight. "I guess you've done stuff like this a hundred times."

"Not with you." His automatic response might have soothed her had it been delivered in a more conciliatory tone. But even he winced at the note of insolence.

Clearly she recognized the contempt in his answer. She seemed to shrink into herself, and the night air was suddenly frigid. Her chin lifted in silent dignity. "I'd like to go to the room now."

She edged past him and he followed her, bleakly wondering why an evening that began with such promise had soured so quickly.

Rebecca concentrated on not throwing up. What had possessed her to think she could keep up with Sebastian Tennant? Her naive attempt to show him she could be outrageous had failed abysmally—unless you counted the fact that each of them had experienced a near cataclysmic orgasm.

Her inner monologue halted abruptly as an even more sickening thought occurred. What if Sebastian had merely faked the intensity of his response? What if he had been humoring her, trying to let her think she had given him a fantastic ride, when in fact the coupling had been an automatic effort on his part, nothing more than a man fucking an available woman.

She stood aside and let Sebastian open the door to their room. Once inside she confronted him bravely, wincing at the dark, almost angry expression on his face.

He simply stared at her until nerves forced her into speech. "I'm going home," she said quietly. "This was a mistake."

He opened his mouth, started to speak, and then frowned fiercely. "You can't go. We made a deal. I still need to check things out."

"You've already told me you never intended to let me do an article. I think that pretty well nullifies any agreement on my part."

"Look, Rebecca . . ." He reached for her, and she stepped back quickly, her skin crawling with humiliation.

"Leave me alone, Sebastian."

His lips twisted unpleasantly. "You weren't so standoffish a little while ago."

She shrugged. "Maybe I just wanted to see if all the stories were true."

His eyes grew dangerous. "What stories?"

She smiled with saccharine sweetness. "The ones about the famous Sebastian Tennant, of course. Legendary lover. Fabulous fuck." She laced her reply with vicious sarcasm, hoping desperately he wouldn't realize that their encounter had completely destroyed her. To go from erotic ecstasy to abject despair in mere minutes was a crushing blow.

He walked over to the bedside table and picked up the hotel brochure. He held it out, his hand rock steady. "Select a suite, Rebecca—now. You're not leaving until I get what I want."

She trembled. "I already screwed you. Game's over."

He walked toward her, and this time she stood her ground. He held out the folder. "Not quite, my sweet," he said, his teeth flashing in a smile totally devoid of humor. "You're my wife, remember? And I want to play for awhile."

The sheer menace in his posture shook her badly, but she was even more appalled by the knowledge that her body was responding not in fear, but in heated excitement. Her nipples were thrusting against the fabric of her dress, and the dampness between her thighs was not merely the residue of their earlier sex. He wanted more from her. He wanted to play.

She stalled. "I'll sue you."

He sneered. "You signed a paper stating you were here of your own free will, remember?"

She grabbed the brochure from his hand and stalked over to the phone. He followed her, grasping her chin and forcing her to look up at him. "Tell them we want the room immediately." His voice was rough.

She licked her lips, and saw with a tingle of triumph that he focused on her mouth. "What if it's not available?"

"You'll think of something."

Sebastian released her abruptly and retreated to the opposite side of the room to watch as she followed his instructions. Her face was completely pale except for two spots of color high on her cheekbones. She still wore his rumpled tux jacket, and it gave her the appearance of a little girl playing dress-up.

He could see red patches on her neck where his late-day stubble had marked her delicate skin. He growled a curse beneath his breath and jerked open the minibar, sending bottles of macadamia nuts and olives crashing to the carpet. The clumsy accident shocked him into taking a deep breath.

He put everything back and then poured himself a single shot of whiskey, downing it with uncharacteristic desperation. What in the hell was he thinking? Why was he pressing the issue of the suite? He'd never forced a woman in his life. His style was more courteous than caveman.

Rebecca picked up the phone and he froze, every ounce of concentration focused on the slender woman sitting on the bed. She spoke in such a low voice he was unable to hear her conversation with the front desk. When she hung up, his senses snapped to alert.

"Well?" he demanded, his palms sweating.

She shrugged. "We have to wait thirty minutes. They're cleaning the room."

"Let's freshen up, in that case. Ladies first, unless you'd like to share."

She eyed him warily. "No thanks." She bit her lip and pulled the coat close about her. "What do we wear?"

He chuckled, a fraction of his good humor returning. "All the suites provide costumes. After your shower, just slip your dress back on. I'll take care of the rest."

She fled to the bathroom, leaving Sebastian to prowl restlessly from one side of the room to the other. He was beginning to regain his equilibrium, aided by yet another shot of really excellent whiskey.

Clearly he had overreacted outside. Rebecca was a damned attractive woman and a natural when it came to sex, despite her limited experience. He was a man with strong appetites. Due to a busier than usual schedule, he hadn't been with a woman in ten days. Screwing Rebecca had been a deeply enjoyable interlude, but hardly out of the norm.

His gut-wrenching climax was the result of deprivation, not some naive little girl's tame teasing. He had nothing to worry about. Rebecca Fraser was a delight to look at and a treat to fuck, but that was all. He was back in control, and he would set the pace for the evening's entertainment.

When she emerged from the bathroom in a fragrant cloud of steam, his heart clenched. She tossed his jacket on the bed. As he had demanded, she once again wore the red dress, and if his luck held, only the red dress. Every inch of her smooth, lovely skin was flushed a dewy pink, and she had washed off whatever makeup she had worn earlier to reveal a face that needed no adornment.

Unfortunately for his libido, she had also erased a good ten years from her age, the result of which was the disconcerting notion that he was planning to get naked with a female who bore a more than passing resemblance to an innocent schoolgirl. She was looking at him with a mixture of apprehension and what he hoped like hell was burgeoning excitement.

He unbuttoned his shirt. "I'll be quick," he promised, his words deliberately soft. Before stepping into the bathroom, he couldn't resist the urge to touch her, a compulsion that he convinced himself was natural. She stood frozen in the posture of an animal sensing danger.

He slipped one strap of her dress off her shoulder, trapping her arm and freeing her lush, plump breast. He cupped it in his palm and squeezed, monitoring her response with intense interest. Her eyelids fluttered shut. She sighed, a tiny puff of breath that he fancied held a note of surrender.

His other hand had a mind of its own, sliding beneath the hem of her dress and up between her thighs. He probed the wet, slick folds of her vulva, thrusting deeply with three fingers. She cried out and her inner muscles clamped down when a sudden, sharp orgasm ripped through her slender frame.

He caught her as she collapsed against him, limp and unresisting. He laid her on the bed and knelt over her, ravaging her mouth in a kiss of possession. Her bare breast pressed against his chest, and he freed the other one, pinching each nipple roughly until her drugged eyes opened in protest.

"Sebastian . . ."

The sound of her voice crying his name made his aching cock even harder. The driving need to make her submit was unusual enough to cause him to back away, stirrings of his earlier unease returning. He was in control, completely.

He stroked her cheek. "Rest for ten minutes, sweetheart . . . and then it's showtime."

Rebecca pulled a corner of the bedspread across her bare chest, shivering from reaction, almost in shock. Her body was betraying her at every turn. Despite her resolve to stand up to Sebastian's sexual challenges, she felt scattered, helplessly vulnerable.

She glanced at the clock and listened to the sound of the shower, realizing with some degree of anger that Sebastian's arrogance was complete. Clearly he thought there was no danger that she might leave.

Part of her wanted to prove him wrong, yearned to put a dent in his colossal self-confidence. The front desk would call her a cab, and unless Sebastian decided to blow his cover, she had every opportunity to leave and never look back.

But a deeper, more disturbing corner of her soul ruled at the moment. Some brazen, fearless part of her personality, never before freed or even acknowledged, was in the driver's seat. That Rebecca never considered sneaking away. That Rebecca needed to test her capacity for pleasure, for sexual fulfillment. That Rebecca had allowed Sebastian to bring her here, had revelled in a brief, carnal act of sex, had ignored feelings of inadequacy and managed to stand up to him at every turn.

And that Rebecca had every intention of seeing this through to its inevitable conclusion. She had no rosy illusions. She was a momentary disturbance in Sebastian's life. A week from now he might have forgotten her name. But despite that, perhaps because of that, she was determined to experience what might be the most profound sexual experience of her life.

The brazen Rebecca insisted that her relationship with

Sebastian was only physical, but the ordinary Rebecca, a bit reserved, a lot inhibited, felt a growing attachment to the man who was so much more than she had ever imagined. A man who played the roles of tender romantic and earthy lover with equal ease.

Her heart played games with her emotions, making her crave him, forcing her to fall deeper beneath his sensual command. If she fell in love with him, her submission would be complete. The brazen Rebecca scoffed. The true Rebecca blinked back tears and waited for the man in the shower.

The room was lonely without his vibrant presence. Her hand traced hesitantly over the curves of first one breast and then the other, delicately scraping the nipples, her skin almost unbearably sensitive. She closed her eyes and moaned as heat gathered once more between her legs.

She clenched her thighs together, and then with a whimper of distress let them fall apart, finding her own secret place with seeking fingers and trying desperately to appease the insistent hunger.

Sebastian discovered her like that, so lost to reality that she didn't hear the bathroom door open. He was drying his hair with a towel, but his hand jerked and went slack, the towel falling unheeded to the floor.

He took an involuntary step forward and then paused, caught by the innocent sensuality of her actions. She cried out, and her back arched off the bed, her lithe body a picture of feminine abandon.

His cock jerked and burned with the driving need to mount her and pound away until this unwilling obsession was finally obliterated. His hands clenched in fists at his sides as he fought to bring his lust under control.

He dragged in a lungful of air and forced himself to lean indolently against the doorway. As her eyes opened, cloudy with the aftermath of her release, she smiled at him. It nearly brought him to his knees.

She showed not the slightest bit of embarrassment, her lips parted slightly, her eyes dreamy and her body boneless and relaxed.

He cleared his throat, his vocal cords almost paralyzed. "I see you didn't miss me too much."

She chuckled, her voice huskier than usual. "I was just warming up."

She sat up slowly, seeming not to notice that her dress was bunched about her waist. Another woman might have looked ridiculous. Rebecca shimmered with an intense sexuality, surrounded with what a less practical man might have called an aura of seductive allure.

Doggedly he maintained his pseudo-relaxed pose, although he was entirely unable to do anything about the bulge in his trousers. He wrestled with the urge to step toward the bed, determined not to give in. "How about a glass of wine before we go?"

She stood, adjusted her dress, and bent to put on her shoes. The dress tightened across her ass, and her long, slender legs taunted him. When she was ready, she mocked him. "Looking for a little Dutch courage?"

Her sassy repetition of his question to her earlier in the day made his lips twitch in amusement. He straightened, a most difficult task, and managed to walk without whimpering to the wet bar. "Red or white," he asked gruffly, refusing to look at her more than he had to.

"I usually drink white," she admitted. "But I think my mood tonight calls for red. I'm definitely not feeling pure."

His hand trembled, and he cursed as wine sloshed over the rim of the glass. He mopped it up and tried again, filling her glass to the brim. When he turned to hand her the cut-glass goblet, she was at his shoulder.

"Thanks, Sebastian." She lifted the drink. He watched, mesmerized, as she drained the contents, and then handed him the empty glass. One slender finger, its polished nail fire-engine red, lifted to trace the contours of his mouth, pressing gently against the fullness of his lower lip until he felt a twinge of pain. Her eyes held a reckless, challenging light. "Showtime, husband . . . isn't that what you said?"

He swallowed. "I'm ready if you are." He wondered if she recognized the bravado in his statement. His innocent little kitten had turned into a tigress, and he wasn't sure how to respond.

Sweat beaded his forehead. He was seconds away from saying to hell with his cover, and pulling her down onto the plush ivory carpet. Instead, he crossed to the bed, shrugged into his badly wrinkled jacket, and gave her his best Sebastian Tennant smile—or was it Edward Edison's? At the moment he wasn't sure which man was in the most trouble.

They stepped into the hall and headed toward the entertainment wing. Suddenly he stopped and put a hand on her arm, turning her to face him. "I forgot to ask, Rebecca. Which suite did you pick?"

She met his gaze hesitantly, once again the slightly shy woman he first brought to the Scimitar. "Number thirteen," she whispered.

"Good God."

Chapter Four

His jaw dropped and his groin tightened painfully. He knew exactly which room she was talking about, and his mind raced ahead, imagining a limitless number of activities he and Rebecca might share.

She misunderstood his reaction. Her face crumpled in anxiety, her expressive eyes uncertain. "Is that bad? Would you prefer something else?"

He rubbed his hands up and down her arms, warming the smooth skin. "It's perfect," he said slowly, brushing a kiss across her forehead. "I'm just surprised, that's all." He grinned. "You realize that in Suite Thirteen you have to do anything I ask for."

She nodded, biting her lower lip until he used his fingertip to rescue her delicate mouth. She nipped him hard enough to make him jerk his hand away. Then she laughed, clearly unrepentant. "I know . . . but I trust you. Remember?"

He rubbed his abused finger and eyed her wryly. "Maybe you shouldn't. At the rate we're going, I may attack you just inside the door."

"Really?" She seemed delighted. "Am I making you horny?"

He assumed an expression of shock. "What a little slut you are. I may have to bring you in line."

Her cheeks flushed, and he saw her nipples clearly defined by the thin silk of her dress. She tugged at his hand, her eyes dark and stormy. "Hurry."

He needed no further encouragement. They walked rapidly from one corridor to the next, not speaking, intent on their destination. When they stood in front of the elegant, polished wooden door with the brass numeral 13, he took a deep breath. "Open the door, Rebecca. This is your show."

He saw her fingers tremble as she reached for the knob. He put his hand over hers, his own none too steady. "Do you want this, Rebecca? Are you sure?"

She leaned her head against his shoulder, the scent of her perfume making him dizzy. "For the next four hours, this is *all* I want."

Rebecca stood on the threshold of the suite and surveyed the interior with fascinated concentration. When they had taken their quick tour of all the rooms earlier, she had been so hyped up and flustered, she had barely registered the contents of this particular setting. But when Sebastian forced her to choose, there had been no doubt in her mind. Possibly because this particular scenario had played a part in a fantasy or two of hers over the years.

Suite Thirteen was an authentic Old West saloon/bordello. The floor was bare wood, scarred and dusty. A dilapidated chandelier hung from the open rafters. Immediately to their left and right as they entered were two decorative folding screens, one for each of them. Costumes hung on hooks behind. To the rear of the large room in the left corner was the bar, fully stocked with drinks and glasses.

On the opposite side, in a partitioned alcove lit by candlelight, a large feather bed stood ready, its vintage quilt and lace-trimmed pillows inviting. Directly in the center of the rear wall was a small raised stage, and a variety of musical choices. But the thing that caught the eye, the one prop impossible to ignore, was the enormous tin bathtub, filled to the brim with steaming water, standing in the middle of the room. A small stool flanked it, with two large fluffy white towels, a bar of plain soap, and various other essentials.

To the naked eye, the room's only concessions to modern convenience were the CD player and discs near the stage, and the hot and cold faucets attached to the tub, ready to replenish the water as necessary.

Rebecca gulped in a mouthful of air, suddenly aware she had been holding her breath. Beside her, Sebastian stood silent and still, his taut frame poised and tense. She breathed rapidly, her senses on overload. Did she really have the guts to carry this out?

She jumped as Sebastian reached behind them and closed the deadbolt with a loud click. He seemed to take pity on her paralyzed voice. "I suppose we'd better change clothes, don't you think?" He cocked his head to look at her, a lazy smile on his face.

She nodded, stupidly mute, more aroused than she had ever been in her life. He shoved her gently toward the screen, his hands deliberately lingering on her bottom. "And don't forget—the pretty little prostitute who comes out in a minute won't be Rebecca Fraser."

She stepped behind the screen and sank onto a stool, her legs suddenly the consistency of spaghetti. She put her hands to her flaming cheeks and listened to the unmistakable sound of Sebastian stripping off his clothes. She peeked and saw one tanned hand toss a pair of tux trousers over the top of his screen.

His voice floated across the distance separating them, mocking her hesitation. "Get a move on, woman. Or I'll be forced to change you myself."

She gasped and jumped to her feet, stripping her dress over her head. She stood nude and shivering as she assessed her choices. The clear favorite was a satin merry widow in emerald green, trimmed with black lace. A matching pair of crotchless panties and garter belt, along with sheer black nylons and heels, completed the ensemble.

She struggled into the unfamiliar garments, using the long cheval mirror to adjust all the bits and pieces. The bodice of the merry widow thrust her breasts into voluptuous mounds, the black lace edging the cups barely covering her areolas. She draped a black feather boa around her shoulders and stepped back to gauge the effect. She looked like a whore—a very young, nervous whore.

She pulled her hair up and secured it with a few pins, hoping that Sebastian would enjoy taking it down.

His voice broke the silence, closer than it should be. "Quit stalling."

Her hand jerked and she dropped the hairbrush with a loud clatter. "Don't look," she cried, unaccountably panicked. "I'm almost ready."

"Well, it's about damned time," he grumbled. "How much can there be to put on?"

She smoothed her hands down over her hips and straightened her shoulders. Then she stepped out from behind the screen and stopped dead, stunned by his transformation.

He seemed bigger, brashly masculine. He wore a traditional brown checked shirt, a vest, and jeans; his legs were covered with chaps that emphasized the intimidating bulge of his genitals. Scuffed cowboy boots encased his feet, and a stained cowboy hat tilted forward over his brow.

Her insides did a funny little dance as she assessed his expression. He had changed his entire demeanor, becoming almost a stranger. His eyes were cold and blank, his mouth set in a curl of arrogance. He stalked toward her, turning her slowly in a circle for his insolent inspection.

His fingers clasped her forearm roughly, biting into her tender flesh. "What's your name, angel face?"

She tried to speak, her throat dry. "I, uh . . ."

He sneered. "It ain't that hard a question."

She licked her lips, her whole body shaking in reaction. "Lola," she whispered. "It's Lola."

"Well, Miss Lola . . ." He slid a finger into her cleavage and tugged, freeing her breasts. "Let's see what you got." He examined her chest with dispassion, his clinical study humiliating. His lip curled as he rubbed his thumb over first one nipple and then the other. "I like 'em with bigger tits, but I guess you'll do."

He took her by the arm and practically dragged her over to the bar, pushing her onto a barstool and uncapping a glass decanter. "How 'bout I buy you a drink?"

"I don't really like whiskey."

His hands stilled over the glasses, his eyes turning dangerous. "What did you say?"

She actually felt a lick of terror, totally cowed by his aura of menace. "I'm sorry," she muttered. "Of course I would like a drink."

He poured her a generous shot and handed her the glass. "Bottoms up."

She tilted her head and recklessly downed the fiery liquid, choking and gasping as it torched her insides.

He seemed mildly pleased by her cooperation. "Another?"

She shook her head, desperately afraid the unaccustomed liquor would make her sick.

He shrugged. "Maybe later."

While she struggled to recover her equilibrium, he reached into his back pocket and extracted a worn leather wallet. Slowly, almost as if he were intent on securing her full attention, he opened it and peeled some bills from an impressive stack. He tossed three of them on the counter. "I believe we have some business to take care of."

She stared at the bills and felt her pulse jerk and race. Involuntarily, she glanced at the bed in the far corner.

He saw the direction of her gaze and laughed sardonically. "Not yet, little Lola. I have a lot of money to spend, and I plan to take my time."

The threat in his voice was unmistakable. The part of her that was feminine, vulnerable, quivered in a mixture of dread and anticipation. She reached for some of her customary spunk. "So tell me, cowboy. What do I call *you*?"

He stood up and stretched, towering over her. He bent his head to whisper in her ear, his breath tickling the tendrils of hair at her neck. "You can call me sir."

Sebastian stepped away from the bar, shoving his hands in his pockets to keep from reaching for her. He had to be careful not to overplay his hand. For a minute there she looked like she might faint. Right now she was staring at him with wariness combined with what he hoped like hell was sexual curiosity.

He nodded toward the three hundreds. "Pick them up and tuck them in your top."

She did as he commanded.

"Now get up on stage."

Her eyebrows rose. "The stage?"

"Yeah," he said, enjoying her discomfiture. "You're going to strip for me. Stand up, Lola."

She rose to her feet, swaying, her face suddenly pale. But she didn't protest.

He pointed to the back of the room, not saying anything, curious to see if she would balk.

She walked gracefully, seemingly comfortable with the high heels that completed her ensemble. The pale globes of her ass peeked out from beneath the ruffled bottom of the merry widow. He rubbed his aching cock and followed her, plopping into a chair just in front of the coming entertainment.

As she stepped up onto the stage, his heart stopped. The damned panties were crotchless. His chin dropped to his chest and he breathed deeply, having a heated argument with his libido. This was Rebecca's night, and he was determined to make it the most incredible, sexual, no-holds-barred, deeply carnal experience of her life.

She stood in front of him, her arms by her sides, so close he could see the faint shadow of hair at the apex of her thighs. She shifted from one foot to another. "Seb—" She stopped. "Sir?"

He lifted his head and reached for a disc, inserting it into the CD player. Heavy, pulsing music filled the air, definitely not from the Old West. More like something from a French porn flick.

He cleared his throat, wishing for water. "Dance for me, Lola . . . and then take off your clothes."

Her eyes were glassy, her skin completely pale. He sensed she had disappeared into a place inside herself, and he hated the distance between them. But he sure as hell wasn't going to interrupt her performance with complaints.

She began to move to the music, awkward at first, and then with more grace and style. Her eyelids drifted shut, and she swayed sensually, her arms reaching above her head as she turned and whirled, playing with the boa. The beat of the music intensified, and Rebecca hesitantly touched her breasts, her fingertips stroking their curves gently.

He nearly came out of the chair. Her lips parted slightly, and a lock of her hair escaped its confinement to tumble across her collarbone. When she lowered gracefully into a squatting position, every last one of her feminine secrets went on display just for him. He absorbed the sight of her, the moist folds glistening with arousal.

Her hands drifted between her thighs, a single finger making the journey where his straining penis ached to be. Just then she opened her eyes and looked at him, her hunger undisguised. He gripped the arms of his chair until his knuckles were white, the temptation almost unendurable.

"Holy shit." He lapsed out of character for a single moment, and then with grim determination remembered that he was in control. Always.

He leaned back, a look of boredom on his face. "Nice pussy. Any chance it's still tight?"

Temper brought brilliant color to her cheekbones. She hissed, she actually hissed. The sound made the hair stand up on the back of his neck. He swallowed. "Enough dancing," he growled. "Ditch the clothes, sweetheart." He made the endearment sound like a slur.

She straightened abruptly, and then turned away from him and bent from the waist to grasp her ankles. It was a damned good thing she couldn't see his face. He watched, mesmerized, as she slid her fingers up her thighs and began to unfasten the hose from the garter belt.

She straightened once more and kicked off her shoes, the force of her anger sending them tumbling across the stage. She shimmied one stocking down her leg and tugged it free, repeating the sequence with the opposite leg—and then she turned to face him.

Her bare feet emphasized her youth and innocence, and his heart contracted. He maintained his pose with difficulty. "You're not finished." He tossed another hundred on the stage. "Speed it up."

He watched as she battled a very clear urge to walk away. For long seconds he wondered if their evening hung in the balance. And then a tiny smile appeared on her face. Her hands went to a row of hooks and eyes hidden in the lace that ran from collarbone to crotch.

She opened them one at a time, gradually exposing inch after inch of creamy, unblemished skin. His mouth dried. The edges of the costume fell back, revealing her breasts, until only a single hook held it together.

She looked up, her face flushed. "More money, cowboy."

He scrambled for his wallet, pulling out a wad of cash and tossing it at her feet. "That's cowboy 'sir,' to you," he muttered sullenly.

She just grinned, and with a flourish unhooked the last of the tiny fasteners. The merry widow tumbled to the floor, hundred-dollar bills fluttering in its wake, leaving Rebecca clad in nothing but a transparent pair of tiny, tempting, crotchless, black-lace panties.

He felt his fingers go numb and wondered what would happen if he hyperventilated. He stood up and slapped off the CD player, determined to act like a man. The resulting silence resonated with tension. Her thumbs slipped beneath the elastic of the panties, but he stopped her with a chopping motion of his hand. "Keep them on," he growled. He stalked to the corner where she had changed clothes and snatched up a red silk robe from behind the screen.

"Put this on," he said, pausing only long enough for her to comply before snatching her against his chest and capturing her mouth in a punishing kiss. She tasted like whiskey and Crest. His head spun. He cupped her ass and lifted her, groaning when her legs wrapped around his waist.

They ravaged each other, breathless, driven. He sensed his control slipping irrevocably away, and it scared him. Badly. He gulped in great lungfuls of air, peeling her away from his body. Ignoring her whimper of protest. With herculean effort, he set her away from him, deliberately stepping back from the dark edge of obsession.

He summoned a smile. "We could screw now, but I think we'd be cheating ourselves."

"I can live with that," she muttered, disgruntled.

His smile was easy, hopefully hiding the churning disquiet in his gut. "Give me a chance," he cajoled. "Let's finish the game."

She huffed, a delightfully feminine sound that turned his smile into the real thing. He felt a shift in his universe, an unsettling, possibly life-altering realignment of his personal planetary orbits. His lust didn't fade even a millimeter, but he felt changed somehow, his feelings for this delightful woman new and compelling.

He held out his hand and she took it, their fingers twining comfortably. "Are we okay?"

She nodded slowly, her eyes glowing. She reached up on tiptoe and kissed his cheek. "I'm having fun, sir."

He slapped her bottom, making her squeal. "In that case, let's get back to business."

She looked down at her robe, a rueful frown on her face. "Unfortunately, cowboy, this sexy little number you gave me is short on pockets."

"I'll think of something," he promised.

He took off his hat and tossed it on the bar. Then he pulled out the billfold once more and extracted seven hundred dollars. Her eyes widened.

He walked toward her, smothering a grin when she stepped backward. He reached out and stuffed the money in her panties, his fingers brushing her intimately. And just that quickly, the game was back on.

She nibbled her lip. "What is this for?"

He pointed to the tub, feeling a kick of excitement when she trembled. "We'll start with a shave and go from there," he said quietly.

And then it was his turn to strip. He ripped off the shirt and vest in one move, watching her reaction. He sat in a chair to remove his boots and then thought better of it. He crooked a finger. "I think this is your job."

She knelt at his feet, her head bowed as she wrestled with the stiff leather cowboy boots. His legs were spread wide, her head between his thighs. He gritted his teeth. She finally succeeded in freeing his feet and looked up at him, her expression suitably submissive.

He stood up and unbuttoned his fly. His hands moved slowly. She watched him, her expression intent. When he stepped out of the jeans and shucked off his drawers, her mouth dropped. He put his hands on his hips and swaggered. "You looked pretty shocked for a hooker." His voice mocked her.

She rose to her feet and wrapped her arms around her

waist, her posture defensive. "I've seen plenty of those."
She looked down at his cock. "Yours is nothing special."

He knew she was playing the game, but her words stung
his pride. "Is that so?" He held his cock and stroked it from
base to tip, watching her watch him. "I guess that remains
to be seen."

He ignored her then, and after testing the bath water
with his hand, stepped into the huge tub. The temperature
was perfect. He positioned a washcloth on the back rim and
stretched out, his head resting on the tub, his knees raised.
"Shave me, woman."

Rebecca watched him for long seconds, enjoying the picture he made. His arms hung loosely over the sides of the
tub, and his face in repose was less intimidating. His tanned
skin was shiny and wet, his broad, hair-covered chest mus-
cular. That part of him he had flaunted so shamelessly was
safely buried beneath the water.

He opened one eye, a frown on his face. "Lola."

"Sorry," she said, hurrying forward to kneel beside him.
She picked up a cup of shave foam and a wicked looking
straight razor. "Seb—sir?"

He opened both eyes. "What?"

She waved the razor. "This is really sharp. Are you sure
we should try this?"

He scratched his chin, scowling. "I don't think I asked
for your opinion. I paid my money. Now give me the damn
shave."

For a moment she almost laughed. He was really good at
playing the irascible SOB. It was so foreign to the real
Sebastian Tennant, but then again, perhaps she had only
scratched the surface of who he was.

She dumped a dollop of foam into her hand and patted his
cheek. His skin was shockingly warm. She smeared slowly,
using her fingertips to smooth around his ears and nose and
lips. His eyes were closed, his lashes long and thick.

When his lower face was covered, she picked up the blade. It was a far cry from a lady's safety razor. With exquisite care, she scraped gently from his right ear down across his cheek to his chin. He didn't move, didn't even flinch.

She tested the bared skin with her finger. It was smooth as the proverbial baby's bottom. Emboldened, she repeated the process, revealing his beautiful sculpted cheekbones and masculine chin a bit at a time. When she was finished, she took a fresh cloth, dampened it, and cleaned away any lingering traces of foam.

He was motionless, perhaps sleeping.

She whispered, "Sir, I'm finished."

This time he didn't open his eyes. His lips moved, his voice rough and gravelly. "Bathe me."

Her nipples tightened at the blunt command. She soaped up a cloth and timidly began rubbing his chest. She paid close attention to his collarbones and worked downward, stopping just below the water line.

"Sit up," she muttered.

He did so, the resultant tidal wave almost sweeping over the side of the tub. His eyes were still closed, and he slumped forward, his head bent. More soap, more rubbing. Her hands lingered over the smooth, hard planes of his back. She was drunk on his masculine perfection, relishing his passive state.

Moments later, she pressed him back to his reclining position and began on his legs. She had to lean far over the side of the tub to reach his feet, and her robe got wet. Impatiently she tugged it off, returning quickly to her task. The hard metal edge of the tub pressed into the sensitive flesh of her breasts.

As she stroked up his thighs, he groaned, a deep, almost anguished sound. She paused and he grasped her hand, urging her on. Finally there was nothing left to wash but that area she had been avoiding.

She sensed he was near the edge, and the burst of feminine power she felt flooded her entire body with knife-sharp pleasure. She dropped the rag and rocked back on her heels.

He opened his eyes, annoyed. "You're not done."

She met his gaze bravely, cupping her breasts with deliberate sensuality. "That will be extra," she pouted.

His stare was hot enough to make the water boil. "Two hundred more. That's it."

She reached for the discarded jeans and fished out the billfold, giving him an unobstructed view of her ass. She pulled out the bills, tucked them in her panties, and got back to work. Despite her bravado, touching him intimately scared her. He was huge, and so thick and long, she wondered almost hysterically how she had taken him earlier.

She soaped him slowly, one hand cupping his balls. When his cock was finished, she used gentle circles to cleanse his balls. His eyes were tightly shut, his face creased with pain or pleasure, or both.

Touching him inflamed her senses almost unbearably. She didn't think she could stand much more. She was hungry for the main event.

She stood up and dried off, watching spellbound as she saw him follow suit. Water sluiced down his body, tiny droplets catching in the hair at his groin. She had halfway expected him to demand she dry him, but he took care of the task himself.

Then they faced one another, his expression stern, only the color high on his cheekbones revealing his mood. "Hand me my wallet," he said quietly.

When she did, he opened it and pulled out the remaining bills, crumpling the impressive stack in his left hand. Unclothed, he was even more intimidating than the fully dressed cowboy. "Go turn down the bed."

She obeyed his request on shaking legs. As she folded the covers back and rearranged the pillows, she was vividly aware of him watching. He turned off the chandelier, plunging the room into semidarkness. When her task was finished, she turned and stood hesitantly at the foot of the bed, waiting.

He stalked toward her, every inch of him the hunter pursuing his quarry. A trickle of her earlier fear returned. She bit her lower lip and wished desperately she had kept the robe, wet or not. She cried out when he scooped her up and tossed her on the bed, then stretched out beside her, his hands gliding over her torso with insolent ownership.

She wasn't sure how a real hooker would act. Did she just let the man do what he wanted, or did she participate? When Sebastian's fingers slipped between her thighs and stroked with deliberate intent, making full use of the crotchless panties, she lost any ability to worry about playing a part. He skidded lightly over her clitoris, backed away to play with her damp curls, and then returned with a steady, firm stroke that sent her arching off the bed in a stunning climax.

Before she had time to recover fully, he forced her to her knees, grabbed a handful of hair at the back of her head, and waved an obscene amount of money in front of her face. "Take me in your mouth, Lola."

She was confused, shaking, still in the thrall of her orgasm, as he lay back, taking her with him. His grip was firm, unrelenting. He forced her to his groin, still damp from his bath. His erection throbbed, swollen and ready.

She opened her mouth, gasping as he forced the head of his penis between her lips. She widened her lips to accommodate his size and struggled to take more.

She heard him curse roughly, and his hand released her head and fell limply at his side. She licked with teasing, tiny strokes, feeling his trembling response. His entire, massive body was tensed in anticipation, his chest heaving with his labored breathing.

She nipped him carefully with her teeth, and then increased the pressure, sucking him slowly, feeling him harden and swell even more.

He was panting now, trembling, so close to losing control, she could see the struggle on his face. She released him abruptly and sat up, crossed her legs in a yoga position, and took a few more hundreds.

He stared at her, his eyes glazed with angry confusion.

She rubbed the bills over her breasts and then sniffed them. "You're running low on cash, cowboy."

"Damn you, Rebecca." His eyes glittered. "Fuck me—now."

She climbed astride him, her hair tumbling across his chest. She took him into her wet, aching passage a scant inch, and stopped, tormenting them both. Then she smiled. "My name is Lola."

Chapter Five

And just like that, he snapped. He shoved her off, rolling her beneath him. "Not like that. Not this time." Rage, passion, and something uncomfortably like fear gripped him. His vision was fuzzy at the edges, his mental capacity impaired. His body was in the driver's seat, not his brain, and he wanted to punish her for that inexcusable lapse. He entered her without preparation, roughly, needing to dominate.

Her shocked cry ate at him as he pounded into her, sweat sliding down his back. "I'll make you come," he ground out between frantic thrusts. "I'll make you want to die from the pleasure."

But he didn't. The suave, ultra-experienced, sexually gifted Sebastian Tennant was unable to take her with him to the edge, because his body betrayed him. With no small amount of despair, he felt his climax bearing down on him. He gave a great shout, his shoulders rigid, his neck taut, and then stinging, mind-numbing release swept through his veins. He pumped into her harder and harder, no longer able to know or care if she was responding.

Rebecca lay unmoving, afraid to rouse the sleeping tiger. Her senses were painfully alert. The smell of sex hovered in the air, and she and Sebastian lay sprawled amidst a collection of crumpled hundred-dollar bills. Most of the covers were on the floor.

Sebastian's considerable weight pinned her to the bed, making it difficult to breathe. She felt as though she had survived a tornado, torn apart, displaced. His fierce passion had first shocked, then aroused her.

She knew she had at last experienced the true Sebastian Tennant, and the experience had marked her for life. She also admitted—quietly, only to herself—that she loved him. How could she not? It would be like trying to sit too close to a fire and not be burned.

His power, his passion, his inventive sexual appetite, first playful, then deadly serious. She stroked a hand down his back, savoring her right to touch him. Now, as in the beginning, she wondered why she was here. What had possessed him to seduce her? What momentary aberration had caused him to pluck Rebecca Fraser from the pool of likely women and take her on a journey of erotic discovery?

She had no illusions about her own sex appeal. She was an attractive woman. She had offers. But she was not the type to keep Sebastian's interest for long. He had strong needs, not the least of which was a penchant for variety. So she would enjoy this while it lasted, and then leave before he could toss her out.

He stirred, rolling to his side, but keeping a heavy forearm clasped across her waist. She met his gaze shyly. He ran a hand through his hair, disheveling it further, giving him a youthful charm. His smile was lopsided, not quite reaching his eyes. "You okay?"

She nodded, mute.

He traced her nipples with a gentle fingernail, making desire curl once again in the pit of her belly. Her eyelids fluttered shut, her breath quickened.

"I'm sorry." His words were terse, uttered through a clenched jaw.

She stirred restively, eyes closed, needing him to concentrate on what he was doing. "For what?" she asked, her voice slurred, not really caring about his answer.

"Because I didn't wait for you to come." He said it as though he had beaten her or stolen her money.

She looked at him again, her hand resting against his nearest thigh, her back arching as he drew lazy circles on her hipbone. "I came a little while ago," she reminded him.

He flipped her onto her stomach, his hands wickedly busy. "It's not the same. I failed you."

She wanted to argue, to dispute his ridiculous statements, but her body took over. He reached beneath her and began teasing in earnest. One big hand rested on her bottom, while the other found, with unerring expertise, every last nerve ending begging for attention.

He lifted her to her knees, granting him better access. She moaned, her face nestled in a pile of lavender-scented pillows as his fingers probed, her eager flesh swollen and tender.

He entered her with his hand, and she caught her breath, sharp spears of sensation gripping her, making her weak. His free hand roamed over her bottom, lightly pinching first one cheek and then the other.

She pressed against his exploring fingers, shaking with need. Suddenly he grasped her hair and tugged her head up, forcing her to look at the mirror on the dresser beside the bed. The candle was still burning, barely more than a stub. In the flickering light she saw him move, and felt the relentless, demanding pressure of his fingers.

Her body began to shake, and still he forced her to watch. "Come for me, baby. Show me how hot you can be."

She screamed as he pinched her clitoris, and then whimpered on the knife edge of pleasure and pain when a climax hit her, more powerful and consuming than anything she had ever experienced. As she rode the first wave, he entered her from behind, his size stretching her, rubbing her almost unbearably sensitive inner flesh. She groaned in submission, lost in the fantasy, almost insensate.

He watched her come in the mirror and then allowed his own release, already planning how he would take her next. In the sudden silence, a tiny pinging noise caught his attention. "Well, damn it to hell and back." Their time was almost up. He himself had designed the quiet reminder that other guests were waiting.

For one long minute he debated revealing his identity to the manager, and offering the couple in question a free week's stay if they would pick another damn room. He looked down at his partner, and his heart turned over in his chest. She slept deeply, suddenly, like a baby. Lust surged again, and he shuddered, wondering about his own sanity.

Regret rode him hard, on many levels. He shook her shoulder. "Rebecca, sweetheart . . ."

She rolled over with a grumbling moan and flung an arm across her face. He laughed in spite of the fact that this moment felt damned serious.

"Come on, little hooker. My time's up—and I'm out of money."

She raised one eyelid and glared. "This had better be a joke."

He pointed at the antique mantel clock on the table. "Our time's up."

Understanding dawned, and she scrambled off the bed. "Hurry up, Sebastian. We've got to leave."

As she raced to the corner and retrieved her red dress, he watched her survey the wreckage of the room.

"Don't worry," he said, trying to erase the look of anxiety on her face. "There's time built in for cleaning."

In moments they were both decent again, albeit a bit the worse for wear. She eyed the stack of hundreds in his hand. "You get to keep that?"

He grinned wryly. "They charge it to the room."

She shook her head in amazement. "You thought of everything, I guess."

The little bell dinged once more, signaling their last call. Rebecca slipped on her shoes and took one last look at the room. Then she looked at him, her eyes such a dark blue they were almost black. "I'm ready to go."

He opened the door for her. She scuttled down the hall to their room like a guilty schoolgirl. He followed a few steps behind, trying not to laugh. She was damned adorable.

Back in their original quarters, awkwardness struck without warning. Rebecca halted in the center of the room, clearly not comfortable with approaching the bed, but unable to do anything else. He tucked the money in her purse and went to her, drawing her into a firm embrace, his heart jumping when she cuddled closer.

He buried his lips in her silky hair, marveling at how fragile she felt in his arms. Yet her spirit was strong, unquenchable. He tipped up her chin. "I want to make love to you again, Rebecca."

She quivered. "Well, I might be a little sore . . ."

Her words trailed off, as he walked her inexorably toward the bed. "I'll be careful," he promised, ignoring her halfhearted attempts to escape him.

"I don't think I can come again," she whispered, her voice agitated.

He tumbled both of them onto the mattress, his eager erection pressing against the vee of her legs. "Just relax," he murmured, nibbling her throat. "I'll take care of you."

He tried to spread her thighs, and laughed unsteadily when the dress hampered his efforts.

He looked down at her, her cheeks flushed, her eyes cloudy with desire. He took the neckline of the dress in his hands and, keeping his eyes locked on hers, ripped it from neck to hem.

Her pupils dilated. "That cost me three hundred dollars."

He lifted her like a doll, sliding her arms free of the straps. "I'll buy you another."

And then he set about taking her to a secret place where nothing existed but the excruciatingly pleasurable, nerve-tingling, completely uncontrollable demands of her sweet young body.

Rebecca lost track of how many times he made her come. He was tender but demanding, refusing to let her rest, mastering her body with a skill honed over years of bedding eager women. It was that last poignant thought that kept her focused, kept her sane. This was heaven, but it came with a price.

When they finally called it quits, sometime after 5 A.M., she watched, fascinated as he fell asleep almost instantly. The force of his personality dimmed as he slumbered, allowing her to carry out her plan. She was quiet as she found slacks and a shirt in her suitcase, but he slept so deeply, it probably didn't matter.

When she was dressed, hair brushed, belongings tucked away neatly, she gazed around the room and had to stuff a fist in her mouth to smother an involuntary sob.

He lay facedown in sensual abandon, the lines of his shoulders, back, and buttocks a picture waiting for an artist's brush. And the man inside was equally beautiful. His sharp intelligence and wit combined with his unselfconscious, tough masculinity added up to a man of incomparable worth.

She dropped the brief note she'd written on a table by the door, stealing one last glance at him before slipping silently away.

Sebastian woke with a pounding headache, but assorted more pleasurable aches in other regions of his body. Gradually, memories of the night before filtered into his consciousness. He reached for Rebecca, and froze in disbelief when he encountered empty sheets.

"What the hell?"

He leaped to his feet, pausing momentarily as the room spun dizzily. He had a head for alcohol, but the sexual excess of the night before was something else again.

He stumbled to the bathroom, promising himself she was there, sure of it. The luxurious room was empty, as empty as the pit of his stomach. He jerked open the drawers and closets, clumsy in his haste, but his nasty suspicions were real. She was gone.

He dropped to the bed, his elbows on his knees, his head buried in his hands. He felt sick, couldn't process the unbelievable information. What had he done to drive her away? Without volition, his mind began replaying scenes from their lovemaking, each one more erotic than the last.

His ever hopeful cock hardened in eager anticipation, leaving him to curse in anguish as his hunger raged unabated, and his love raked him raw. Rebecca was gone. He gazed bleakly toward the door, willing her to reappear. And then he saw the slip of paper, flanked by a neatly stacked pile of hundred-dollar bills.

He unfolded it with shaking hands, and read the brief message:

Thank you, Sebastian, for the magic. I will never forget our time together. Your secrets are safe with me. Fondly, Rebecca.

He crushed the note in sudden rage. Fondly? What in the hell was *fondly*? He'd turned her inside out, given her more of himself than he had given to any other woman, ever. And she'd had the temerity to walk away.

His lips thinned and his shoulders straightened. She clearly didn't understand the big picture. She was his now, no arguments, and he would do whatever it took to convince her of that—just as soon as he came up with a plan.

* * *

Rebecca returned to work Monday, only to find herself fired when she refused to write even the most innocuous article about the Scimitar. Her boss threatened and blustered, but nothing he said could even dent the careful shell she had constructed around her dangerously fragile emotions.

She got online and checked her savings and checking balances, calculating that she could exist frugally for about ten or twelve weeks while job hunting. The problem was, she had no idea what she wanted to do.

Her earlier desire to prove herself at the magazine now seemed immature, juvenile. She was a good writer. There were other choices out there.

Tuesday she bought a paper and went through the want ads, circling possibilities. Perhaps she should change her focus entirely, explore new opportunities.

When her doorbell rang around five o'clock that evening, she opened it automatically, holding the cash and tip for the pizza delivery boy.

Sebastian glanced down at the money and smiled, a nasty smile that made her sweat. He pushed his way in, not waiting for an invitation. "I think I'm the one who's supposed to pay for sexual favors, not you, Rebecca."

He was dressed as he had been at their first meeting, his elegant attire making her bare feet, ancient T-shirt, and jeans embarrassing, despite the fact that she was in her own home. Already she felt at a disadvantage.

She wasn't entirely surprised to see him. Sebastian was a man of great pride, and she had acted with unforgivable rudeness. She waved a hand. "Have a seat. I'll make coffee."

Suddenly the doorbell rang again, and this time it really was the pizza boy. As she settled up with him and set the fragrant box on the table near the door, she was aware of Sebastian prowling around her modest apartment, pausing now and then to pick up a figurine or a photo.

When she closed the door, she gestured to the steaming

box. "You want something to eat?" It was a polite question, not a real invitation.

He nodded, slipping off his jacket and making himself comfortable on her worn sofa. He cocked an eyebrow, reacting to her surprise. "Is it so hard to believe that I might want to share a pizza with you?"

She shrugged uneasily, rubbing her arms. "I don't really see Sebastian Tennant as a pizza sort of guy."

His face darkened, his eyes stormy. "I would have thought you knew me a little better by now."

Was she imagining a fleeting note of hurt in his voice? She ignored his loaded comment, escaping into the kitchen for plates and glasses. Alone, she would have settled for a soft drink. But what could she serve Sebastian?

She rummaged to the back of the fridge and found a beer left over from a neighborhood get-together. She examined it doubtfully, wondering if beer had an expiration date. She did have some wine, but at $3.99 a bottle, she guessed that the beer might be the better choice.

She loaded the stuff on a tray, and returned to the living room, wondering how quickly she could get rid of him. Having him here, dwarfing her small apartment, threatened to pick away at her carefully constructed calm.

She smiled cheerfully, her jaw tight with the effort. "Here we go. Dig in."

They ate in silence for several long minutes, the tension in the room increasing steadily. Just watching him chew and swallow, seeing his long elegant fingers holding the pizza slices, made her want to drag him to the floor and jump his bones.

They both sat on the sofa, but the box kept a safe distance between them. Sebastian finished off his third piece and wiped his hands. He leaned back, as far as she could tell, completely at ease. His conservative white shirt was tucked into the waistband of dark slacks, his abdomen taut and flat.

She refused to look any lower. She cleared her throat. "Why are you here, Sebastian?"

He reached into the pocket of his jacket and drew out a stack of bills, tossing them carelessly into her lap. His smile wasn't pleasant. "You forgot your money."

She shoved it to the floor, scowling. "It was just a game. I'm not taking your money."

His iron control slipped momentarily and she saw the depth of his anger. He sneered. "You earned it, sweetheart. You were fabulous." He uttered the compliments with a total disregard for sincerity, making them sound like the insults they were meant to be.

She bristled. "It was your idea to go to the hotel. You could have just told me no from the beginning."

His lips tightened. "I was under the mistaken assumption that you might enjoy my company for a weekend—but clearly I was wrong."

She sighed deeply, unable to fight when she loved him so damned much. "Don't be an ass, Sebastian. You were great. We were great. What more do you want me to say?"

He stood and paced, his stance betraying his agitation. "I want to know why you left."

His quiet words pierced her heart. He was deliberately making himself vulnerable, letting her see that it mattered, that she mattered. She had hoped to evade a confrontation, but she should have known better. Sebastian Tennant wasn't the type to let well enough alone.

She clasped her hands in her lap to still their trembling. She looked at him, debating how much of the truth to share. He stared at her, waiting for her response.

In the end she settled for a half truth. "I needed to leave. Things were getting pretty intense. You're a very attractive man, and I didn't want to lose my perspective. I don't have your experience."

He frowned. "So you were upset because I have more experience than you have?"

She shook her head. "You're being deliberately obtuse."

He cursed. "Well, hell, Rebecca. Don't sugarcoat it. I didn't realize you had such a high opinion of me."

She cringed at the animosity in his voice. This wasn't going well. She tried again. "The thing is, Sebastian, I don't ... I didn't want ..."

He knelt at her feet suddenly, startling her, taking her icy hand in his and warming them. "What, Rebecca? What was it you didn't want?"

His deep brown eyes were shadowed with emotion, lines of strain around his mouth a testament to how deeply she had hurt him. She bowed her head in defeat, leaning forward until their foreheads were touching. "I didn't want to fall in love with you."

He froze, his shoulders rigid, his hands clenching hers so tightly her fingers began to go numb. He released her hands to cup her cheeks. "But what if I fell in love with you?" he asked huskily.

She quivered helplessly, seduced once again by the touch of his hands, the timbre of his sexy voice. She wiggled free and retreated to the other side of the room, desperate to believe, but clinging to a healthy instinct for self-preservation. "What do you mean?"

He laughed softly. "It's not that complicated, Rebecca. I'm in love with you. I want to marry you."

He said it bluntly, without adornment. Even so, the words hit her at her weakest spot, flooding her chest with warmth, making her yearn for miracles.

She held grimly to her resolve. "I'm flattered, Sebastian, honestly, but I imagine any residual feelings from this past weekend are based more on sex than on love."

He grimaced. "I'm thirty-four years old. I think I know the difference."

Her teeth dug deeply into her bottom lip as she tried to make him understand. "We wouldn't work, Sebastian. You're you and I'm me. I'm not one of your usual women."

"Exactly." The quiet satisfaction in his voice jolted her, undermined her determination.

He crossed to where she stood, and held her waist, his fingers burning through the fabric of her T-shirt. "I'll make you a deal," he said huskily. "Go to bed with me right here, right now, and afterwards if you can tell me it was just sex and not love, I'll leave and never bother you again."

He kissed her passionately, not waiting for assent or refusal. It was a moot point anyway. Clearly, he had only to do that little thing with his tongue, and she would dissolve in his arms.

He held her carefully, as though anticipating a retreat on her part. She leaned into his warmth and strength, not afraid to be alone, but so much more a woman in his embrace.

"Yes," she whispered against his insistent mouth. "I want you."

She led him to the bedroom, swamped with conflicting emotions—love, fear, a heavy sense of doom. She closed the drapes and looked around, mildly surprised to find the room was neat. She wasn't the best housekeeper.

He stood quietly, allowing her to make the first move. She shrugged, feeling miserably unsophisticated. Having sex at the hotel was a romantic fantasy. Having sex on discount store sheets in her tiny bedroom with water spots on the ceiling was something else again.

He smiled whimsically. "Tell me what you want, Rebecca."

"I want you to be in charge," she blurted out with appalling honesty.

He took her gauche outburst seriously. "Okay," he said slowly, a tiny frown creasing his forehead. "Just as long as you know it won't always be like that. Friday night was a game. But I might be inclined to trade places on occasion."

She flushed as she gleaned his meaning. The thought of having Sebastian at the mercy of her sexual commands was wickedly appealing. He picked her up gently and lowered her to the bed in one smooth motion. She closed her mind to the evidence of his expertise.

He began to undress her, his face intent, his hands unhurried. He murmured his approval to see she wasn't wearing a bra beneath her T-shirt. He lifted her hips and peeled away her jeans, his fingers leaving streaks of heat every time he brushed her bare skin.

When her panties disappeared over his shoulder, she resisted the urge to cover herself. She let him look his fill, his eyes hot and eager. His own clothes vanished more rapidly, and she couldn't quite suppress a moan of appreciation as his boxers went the way of her panties. Lord, the man was gorgeous.

He rejoined her and began to relearn the contours of her body. She closed her eyes, unable to watch his hands on her skin. She was already trembling, unbelievably on the brink of orgasm. He handled her with infinite care, his hands gentle, worshipful.

When he spread her legs and entered her, a keening cry escaped her lips. He lifted her arms over her head, holding her wrists in his left hand as he stroked her breasts with the other. He moved slowly, making her writhe beneath him, denying them both release.

It was completely different from their fantasy love play at the Scimitar. This was straight, conventional, missionary position intercourse. Which didn't explain why her body was humming with erotic pleasure, ready to explode with the slightest encouragement.

He stroked a tentative finger over her eyes, ruffling her lashes. "Look at me, sweetheart."

She obeyed, resenting his control. She glared at him. "Is this some kind of damned contest? If it is, I give up, you win." She wriggled her hips, trying to force him deeper. "Just don't stop now," she whispered, unable to mask the pleading in her voice.

He was tense, ready to find his release. She knew it. But

he only smiled, his face filled with warmth and what looked suspiciously like amused affection. He brushed her lips with a barely there, butterfly kiss. "I love you, little Lola. I swear I do."

He let go of her wrists and rested his weight on his forearms, leaving him the freedom to sink his teeth teasingly into the soft flesh below her ear. She gasped as he moved his hips at the same time, sliding in and out, waiting for her to match his rhythm.

He grunted, burying himself to the hilt and groaning as her inner muscles gripped him. "Tell me you believe me."

She remained silent, her heart breaking.

He withdrew almost completely, threatening to break the physical connection that was their only real link. "Tell me, dammit."

She panted. "I believe you love me at this moment, Sebastian."

He tried to stop, he really did. But the driving urgency to possess her took precedence over their verbal battle. He changed angles, putting pressure where it mattered. He felt the beginnings of her climax and gave up the fight, thrusting harder and deeper as his body claimed its release.

In the aftermath, the ragged tenor of their breathing was the only sound in the room. He brushed her hair from her forehead, his face troubled. "Why is it so hard to believe, honey?"

She found it difficult to carry on a conversation when their bodies were still joined. She shoved him off, and he allowed it, watching as she escaped to the bathroom to clean up.

She returned, wearing her most ratty, non-sexy bathrobe. She grimaced, denting his ego. "Please go, Sebastian. I don't have anything else to say."

He scooted up and leaned against her headboard. "Not until you tell me why you can't believe me."

She stared at the floor, realizing that her pride was about to go the way of her virtue. "I know you'll get tired of me and move on to someone else."

"Damn, you're stupid."

His blunt comment shocked her. "Hey, that wasn't very nice." Her lips trembled, tears spurting to her eyes.

With a long-suffering sigh he clambered from the bed and grabbed her around the waist, hoisting her over his shoulder and dumping her in the pile of rumpled covers. He sat beside her, stroking her arm. "How many women do you think I've proposed to, Rebecca?"

She shrugged, her expression mulish. "I don't care."

"One," he said softly. "Including you."

"You're infatuated, thinking with your cock."

He chuckled. "Well, that last part is probably true," he admitted, grinning. "But I know what I feel. I love you."

"I'm afraid. I'm young and naive and you're . . . sophisticated."

He wiped his brow with mock relief. "I was hoping you weren't going to say old and cynical."

His gentle teasing made her want to weep. "You're not taking me seriously," she wailed.

He reached for his pants on the floor. "Maybe this will convince you."

He handed her a sheaf of papers, helping her sit up as she studied them.

She rifled through the lot, reading a paragraph here and there. "I don't understand."

He shrugged, his face rueful. "It's the deed to the Scimitar. I'm giving it to you—the hotel, and my heart. I trust you to keep them both safe."

"My god." She looked from the papers to his face, and back again. "You really mean it."

He nodded. "Yes. And I'm known for never changing my mind."

She started to laugh, a bubbling joy spreading through her veins. "Well, in that case, cowboy, call them up and tell them we want Suite Thirteen taken off the market."

He pushed her back, the papers forgotten. "Whatever you say, ma'am. You're the boss."

Voices Carry

Morgan Leigh

To Mom: my hero.
Dad: I miss you every day.
My family: Thank you for the love and support.
To my very special circle of friends:
Thanks for the push . . . and the closet.
And to Lori Foster and Kate Duffy:
Thanks for the invitation to "The Show."

Chapter One

"How am I going to do this work here?" Camelot Reeve muttered to herself as she looked at the cassette tapes lying on her desk. More and more work was coming her way lately because her performance was exemplary. She wondered how she'd gotten herself into this predicament, and then she closed her eyes, shaking her head. She knew *exactly* how, but just couldn't believe her stupid luck, or rather, her lack of it.

She'd signed on with the law offices of McCauley, Parrish, and Hawke two months ago as an assistant's secretary, and Camelot was told that she'd mostly be doing final preps of documents, but occasionally she'd be taking dictation, transcribing, and perhaps sitting in on meetings when Barbara, her direct supervisor, was busy with other assignments. There was plenty of work to do, and she was chosen because she was an ace in the secretarial field. They needed her.

What Camelot got in return for her expertise, besides a good paycheck, was a very unhealthy addiction to the voice of one of the partners. And he just happened to be her new boss: Jonah McCauley. Every time she heard his deep tenor, it was like being wrapped in a warm blanket, her nerve endings and senses caressed and stroked until her skin felt raw with arousal.

It would have been fine if she'd heard Mr. McCauley speak *before* lobbying so vigorously for the position. She would've known that taking his dictation, or other assignments that required she listen to his voice, wasn't such a good idea. If they insisted that those things were part of her job description, then she could've bowed out gracefully, declining the position when they offered it.

But after interviewing with Barbara Dimera, Mr. McCauley's personal assistant, Camelot had liked the woman immensely, and had knocked Barb's socks off with her skills to get the position. Unfortunately, Mr. McCauley didn't enter the picture until her first day on the job. She felt that pull at the moment of their introduction, but she shook it off, attributing it to nerves and being a part of such a prestigious firm.

Now she was stuck. She'd painted herself into a corner that she just couldn't get out of without leaving a bad impression of her character and a permanent stain on her performance record. That wasn't something she was willing to do.

It shouldn't have been a problem, really, Camelot mused. She knew that if something wasn't good for her, then she should simply avoid it. She'd just decline any assignments where she had to listen to that sensual voice hum in her ears, creating an inferno every time she donned her headset. She'd do all the other grunt work, but refuse to do that one thing. Right?

Wrong.

Her boss was the senior partner at the firm, and what Jonah McCauley wanted, Jonah McCauley got. She was hired because she was the cream of the crop in secretarial work, and because no one else could manage the demands that would be placed on the assistant's secretary. Camelot shook her head. While she took great pride in the reputation she'd fought hard to build, sometimes being the best really sucked.

Heaving a sigh, she stared defiantly at the note Mr.

McCauley had attached to the tapes, stating that the assignment be completed by open of business tomorrow. Her eyes slid to the clock on the bottom of her computer screen. It was almost quitting time anyway; she'd sneak them home and suffer her odd obsession in private. Her body had already begun to burn, imagining what his voice would do to her once she put those tapes in her stereo and began transcribing.

No one except Mr. McCauley, Barbara, and Camelot herself knew what her assignments were each day. That was one of the perks of being the boss's Girl Friday: no one peeked over her shoulder to see that she was doing her job. As long as it was completed on time, she wasn't a concern to the powers that be. *A good thing, too!* she thought.

Camelot was pretty sure that taking confidential documents or files out of the office was a huge no-no, but she wouldn't bother to ask. She'd claim that she was ignorant of the rules if anyone happened to catch her. The documents she'd signed when she was hired didn't say anything about not taking work home . . . she didn't think. With the credentials she brought to the job, she should know better, but it had never come up. And if Barb or Mr. McCauley asked her why she wasn't staying late at the office to complete the reports—well, that didn't even bear thinking about! While they'd be thinking corporate espionage, she'd be mortified if they learned the truth. She could imagine them looking up a similar case in the tomes of the law books all over the building. But she was virtually positive that "sexual arousal by voice" *wasn't* a defense this state had ever had presented in court.

She slid the cover over her computer and closed the smaller laptop, locking it securely in her desk drawer. She had her own PC at her apartment, thank God, so there was nothing to taking work home discreetly. The tapes were all she needed, really. She slipped them into her leather briefcase and snapped off the small lamp as she left her cubicle.

Waving good night to the others in the secretarial pool, she made her way out of the office and into the lobby.

Camelot gave a distracted grin to nameless associates as they passed; the lure of her boss's voice was forgotten as she walked along the corridor. She'd been so enthusiastic this morning to wear her new shoes to work, but now, hours later, her feet were swollen and each step felt heavier than the last. They pinched in spots and she felt like she was walking on shards of glass.

Before she'd even left her cubicle, Camelot had determined that she was ducking into the ladies' room when she got to the ground floor, taking off her shoes and hose, and walking home barefoot. It was only a three-block trek to her studio apartment; she'd be able to walk without the agony she'd been in since nine A.M. Every minute she remained standing was torture.

She waited at the bank of elevators for one of the many doors to slide open and take her down. Impatience gnawed at her, but tapping a foot in annoyance would only send needles of pain shooting up her legs, so she gritted her teeth and endured the wait. One thing was for certain: she didn't care if the next elevator was stuffed to capacity, she was boarding it. So what if the car dropped from excess weight and she plummeted to her death? *At least I'll be off my feet*, she thought.

At the ping, she turned as the doors to the executive elevator opened and let two men in suits out. Camelot bit her lip and looked around, considering. She wasn't supposed to use that one; it was reserved for the executives and clients. But then she snickered to herself. A minute ago she'd been willing to risk free-falling to her death to get to the ground floor; getting the boot didn't seem significant in comparison. With a decisive shrug, she hurried to get on before the doors could slide closed without her.

It was cramped inside the small space, but she couldn't care less. Silently cheering when the elevator began its descent, she inwardly groaned, realizing that they were nine stories up, and damned if it didn't stop at every floor! Execs and lawyers scrambled to get through the crowd at each stop, but thankfully, no others got on.

She was jostled and nudged, poked with briefcases and the elbows of men speaking into cell phones. She wasn't sure, but at least once she thought she felt a hand sweep across her bottom when one man or another edged past her to exit. She was beyond feeling indignant. A little sexual harassment was a small price to pay for her liberation from the atrocity some Italian designer called High Fashion.

She was squished against the wall, but as more and more suits got off, the elevator finally cleared enough for her to breathe and take in the opulence of the space. The walls and doors of the elevator reserved for the higher-ups were gold-plated and reflective. If she were an executive, she imagined her morning prep time could be cut in half by doing her makeup in here on her way to the office. She knew she wouldn't really dare such a thing, but the thought of it made her grin.

Turning toward the shiny wall, she smirked at the absurdity of the occupants behind her; they faced front like toy soldiers in business attire of muted gray and black. Camelot ducked her head, trying to appear as inconspicuous as possible, though the assault to her posterior was proof that she hadn't gone unnoticed. But she'd rather not be called on the carpet for illegally hitching a ride.

Speaking of carpets, the floor was covered with a plush fleur-de-lis design in blue and white, and she was sure it had extra padding underneath. When she stepped into the elevator, her narrow heels dug into the thick pile; she sank into its richness like stepping on soft earth.

Absconding with confidential documents, utilizing the executive elevator. Those were two rules she'd already thrown out the window. Could the shirt and shoes policy really matter that much? Camelot hesitated for a split second, but the urge to slip off the strappy shoes was too appealing. *Ah, well. In for a penny, in for a pound*, she thought, and stepped out of them.

Standing on tiptoes, she lowered her feet by degrees into the lushness that covered the floor. The simple pleasure of it was ecstasy, and her eyes closed as she gripped the rail for support. It made her think of sex, or more accurately, that feeling of buoyancy that comes when tumbling over the edge in explosive climax.

Camelot tried to deny the comparison. She didn't want to think about sex right now, but the relief felt so good, sex was the only thing that even came close to this euphoria.

She opened her eyes and her heart skipped a beat, then tripped over itself, trying to catch up. In the reflection of the gold wall, her eyes locked on the shrewd green ones of Jonah McCauley as he stood at the opposite end of the car. They were the only occupants left now, and he focused on her with the intensity of a predator stalking his prey.

And Camelot, unlike other self-respecting creatures about to be devoured, stood frozen in his riveting gaze.

She needed to flee, but where would she go? He had his thumb pressed on the STOP button; the only muscle he moved was the one that leaped in his cheek. He simply . . . watched her. His tall, lithe frame was rigid but calm, and though he remained where he was, Camelot instinctively knew that if she so much as blinked, she'd see firsthand just how fast that powerful body could lunge with catlike grace.

A stirring began in her belly, quickly branching out and engulfing her in a heat that raced to all the right places. Her nipples stiffened and a pulsing throb concentrated at the juncture of her thighs.

His face was hard with restraint, and raw hunger burned in his eyes. He held her captive with just a look, one that brought every erotic thought she'd had of him to the forefront of her mind. Like a startled doe, she was mesmerized, remaining stock-still. She couldn't break away from the force of that stare if they *were* plummeting to the bottom of the elevator shaft!

Why did it have to be this *man?* she thought miserably. *Please, please don't let him speak,* she prayed. If he said even one word, in the state she was in, Camelot knew she couldn't be responsible for whatever followed.

Sizzling, lusty sex here in the corporate elevator was a reckless thought, but once it took hold, it wouldn't let her go.

Neither she nor Jonah blinked, but his eyes hunted her, and as he watched, she waited.

Her pounding heartbeat echoed through her ears, dulling her ability to distinguish what was real and what her mind conjured up. She didn't understand it, but she couldn't break away from the heat of his eyes to ponder it. She couldn't stop what was happening, either. It was as if the figments of their imaginations were one thought, and as real as a physical touch. In the depths of their unwavering honed link, Camelot sensed that they'd gone to a place where thirsts would be quenched, clawing hungers, fed.

This transformation that was so familiar to her now took over. She went from quiet and poised law secretary to needy sexual being under his hard stare. Too late, she realized that it wasn't merely his voice that set her off. It was Jonah himself, his spicy scent, his body, his masculinity, everything. That scared her even more than the things she'd been doing to appease the ache.

Her vision blurred except for her pinpoint focus on his eyes, the overpowering attraction driving all other thoughts far from her mind. Her dreams swept her away and she went with the tide, unable to veer off the collision course they were on.

Her body hummed with excitement. The erotic delights she'd pictured a thousand times with Jonah McCauley came to life before her very eyes.

*   *   *

When Jonah caught the flash of color as she entered the elevator, he turned his head, and clenched his jaw against the rush of adrenaline he felt when he realized it was Ms. Reeve, his personal assistant's secretary. He'd recognize that fiery red hair anywhere. *Damn! Why did it have to be her?*

She bowed her head as if trying to make herself invisible in the cramped space. She knew she wasn't allowed on this elevator, but he wouldn't discipline her for it. He couldn't. He didn't want anything to do with that woman. She had a way of making his gut tighten and his cock stir to a painful erection whenever he saw her. Like now.

But as the senior partner, Jonah made it clear that neither he, Sam nor Elliot date anyone within the firm. Company liaisons rarely worked, and he didn't want to lose good people because of a romance gone sour.

Despite his resolve, Jonah couldn't dictate his physical reactions to her.

He recalled their ten-minute meeting two months ago, when his assistant hired her, and that was when he knew this one was trouble. He'd taken her hand in his to welcome her to the firm and he'd felt a jolt, like a shock, but charged with an energy that awoke every sexual need in him. It was all he could do to sound unaffected by her touch, though his cock throbbed painfully, and he'd broken out into a cold sweat. He suspected she'd been struck by the same sense of awareness because her eyes collided with his in surprise and confusion before sliding away, but he couldn't be sure.

From that day on, all correspondence between him and Ms. Reeve had gone through Barbara. Jonah planned to keep it that way. He couldn't afford to lose her; she was the best secretary the firm had ever hired. But that memory of their introduction had come to him more than once in the past eight weeks, and it was getting harder and harder to dismiss her as just another pretty face that any red-blooded American man was susceptible to.

He watched her from his corner of the tiny space, but she

hadn't spotted him among the other clones in dark suits, so he looked his fill while she was unaware of his scrutiny. He could do that, at least. *Staring and fantasizing isn't against the rules*, he justified to himself.

With a few others still blocking his view, Jonah couldn't see that far down, but she must have taken off her shoes because she sank a few inches as he watched her face in the reflection of the wall. His cock grew thick and hard behind the placket of his trousers when she sighed softly and closed her eyes. Her faint smile invoked images of fantastic sex, the languid, liquid, warm satisfaction a woman reveals at the height of her pleasure. How many nights had he lain awake and wondered what she'd look like at that moment of completion? Jonah stifled a groan that rumbled in his chest, guessing that this was it. That look was a temptation even his hard-won resolve couldn't resist.

When only the two of them remained on the elevator, Jonah hit the emergency button between floors, but kept his finger pressed to it so the alarm wouldn't sound and alert others that they were stopped. He knew this was lunacy, but she was what fantasies were made of. In the months since she'd been on the payroll, his dreams had been filled with visuals of that glorious hair cascading over her shoulders as she tipped her head back and rode him hard until they both shouted their release. She exuded a sensuality that was palatable.

As she stood there, unaware of her allure, Jonah catalogued every inch of her for recall later in his lonely bed. His eyes raked over her in the wall's reflection. Her body would complement his in bed, he thought lazily. He was average at just over six feet, but her long silky legs gave her height; even without her heels, her head would reach his shoulder.

Her cream-colored blouse was thin and nearly transparent. God, he loved silk on a woman! She'd discarded her jacket and left less to the imagination, more to the absolute.

He saw the thin straps of her bra, the delicate line of her spine.

He'd trace his fingertips along her bare skin, and she'd shiver and moan for him, he thought. He ached to hear it. Her responses would make their lovemaking spectacular.

His gaze settled on the sweet curve of her buttocks. He'd cup and squeeze the soft cheeks and grind against her belly. *Yes,* Jonah silently sighed. They'd be amazing.

Too damn bad that was impossible. Jonah cursed his own stupidity of setting the "no intra-office dating" policy in stone. His hands were tied, but this one temptation, this one pleasure of watching her, dreaming of the heights he'd take her to, was irresistible. Especially when he looked back at her face in the mirror just as her eyes opened, and a carnality that matched his own was reflected in the bluish purple depths of her gaze.

Her eyes widened when she recognized him and realized that they were alone in the space. She was startled, but Jonah saw the desire in those eyes. She knew she'd been caught red-handed breaking company policy, but that fire didn't diminish one bit. Whether it was his steady gaze or her surprise, Jonah didn't care. She didn't look away. He watched, and she waited.

A sensation came over him, as if he were moving toward her, though he knew he stood rooted to the spot, his thumb still pressed to the button on the panel. But like in a dream, he did move, closing the distance and bracing her as she leaned back against his chest. In her eyes, there was passion, and in the tiny space of the elevator, there was heat, energy, arousal.

Camelot let go of the rail, swaying slightly as he approached. His hands slid up her sides, molding to her curves. She held her breath, willing his hands to cup her swollen breasts and ease the ache. But he abandoned her rib cage, one hand gripping the rail where hers had been, the other sliding down and splaying wide over her belly. He drew her back against his hard, heated frame. Her sigh echoed his as they both reveled in that first intimate contact.

His mouth opened on the column of her throat, sucking gently at her soft flesh, and she shuddered almost violently. He took teasing nips with his teeth, his tongue then darting out and soothing the spot. Forging a path up and down the pulse that throbbed there, she went weak in the knees when his late-day beard abraded her already super-sensitized skin. His touch seared like a brand, possessing her, marking her as his own.

His hand kneaded her belly, and Camelot stretched up and up, as if pulled by a string, back arched, pressing her shoulders against the wall of his chest. She'd never been so aroused with barely there strokes, and the heat he gave off encompassed them in a cocoon of need and lust.

She was still rational enough to fear what would happen if he started talking. Hearing his voice was one of the reasons she'd given him a wide berth these past months. When it filtered to her ears, she did things that would make even a prostitute blush. As delicious as his attentions were right now, Camelot hoped he never learned that insane power he had over her.

She prayed he'd stay silent and allow her just a moment or two more of his sensual assault before she put a stop to this madness. Where they were was so inappropriate, so wrong, that they'd surely be caught if things went much further, not to mention that she was his secretary. He didn't seem to be able to help himself any more than she could, but Camelot knew the other partners would frown upon their association. But, oh, he felt so good!

His eyes focused on her as his tongue made one last sweeping stroke, intent on witnessing every reaction from her. She reluctantly rewarded him by shivering under his hot stare, and gasping as his breath fanned her moist skin.

He grinned wickedly, arrogantly gloating over her every reaction, but instead of taking pleasure, he was giving it, cele-
brating it.

One hand still bracketed her by gripping the rail, but the
other slid from her belly, fingers traveling up her blouse.
Then he began the slow process of starting back down,
plucking open buttons along the way. First one, then another, his fingers dipped into the valley between her breasts,
his palm lightly skimming the tightened bud of her nipple
before continuing on. Both breasts swelled under his idle
foray.

Camelot wanted to grip the collar of the garment and
tear it open if it meant he'd put his hands on her. She
silently pleaded with Jonah to do just that. She'd lost her
ability to speak, or maybe they both knew that in this vac-
uum of illicit passion they were sequestered in, words
would sever the fragile link they shared.

He acknowledged her desperation by chuckling under
his breath, but he didn't pick up the pace one bit. He just let
his fingers roam over her flesh and enjoyed her shivers in response to his attentions.

Camelot knew he wasn't as unaffected as he wanted her
to think he was. With every bit of flesh he revealed, his erection prodded her backside more insistently. She wriggled
back against it, intending to inflict a little torture of her
own as she stared back at him. She succeeded, his eyes half
closed momentarily, and his breath hissed through his teeth.

Reaching back, she dug her nails into the seams at the
outside of his trouser legs, twisting the material in her fists.
It tightened over his hard arousal. But her victory was
short-lived. She nearly whimpered when he shook his head,
grinning at her like he was scolding a naughty child, and
covered her hands with his own, prying them from him and
placing them both on the rail, his eyes bidding her to grip it.
One brow rose, waiting for her nod of compliance, and
Camelot was too caught up to do anything but follow

wherever he led her. She bit her lip and nodded, signaling her acquiescence in the mirror. But she just *knew* she'd start begging any second if he didn't hurry.

The shrill bell of the alarm abruptly yanked them out of the impossibly real visual fantasy they'd been sharing. Jonah's brows furrowed, seriously doubting his sanity as he scrutinized her face from the far end of the elevator.

She was unstrung, embarrassed even. The elevator moved, but he hadn't, except that his hand had dropped off the STOP button, signaling the alarm to sound as the car reengaged and continued to the lobby.

She remained at the opposite wall, one hand still gripping the rail, just as she'd been when his eyes caught hers in the reflection. His *most* erotic experience wasn't real? But how could they have had the same fantasy? he wondered.

She hurried to the exit and gained her freedom as soon as the doors slid open. He had to know.

"Ms. Reeve, wait . . ." he said above the bells that still wailed.

She whirled around to face him just outside the door, her jaw slack, and her beautiful eyes wide and so hurt. He cringed, and she turned and melted into the crowd that had gathered around the elevator, gawking to see what the trouble was.

Oh, she'd felt something, all right. They'd been intimate in this elevator somehow. He knew it. The only confirmation he needed was the look on her face when he didn't use her first name.

"If I could remember it, sweetheart, I'd have said it," Jonah muttered, slapping the panel and effectively shutting off the alarm.

He glanced over to where she'd been standing. Her shoes lay on the floor, forgotten when she'd made her escape. They were proof that she'd indeed taken them off. *Hmmmm. Interesting.*

Chapter Two

She was the best typist around, but Jonah rued the day that woman was hired. He hadn't felt this aroused, this *often* since he was a horny teenager.

She'd left the lobby of the building at breakneck speed. *After* she'd shot him that crushed look, that is. Even if he'd wanted to pursue her—which he didn't; any further contact would only lead to disaster—she'd taken off so fast, he wouldn't have been able to push through the crowd surrounding the doors to catch up with her anyway.

He took the elevator to the garage level and racked his brain to come up with that siren's first name as he got into his car.

Siren? Is that what she is? he wondered. Was she luring him with her at once shy and provocative nature? In every instance, he felt a pull so powerful that he couldn't even fight the fantasy when it popped into his head. What just happened was too close for comfort.

Three months ago, Jonah asked his personal assistant to shop for a person who could help her with the overload of work. They needed someone who was smart and fast on the keys. Barbara still acted as his assistant, but he didn't want her to feel threatened by a new hire working so closely with them, so whomever they chose had to be willing to work in the pool with the secretaries and interns, though the job would entail a much broader scope.

He'd tried to hire in-house, but they hadn't found anyone suitable for the job. Jonah had finally resigned himself to advertising outside the firm for the perfect applicant.

Perfection came in the form of Ms. Reeve. Her resumé indicated that she was overqualified for the position, but Jonah never begrudged anyone for having too much knowledge, so he told Barb to interview her on the phone. If Ms. Reeve could keep her cool with the woman who would be her direct supervisor, then they'd go to the next stage in the hiring process.

She passed with flying colors, and Barb met with her for lunch one afternoon that week. When she got back to the office, Barb informed him that she'd already offered Ms. Reeve the position and she'd accepted. And all before he'd even laid eyes on the woman! But his assistant's judgment was accurate about people; when she said Ms. Reeve was "the one," Jonah went with her decision. Now he wished he hadn't been so quick to give her such leeway. He might have been able to cut this off at the pass. Hindsight was twenty-twenty.

After a half-hour drive home, he let himself into his two-bedroom Cape, dumped his keys on the table by the door, and hung up his coat. He walked down the hall, flicking on lights as he went.

In the den, he tossed his briefcase onto the sofa and hit the REWIND button of the answering machine.

As he waited for his calls to play back, the phone book on the corner of his desk brought Jonah's thoughts back around to Ms. Reeve. Her first name was still elusive to him. When he'd heard it, he thought it couldn't possibly be her name, but Barb assured him it was. If he saw it in the listing, he knew he'd recognize it. Strange that he couldn't remember it now, except that it was unique. When Jonah saw her stricken face today, he felt like he'd been sucker punched. He *should* know it, dammit! She deserved that much. In his erotic visions and nighttime dreams of her, she was a fantasy, an apparition, never real to him. And when he awoke, her face was still vivid, and he always ached, but knowing her name would make it personal, intimate even, and he couldn't afford to let her be that important. He'd made himself not care. *Until now.* For his own peace of mind, it was imperative that he know it, but Jonah staunchly refused to look too closely at the reasons why when he had no intention of ever being this personal again. Today was a fluke. A chance meeting. But he didn't think he'd sleep until he solved the mystery.

He thumbed through the white pages, turning to the R's.

Reeve, C. 555-0818
511 Highview St.

Well, the address was close to his office building, he remembered that much from her personnel file, so C. Reeve was the listing he was looking for. But it didn't help him in the least trying to determine her first name!

Jonah shrugged, deciding that requesting Ms. Reeve's personal file was first on his agenda in the morning, and went to the kitchen. He started a chicken stir-fry, but it didn't require thought to put together, so his mind was free to roam; inevitably, her image crowded in. His body responded typically. *Great!* He'd finally gotten himself under control on the way home, and here he was hard and aching all over again. Every time he thought about the way her curvy bottom swayed as she walked away from him, he was hard as steel. It was infuriating, especially since she was off-limits.

Jonah stopped stirring the food and cocked his head, recalling how many times he'd seen that sweet ass. It was a wonderful distraction, but he realized that in getting the rear view, he rarely saw her face.

Up until today, Jonah had assumed she was simply timid,

and he liked seeing her without drawing attention to his own ogling, but now that he concentrated on their encounters, he realized that she didn't lower her head to avoid eye contact, she turned her back on him altogether. Her about-face reactions were strange in their extremity. In fact, her back was to him earlier, too, but the mirrored wall gave her away and let him glimpse her face. He remembered every expression from the depths of those gorgeous eyes, every movement of her supple form. Her body language spoke louder to him than any words ever could. Whatever her initial reaction to his presence might be, it always changed to something else. Something that was too weird to even define. This afternoon in the elevator was just another example. She feared something, but the desire in her eyes told Jonah it wasn't him. Or at least not entirely, anyway.

"Very odd," he said out loud. Given that she was his own personal assistant's secretary, they'd been in contact a scant few times, but that was partially his doing. It was his idea to put her in the secretarial pool—and after that initial meeting, he was glad for the forethought—but it was strange that when they did have to be in close proximity, it was always in retreat, rather than approach. That wasn't right.

Of course, it never bothered you until now, his inner voice reminded him.

He was sure of one thing, though. Other than the peculiar behavior she displayed around him, she was a hard worker. One of the reasons he didn't protest when Barb hired her was her impeccable track record. She was hired as a secretary, but she was an ace at it and had the potential to be so much more. He knew he shouldn't avoid her, but for his own good, and hers as well, he was justified. His curiosity was piqued. Things didn't add up, and he wanted to know her motives behind *her* evasive tactics.

Jonah ate his dinner without tasting it. Finally giving up trying to enjoy it, he went to the sink and dumped it all down the disposal. A perfectly created meal was ruined, and she was the cause.

After shoving the plate in the dishwasher, he strode back down the hall to his bedroom. He was restless and his groin was tight with need. A shower would relax his muscles and relieve the tension.

He started the water, turned it to hot, and padded through the bedroom to grab a towel from the closet in the hallway. His eyes honed in on the portable phone on the dresser.

He couldn't call her. Could he? What the hell would he say if he did?

"No!" he said out loud, with conviction. That would be a breech of policy. No executive messed around with the staff. Jonah knew it. Hell, he'd helped write the rules with Elliot and Sam when they signed on at the firm. How could he be the one to defy it?

But Christ, she was always in his thoughts lately, and there wasn't a thing he could do about it. And today, his obsession was apparently strong enough to pull her smack-dab into the middle of his fantasy.

Before Jonah could think about what he was doing, he'd already dialed the number he memorized downstairs. The enormity of it hit him on the third ring.

She answered on the fourth.

"He-hello?"

"Ms. Reeve?" he asked, feeling like an ass, still having to call her by her surname. "Are you all right? You're out of breath." He could hear her fumbling with the phone.

His hand traveled to the fly of his trousers. He began to undress for his shower as he listened to her shallow breathing, thinking up the most erotic of scenarios. His mind conjured images that were too much to hope for, but he imagined them anyway. He closed his eyes as he listened to her breathe into his ear.

"Mr. McCauley?" she said, nearly choking on his name

when she realized who was on the other end of the line. Then she whispered, "Oh God."

She recovered quickly, asking in a less sexy voice, though not much, "Uh, y-yes, sir. Is there something wrong for you to be calling me at home?"

Jonah got a sick feeling in the pit of his stomach. He didn't even know if she was married! It hadn't occurred to him to look in her file when Barb hired her. And even though he hadn't spotted a ring on her finger this afternoon, she could be in a relationship. Imagining her there with a lover didn't diminish the state of his arousal, but it did make him feel like a heel. As a rule, he'd never dated a woman exclusively. He'd never been very good at commitment. He had so many siblings that the boys were lost in the shuffle when it came to love and affection, and security. But it was possible that *she* was involved with someone. Damn! Why hadn't he thought about this before?

Because an hour ago, you had a grip on your hormones, you thought with the head above your neck, and you followed the rules, his little voice mocked him.

"Mr. McCauley?" she prompted.

Jonah cleared his throat, gently probing for information, saying, "I didn't interrupt a private moment, did I? I'm sure your husband wouldn't appreciate it if I called during your personal time with him, would he?" *Smooth, McCauley.* "I'm sorry if I did, it's just that I—"

"No, sir," she said, cutting him off. "I'm not married, and I don't have a boyfriend, so don't worry about calling me at home. What is it that you wanted to talk to me about?"

Jonah noticed that her voice was stronger, but she covered the phone between every sentence. What was she doing? The possibilities were endless to his sexually charged brain and body. And the relief he felt that she was unattached mattered more than it should've.

The muscle in his jaw flexed as he sat down on the edge

of the bed, clad only in his boxers now, and tried to focus on the questions that swirled in his head through the haze of lust his imagination was creating.

He tried to come up with something to say that didn't sound sexual. One second, two . . . *Think, McCauley!* "I, ah, I wasn't sure if this was the right number. Your first name isn't listed, and I didn't know I'd be calling you until I'd already left the office." *Shut up now, Jonah, spare yourself the humiliation*, the voice mocked again. "I looked you up in the book. For the life of me, I can't remember your first name."

Jonah could barely keep his mind on track. He kept picturing her naked on her bed, alone and doing things that made her breath rush, her voice coarse like it had been when she answered the phone. He'd never buckled under pressure, but he found himself struggling to suppress a groan that rose in his chest when she chuckled deeply, seductively.

"How could you forget *my* name, Mr. McCauley?" she asked, amusement in her voice.

Jonah winced, knowing it was something he should remember because it was so unusual. Not only that, but she had the upper hand because of it. It wasn't in his nature to let anyone get the better of him.

"Yeah, well, I'm sorry about that, and about what happened in the elevator today. I can't explain it." He sighed long and low, wishing he understood it himself.

"I was there, too. And I don't know why I behaved that way, either," she whispered. "That woman was someone I don't know, Mr. McCauley."

Jonah had a gut feeling that she wasn't being completely truthful about that. He had a sneaking suspicion that she did know the woman she'd become today, but he let that slide. He could tell that she wasn't comfortable discussing it, but he was hoping that it would become easier. He had her on the phone, and he wasn't going to get any sleep until he had her name.

"Call me Jonah," he blurted out, grinning as her breath caught. *Now there's a distraction for her,* he thought. *Get right to the heart of it.*

She fumbled with the phone again. "Oh no, I—I couldn't do *that,* sir," she rasped when she had the receiver back to her ear.

Why not? he wondered. Professionalism aside, she'd been affronted that he hadn't called *her* by name this afternoon.

"I'll tell you what. When we're in private"—her breath caught again, and he thought, *Did she just moan into the phone? Jesus! Concentrate, ol' boy*—"you call me Jonah, and I'll call you by your first name." His free hand swept down and stroked his full arousal through his boxers. Hard and ready. Damn, what she did to him! He had to force himself not to touch it again.

Jonah couldn't help the gruffness of his voice. "Give me hints. I'll be able to figure it out."

"All right, then. I'll try." She did moan this time, though she'd covered the mouthpiece. Jonah heard it and his body reacted accordingly. His felt mass amounts of his blood supply rush south, and he gnashed his teeth.

He was drawing her out, and this was the safest thing for both of them. He'd never played like this before, but he couldn't think of a more enticing woman to have fun with.

"Think . . . magical," she said timidly.

He sighed into the phone, but he didn't want to spook her by pushing too hard, too fast, so he let his imagination take him away. He listened to the tone of her voice, hesitant still, but that *something* that he'd been feeling for her was mutual, whatever it was. He didn't want to examine it too closely right now. They both knew there was an odd connection between them, and perhaps it was wrong, but Jonah would bet his last dollar that she couldn't help herself any more than he could.

He squeezed his eyes shut again, freed his cock, and let it rest loosely in his fist. "Another."

Again came her sweet, stirring voice. "Think . . . forbidden love."

She whispered to him like a lover. Jonah fell back onto the bed, his cock firmly in hand now. He stroked it with every seemingly innocent but sensuous word she uttered. Her intensity increased with his low groans, his encouraging yeses, urgings that had nothing to do with her giving him clues. She told him she couldn't call him by his first name, but her brazen "Think of an enchanting place, Jonah" put him right on the precipice as his name rolled off her tongue.

Damn, but she aroused him with her PG version of phone sex more than even his most active partners ever had! That *should* worry him, but Jonah hadn't shared his bed in months, which probably contributed to his overactive imagination. That, and the fact that he'd made her inaccessible with his office policy. She was forbidden fruit, and he craved the one thing he knew he couldn't have. But he was talking to her now, dreaming of being with her, hearing her sweet, sensual voice. And she was so beautiful. He loved that she seemed unaware of her allure, even as she turned heads everywhere she went. He was no exception. He thought of those high cheekbones, full kissable lips, and her—God, she made him crazy! And that hair. Jonah was wild for her hair. He ached to use it during their lovemaking.

"More," he rasped, breathing so harshly now, he knew she could hear his excitement. His arousal throbbed in his fist and every pearl of fluid that formed at the tip, he swirled with his thumb, making his strokes smoother, the shaft ultrasensitive. Listening to her voice rise and come quicker was getting him so hot, he knew one more clue from her would put him over the edge, name or no name.

"Think . . . a sharp, piercing sword. Excalibur."

It came to him just as he came.

"Ahhh, fuck, Camelot!" Jonah shouted at the top of his lungs, dropping the phone away from him. His eyes rolled back in his head as his body stiffened, then shuddered in pleasure. He rode the waves of his climax, milking the essence of it from his cock as it pulsed and spilled the hot stickiness of his seed all over his chest and stomach.

He couldn't move for a full minute when it was over.

His body relaxed slowly, and his breathing struggled to return to normal. His groans had drowned out any sounds coming from the phone that had fallen to the floor. He'd had enough sense not to shout in her ear when he felt his orgasm approaching and let go of the receiver, but he knew she heard.

He was left weak and drained. Gathering his strength and rolling over, he reached for the phone. As he brought it to his ear, all he heard was a dial tone.

Shit! Did she hang up? he wondered. He could've sworn she was with him at the end, but maybe not. Was she embarrassed? If Camelot . . . God, now that he knew her name, he loved it.

By rights, Jonah thought maybe *he* should feel embarrassed by the unorthodox encounter with an employee, or at least contrite, but he couldn't summon up a single regret.

He might pay for it tomorrow, though. He'd call Camelot up to his office to gauge her reaction to seeing him. His only worry was that she'd quit, thinking he was a pervert, maybe even a sexual deviant.

"Shit!" Jonah barked out loud now. He sat up on the edge of the bed, still feeling the ripples of sexual satisfaction, wondering what the hell had possessed him to call her and do something so damned unprofessional. Until this moment, he hadn't realized just what an impact she had on his desires, or how much he'd underestimated his weakness in resisting them.

When she said she didn't have a husband or a boyfriend,

he'd jumped in with both feet, and dragged her down into his lusty fantasies yet again.

What had come over him? He had no excuse, but the only shame he felt was in not making sure that she'd derived the same pleasure that he had. Jonah realized that laying his reputation on the line didn't matter to him in the least. But having Camelot Reeve thinking badly of him made him absolutely sick to his stomach.

He cleared his head, fighting the urge to call her back. No, two sexual encounters in one day where he never got to touch her were enough. He didn't think his body could take much more, and he didn't trust himself not to pull her back into another fantasy, even if it was only to make her come for him.

He got up and padded into the bathroom. The small space was filled with moisture, but he howled like a wounded animal when he stepped into the still-running shower. The water had turned icy while things had heated up in his bedroom. He shivered under the bitter cold spray, enduring it as punishment, washing as quickly as he could. He used his terry robe to dry his chilled skin since he'd forgotten the towel when he spotted the phone. Even now, fresh and clean from the shower, his mind clear of erotic images of fiery red hair, piercing swords, and enchanting places, Jonah wanted his new employee with the passion of any knight fighting for his queen.

In the span of one wild, unpredictable, amazing day, Camelot Reeve had become *his* quest. In the two months since he met her, he'd kept his distance, but it didn't dispel the want, the need for her. He'd marked her as trouble to his career, and even that hadn't mattered. His subconscious still wove her into every sexual fantasy he'd had since the day he welcomed her into the firm.

Jonah was beginning to think that she might never be out of his system. He understood that his attraction to her was the catalyst, but what worried him was that sex wasn't the goal. No, his goal was to know her, and know what it was about her that made his heart pound, along with other parts, and made thoughts of her come unbidden at any time of the day. There, he'd admitted it to himself, and finally acknowledged what he wanted. In a fantasy, any woman should do, but not for him. It was always Camelot's face that haunted him, intrigued him, and he hadn't even been able to remember her first name without her help! What they'd experienced so far didn't happen to just anyone. The questions were like a scrolling marquis in his head. As a lawyer who searched for the truth, he wanted answers to them. He was finally being honest with himself, but until he understood what made her sidestep him and turn her back to avoid him, getting information would be difficult. He'd dig until he was satisfied.

He stepped into a clean pair of boxers, put the phone back on its cradle, and began to devise a strategy to convince Camelot that he was actually a good guy. He'd deal with the fallout of breaking company policy later.

He smiled, feeling better now that he had a focus and a direction. He headed back down to the kitchen. Suddenly, he was starving.

Chapter Three

"God, what have I done?"

Camelot lay sideways on her bed, legs still clutching at the hand that had found its way between them when Jonah started groaning and pushing her to further their game of "what's in a name" with each "yes" and husky demand for more.

Had she just talked a man into coming over the telephone? And had that man been *the* Jonah McCauley? It was one of the fantasies her mind latched onto when she listened to him on the tapes, but she never dreamed it would ever be real.

Damn him for calling right when she'd been on verge of a climax that his voice had been driving her toward!

She lay there and replayed it in her mind, still unable to believe what had actually happened. Like this afternoon in the elevator with him, she was confused by this power, this pull that had her in its grip.

When she got home from work, she'd changed into her robe and sat down at her computer. For nearly an hour she'd worked, valiantly ignoring the way his voice teased and beckoned her. She'd typed exactly what he dictated on the tapes. But it wasn't long before her imagination created

a world of sensual delights and erotic words, and it demanded recognition.

"The above mentioned plaintiff, a client retained by this
firm shall hereby . . ."

He was unquestionably professional and articulate, but
she'd become aroused by the sound of his voice as he
droned on. He slurred certain words, gave sharp resonance
to others, and all the while, the deep tenor stroked her
erogenous zones like an experienced lover.

Eyes closed, her fingers had skimmed her breasts, lost in
the thought that they were his lips brushing over the taut
nipples. She slid a hand over her belly, imagining his mouth
open over her navel, his tongue delving into the hollow.
She'd sucked in her breath at her own ministrations, but in
her mind, it had been Jonah doing those things. It was his
voice, his phantom body that made her strain forward as
her own fingers stretched to reach their goal. She was wet
and swollen, and she arched in her chair as her hand sank
into the heat and pulsing ache he'd unwittingly summoned.

"Mmmmmm, Jonah," she'd sighed, her moans rising
above his voice booming from the speakers.

Riiiiinggggg . . .

"Wha—?" Camelot had jerked upright in the chair; her
feet, propped up on the edge of the desk, dropped to the
floor in front of her. She'd turned down the stereo that
blared out her boss's legalese and sat frozen, staring up into
the loft at the phone. It trilled from the nightstand next to
her bed, effectively jerking her from the fantasy that pulled
her under like a drug.

On shaky legs, she'd made her way up the stairs, finally
picking up on the fourth ring.

She'd nearly groaned out loud, hearing Jonah's voice on
the other end. Already on the cusp of a mind-blowing orgasm, no matter what he said, Camelot felt its effect. He'd
told her to call him by his first name when they were in pri-

vate. *In private?* When would they ever be together in private? she'd wondered.

When they began their guessing game, that smooth timbre seeped into her pores all over again. But it was Jonah himself, not a reproduction of his voice; the memory of his stalking look in the elevator today was too much for her taxed resistance, and she played the game. Even in her heightened, aroused state, she was shy. She wasn't able to take the game very far into a sexually worded realm. But from the sound of things on Jonah's end, it didn't put a damper on his imagination at all. She'd heard his excitement as she gave innocent descriptions of the legendary tale, amazed that she was able to keep giving hints from Arthurian folklore. But she'd shivered at his whispered one-syllable replies until she was teetering just as precariously on the edge as he was.

He'd dropped the phone away from him as she reached the summit at the same time. He'd shouted in the distance, but his voice roared in her ears as her name finally wrenched from his lips. She'd undulated and cried out, her inner walls gripping her fingers, imagining that it was Jonah filling her. She'd erupted like a volcano that flowed lava, an intense, molten heat of pleasure.

Then there was silence on the other end of the line. That couldn't be good.

Reality crashed down hard on her. She'd been too rattled to call him back to the phone. Not that she was capable of shouting anyway. She was spent, lethargic; her belly fluttered from the excitement of the exchange.

It took precious energy to hit the OFF button and sever the connection. But as she lay there, her mind jumped ahead, even more wary of having to face him at work tomorrow. Camelot didn't fool herself into believing that Jonah was going to let this go.

The call had gone from professional to casual to sexual

in the blink of an eye, and Camelot knew she was partially to blame. She'd answered the phone with a shaky voice, and her deep-throated chuckles at his forgetfulness of her name had started their conversation, but he was as much to blame for the outcome as she was. The guilt was even more solidly placed at his feet because it was his voice on those damn tapes that had been arousing her for more than an hour before he called.

Okay, it wasn't exactly his fault there, she admitted. But *he'd* called *her*. And didn't call her back. *That can't be good*, she thought again.

Camelot closed her eyes, troubled by the Pandora's box Jonah had just opened without even knowing it. Now every time she took dictation for him, she'd think of tonight; his groans, his heavy breathing in her ear, and his soft-spoken pleas for her to push on and keep going until he . . . well, until he came, she supposed. With or without her name, Camelot was positive he'd been reaching for more than his memory.

Out of the pan and into the fire. Lately, that was more the rule than the exception, she thought irritably.

She dragged herself to the middle of the bed and burrowed under the covers. She was anything but hot now. The icy cold grip of uncertainty spread like a virus through her veins, and she wondered if she'd ever feel balanced again. Not being in complete possession of her faculties made her tense, edgy, and high-strung. She hated it. Something had to give, and soon!

She stared at the ceiling, attempting to clear her mind, but it was useless. He was still there, his face lurking just behind her closed lids. Sighing heavily, she resigned herself to a night filled with images of Jonah.

The alarm clock buzzed precisely at four-thirty, and she slapped the snooze for nine more minutes of blessed slumber. Sleep hadn't come until well after one, and she felt the effects from the lack of it.

Light-headed and feeling hungover, she crawled out from

under the warm covers. The events of the night before slowly filtered into her sluggish brain, and she found herself shaky for another reason.

"Oh, no, no, no. Oh shit," she cursed as she bolted from the bed and ran for the shower. Last night's illicit pleasure wouldn't get her canned, but not having those tapes transcribed on paper this morning sure as hell would! When Jonah called last night, she'd completely forgotten that she'd left the report only half finished downstairs.

She frantically got ready, formulating a plan for the day. She'd go to work early, use the extra computer that was set up in Jonah's office and complete the report there. The moment it was finished, she'd leave it on his desk, slip out, and be back to her cubicle before anyone was the wiser. She couldn't take any chances by working on it down in the pool. She didn't trust what the combination of his voice and her memory of last night might do to her. For the good of her own reputation, and that of the company, working at her own desk was out of the question.

Just don't panic, and this'll be a walk in the park, she thought.

If she played her cards right and stuck to her schedule, she'd be back down in the pool by the time Jonah even woke up and had his first cup of coffee. Camelot hoped he needed a little extra sleep this morning.

Locking her apartment, she tromped downstairs, avoiding any thought of what she might say if she saw Jonah today. She didn't leave herself any time or energy to be distracted. Completing her assignment was tantamount. Her belly twisted in nervous knots. No matter what the circumstance, Camelot had never missed a deadline, and even with her libido spiraling out of control, she'd be damned if this would be the first time. She had to own something, and she latched onto her performance record like a lifeline.

Wearing comfortable heels today, she picked up her pace as she hurried up the street.

On the eighteenth floor, the security guard nodded as she flashed her badge and breezed by him. She'd been given access to the offices on that floor when Barb had handpicked her for the job. For once, she was grateful that it gave her clearance instead of the raised brows her "special" status got her down in the pool.

Hastily settling in and plugging in the headphones, she typed without a single glitch at first. Camelot was so focused that the oral notes did nothing to stop her flow.

It wasn't until she finished typing and was reading it over to make sure it corresponded with everything Jonah had dictated, that she started to feel the unwelcome yet too familiar curling in the pit of her stomach.

Camelot listened as Jonah's voice rose when he started speaking, and had to strain to catch the end of each sentence as it fell away, like he was projecting ahead to the next thought before he'd finished vocalizing the last. The melodious timbre played over her body like a musician lovingly strumming his instrument.

She hadn't thought that anything could make her lose her focus this morning, she was so stressed, but she hadn't counted on the atmosphere in his office or being surrounded by his things when she decided on her course of action.

Her eyes drifted around the room. They landed on the comfortable chairs, worn with age and use, facing his huge mahogany desk. The walls were lined with law books, their spines polished to a fine sheen on the shelves.

Oh, and the smells of the room! She breathed deep, her senses reveling in the combination of old leather, lemon oil, and Jonah.

She'd been up here on the day she'd started working at the firm, but it had been very brief. Jonah had seen to that. Camelot was beginning to think that maybe he wasn't completely oblivious to what she'd been living with these past months.

This time, however, she was alone and her senses were on alert. The potency of a space that Jonah occupied for hours a day was a ticking bomb, and Camelot discovered it too late to stop the detonation. The urgency to finish the job was past, and her sexual appetite demanded sustenance.

"Oh God, it's happening," she murmured, her eyes drifting closed. The sensual dance with her phantom lover and his hypnotic voice began again.

Jonah let himself into his private rooms next to his office and threw his briefcase onto the futon. He'd awoken with more energy than he'd had in months and he was anxious to start his day. He grinned; the last time he'd been to the office at six A.M. was when he was just a clerk, trying to get a jump on the day and impress the judge who had hired him.

He was going to see Camelot today, and Jonah found himself smiling like a kid with his first crush. As long as no one found out why he was so cheerful, they'd be fine. For now. He'd have to face the reality of breaking policy eventually, but it wasn't urgent. It could wait.

A noise in his office next door drew his attention. No one was supposed to be here this early. Jonah's brows furrowed with suspicion. Even Barb didn't come bustling in until well after eight. He crossed the room and pressed his ear to the door. The sounds were muffled but he could hear someone talking. The answering moans were what put Jonah on alert.

Was someone hurt in there? Should he burst in and confront whoever it was on the other side of that door? Adrenaline began to surge through his veins as his mind raced ahead.

If whoever was in there had a gun, he wanted to be prepared for whatever he was about to face. He reached for the phone to call security, but stopped midway to his ear. Of course! He put the receiver back down, realizing he could see precisely what he was up against without even entering the room. He'd have a bird's-eye view of his entire office.

Striding across the room again, he hit the ON button of the monitor that sat on the cabinet near the connecting door. Security cameras had been installed in all of the executive offices when his files and some of Sam's had been rifled through about a year ago.

In that instance, it turned out that his former security officer and a custodial worker were conspiring in search of documents related to a large corporate case for which the firm was on retainer. The men had been bribed and were stealing information for the competition. The partners and their personal assistants were the only ones in the building aware of the surveillance he'd had put in subsequently. Barb had the responsibility of making sure his camera was recording when she left each day, then labeling and cataloguing the tapes each morning. Kat was responsible for the one in Sam's office, and Summer for Elliot's. Now he felt like a genius for insisting on the expense.

The screen began to fade in, and his office came into view in stark black and white. What Jonah saw made his jaw drop, his eyes go wide and glassy; he blinked several times, not sure he was seeing right. He bent closer to the screen.

"Holy shit!" he whispered reverently.

It was just too incredible, too *"Twilight Zone* meets Playboy Channel" to be believed. It was something so private, and to Jonah, so arousing. And she was doing it in his office! Jonah was hard before he even realized *who* it was.

The screen's lack of color took away from the vividness of the image, but he groaned when she rolled her head to the side, exposing her luscious throat and partial profile. Jonah knew that hair would be fiery red, those eyes bluish purple and glowing in forbidden passion when her face tipped up for the camera to capture.

"Wow . . ." he whispered in awe as Camelot pleasured herself right before his eyes.

She was sitting at the computer in the corner of his office. Her dainty feet encased in heels were propped on the desk's edge as she reclined in the chair. Her already short skirt was twisted up nearly to the waist, giving her hands access to the space between her legs. Jonah watched, transfixed as her hand skimmed up one thigh and down the other, slowing every time she reached the juncture; he wasn't sure because of the bad angle of the camera, but he thought her fingers skated across her panties with every pass.

What if she's not wearing panties? *"Jesus,"* he growled, torturing himself with his rampaging lusty thoughts.

He couldn't take his eyes off her as she slid a hand up her body, over her breasts, up her neck to drag the earphones from her head. She must've pulled out the plug when she leaned back in the chair, and that was the talking he heard. Jonah gnashed his teeth to keep from coming right there. It was *his* voice booming from the speakers as she plied her body, taking her pleasure, listening to the dictation he left for her to transcribe.

Things began to click into place and confirm what was only a suspicion yesterday: sexy, quiet Camelot Reeve got off on the sound of his voice! He'd hoped it was true last night, but they hadn't said a word in the elevator, and they'd played a sensual game of cat and mouse. He hadn't been sure. *Until now.*

Even as he absorbed that piece of information, his eyes remained glued to the screen, murmuring softly to her, knowing she couldn't hear him over his own voice reverberating in the next room, but her moans were turning him inside out.

"Oh Christ, what are you doing, babe?" he murmured. "I'm sorry, sweetheart. I shouldn't be seeing this, I *know* I shouldn't . . . Oh, you're beautiful but, ah God, Camelot . . ."

Her hips rocked, her body strained, building toward her climax, her head rolling from side to side. Then she shot forward in the chair, shuddering and biting her lip to hold in a scream of pleasure that would have brought security running to investigate. But her whimpers reached him through the door.

"Oh, Cam," Jonah whispered, shaking so badly he could hardly contain himself. His hands were braced flat on the table on either side of the monitor, elbows locked, and his jaw clenched in the worst pain/pleasure he'd ever endured. His cock was so hard, it throbbed in his trousers, but he couldn't tear his eyes from her. Last night, on the phone, he'd wondered if she writhed or thrashed when the pleasure overtook her. Now there she was, filling in all the blanks.

Jonah needed relief, badly, but he couldn't bring himself to ruin her beautiful climax by touching himself like a pervert in a darkened theater. He couldn't taint what she'd unknowingly given him.

Camelot's moans died down, and all he heard now was his own muffled voice from the speakers. She tipped her head at an angle that brought her radiant face into near full focus of the camera lens. With her eyes closed, a soft smile on her sweet, swollen lips, they formed his name. *"Jonah."*

"Oh God!" He thrust himself away, using colossal will to turn his back on what lay just beyond that door. Cursing under his breath, he braced his hands on the wall at the other side of the room. He stared at the floor and he took deep breaths, shaking like he was naked in a blizzard. But he was hot. So damned hot!

That woman could make a saint hot, and I'm no saint! Jonah thought desperately.

He concentrated on the most mundane things: trial proceedings, baseball, the spin cycle on the washer, anything that would bring his body to heel.

Finally able to pull himself together enough to breathe, he hauled himself over to the futon and sat down. He glanced at the monitor to see Camelot get up, hit the PRINT button, and straighten her clothes. The ravaged look on her face wasn't passion anymore, but despair. She was embarrassed and ashamed, and Jonah shared her anxiety that she couldn't seem to control her behavior. He'd barely been able to control his own. Not when his thoughts and sights were filled with her.

"I know, baby, I know," he whispered to the image, nodding his head, sympathizing with her. Jonah didn't think she took defeat any better than he did, however erotic it might be.

He wished he could tell her that he understood. It made him all the more resolute to find out what else they had in common besides this odd infatuation that held them like prisoners. It was as if their lust controlled them like puppets on a string.

She slid the documents into a folder and placed it and the tapes neatly in the center of his desk.

He stood as she left his office, shutting the door behind her. Popping the tape out of the VCR, labeling it with her name and dating it, Jonah stashed it in his briefcase for safekeeping. He might not know much about this woman yet, but for his own peace of mind—and apparently hers, as well—starting today, he'd begin the process of finding out what made her tick. But in the meantime, his first priority was to protect Camelot's reputation and her privacy.

Chapter Four

Camelot was typing a brief at her computer when Kat Murphy, Mr. Parrish's assistant, peeked her head around the corner.

"I just saw Barb, Cam. Mr. McCauley wants to see you in his office."

Camelot's hands suspended over the keys for a heartbeat; no one even should have noticed as she muttered a "thanks" without even looking up. But Kat was a friend. And she noticed everything.

"Hey, are y'all right?" she asked in her slight Southern drawl. She was Camelot's age, beautiful, and she had a heart of gold.

Camelot looked up. "Sure, I'm fine. I just had a long night, that's all." She wasn't about to tell Kat about her adventures into the sexually depraved and borderline kinky. Flashing her a bright smile, she hoped her friend would drop the subject.

"I don't buy it."

Camelot rolled her eyes and sighed. She'd never been that lucky.

Kat came around the cubicle, pulling up a chair and sitting down. "You can try and fool everyone else around here, but I know you." She leaned over and whispered low,

"Something's going on with you, and it's got to do with the boss man."

Camelot winced.

Kat gasped. "Aha! I'm right! I knew it!" She leaned in ever closer with rapt attention. "Tell me everything."

Camelot inwardly groaned. No way could she tell Kat the events of the last twenty-four hours. She was already a little freaked out that Jonah even had an inkling of what was going on. And she could feel herself blushing as her appalling behavior in Jonah's office earlier popped into her head. It was going to be hard enough facing *him*!

Her nerves were shot, but she was curious enough to ask some general questions. Pursing her lips, she glanced tentatively at her friend. "Kat," she asked, carefully avoiding direct eye contact. She was too perceptive. "Have you ever had an obsession?"

"What, you mean like all things chocolate?" Kat chuckled. But she noticed Camelot's brows furrow and became serious. "No, Cam. I don't think anything has ever overwhelmed me so much that I can't control it." She shrugged. "Sure, I want things, but not to the point where I can't stop myself from getting them any way possible. Why?"

Well, don't ask if you aren't gonna like the answer, Camelot thought. She shouldn't have even hinted that anything was bothering her, but she'd hoped that Kat would tell her that she wasn't alone.

Strike one.

It was just that every time she heard Jonah's voice, she could barely breathe. Looking at him had the same effect on her, but up until now, she'd easily remedied that by turning her back on the temptation. Not so easy when he called her on the phone, stared at her in elevators, or spoke with such lazy sensuality on those tapes. *Did they have a twelve-step program?* she thought with sarcasm.

His sometimes rough, sometimes smooth-as-silk voice engulfed her until she was under siege. And his quick wit and easygoing demeanor didn't help much, either. Add to that his black hair, his strong, square jaw, Roman nose, and deep green eyes, and Jonah McCauley was a prime specimen for any woman's unbridled fantasies. But that wasn't the problem. What plagued her was that it wasn't late at night in the privacy of her bedroom when the sensations flowed over her like a river. And it wasn't some abstract dream that played with her subconscious. It consumed her, dominated her. It was real. And it was ruling her life.

"Cam?" Kat asked, concerned.

Camelot waved her off, saying, "It's nothing. I've just been wondering what makes people do the things they do, that's all." She shrugged, pretending to give it less importance than it deserved.

She locked up her desk and rose from her chair, prompting Kat to do the same. "I'd love to stay and talk, Kat, but I'm going to be late. If Mr. McCauley wants to see me, I can't keep him waiting."

Kat was astute enough to know when she was being dismissed, but she didn't take offense. She wasn't going to let Camelot off the hook entirely, however. "This discussion isn't over, Cam. Something's been bothering you lately, and it's getting worse instead of better."

Don't I know it, Camelot thought wryly.

Kat put a hand her shoulder. "Hon, you can tell me anything."

"Not this, Kat. It's private." She didn't want to hurt her friend's feelings. Her eyes begged Kat to understand and not push for explanations.

Kat sighed and dropped her hand. "Well, I'm here if you need to talk. Even if you just want to vent, okay?"

Camelot nodded, but if she were to talk to anyone, it would have to be Jonah.

"You know, Cam"—Kat lowered her voice again, wriggling her eyebrows—"as long as you don't break any rules, there are worse things than lusting after Jonah McCauley."

Camelot could argue that point, but she let Kat leave on that parting shot. She had too many things churning through her brain to discuss the wheres and what-fors of wanting her employer.

Camelot squared her shoulders and raised her chin, mentally bracing herself as she left the pool and made her way up to Jonah's office for the second time that morning.

Jonah read the same court transcript for the third time and he still couldn't comprehend a damn thing it said. That chair across the room sat empty, but he couldn't forget Camelot reclining in it, struggling to stay quiet as she reached her peak of pleasure.

God, what an image.

He was tempted to watch the videotape and immerse himself in the beauty of her body language, how it had spoken to him in breathy pants and lusty expressions. But his conscience barked at him that he'd invaded her privacy once by watching her the first time; to do it again would be a violation beyond any hope of forgiveness.

Besides, she was due here in just a few moments and he couldn't risk what seeing her in the flesh after watching that tape would do to him. He'd be lucky if he could stand when she walked through the door if he watched it again. Just remembering it was driving him insane.

He raked his hands through his hair as he sat back in his chair. "You really should have come up with a plan before you sent for her, McCauley," he muttered to himself. In the three hours since she left his office, he hadn't been able to think of a single valid reason to summon her, aside from the obvious: he *needed* to see her.

When he'd pulled himself together last night and finally drifted off to sleep, he'd dreamed of her. But he'd also envisioned the yarn her few words had woven into his subconscious. Not since he was a kid had he thought of kingdoms and queens, rogue knights, and forbidden couplings. His mind spun a very adult version of the mythical legend. He dreamed that he was Lancelot, and she, his Guinevere. Visions of swords and sorcerers, magical lovemaking, and Camelot, with her creamy skin, her hair wild as fire, her body supple and pliant as he knelt behind her, staring at her radiant face in a mirror as he took her in a most primal way. It was no wonder Jonah awoke sweating and so hard he ached. Damn the things she did to him without even trying!

A knock interrupted his thoughts, yanking him out of the dangerous territory his mind was entering.

He cleared his throat. "Yes," he said roughly, sitting upright in his chair as Barb peeked around the door.

"Ms. Reeve to see you, Mr. McCauley."

Jonah nodded, and stood as Camelot crossed the threshold. *Aw, damn*, he thought. *Why* did she have to glance at the computer as she walked past it?

His eyes sized her up: her nervousness, her head bowed slightly as she hid her embarrassment from him. Jonah bit back a curse. He hated that she was ashamed. What he'd seen had been so exquisite, so . . . beautiful that he could barely breathe even now. He wanted to tell her that, but if he thought she was embarrassed now, he could just imagine how she'd react if she learned that she'd had an audience. It was an act so private and personal that some married couples never even shared that part of their sexuality.

No, he decided, he wouldn't tell her about the security camera capturing everything on video. He wanted to put her at ease with him. If the truth came out, he'd be the last person she'd turn to. He *would* tell her . . . eventually. But he wanted her to trust him first. It was so important that she see *him*, not the fantasy of what she thought he was.

He cast her an approving look, loving the way she dressed. His eyes took in her short skirt and long business jacket that perfectly matched the color of her eyes. Her ability to dress professionally and still be so sexy was one of the reasons Camelot caught his attention in the first place. There were plenty of beautiful women at the firm—Kat, for instance. But Camelot was a supreme employee; her resumé was as long as his arm and every assignment was turned in on time without a single error. The combination of beauty and brains was an aphrodisiac to his analytical mind and voracious libido. And he was just a man, after all.

She seemed unsure of herself, but she concealed it well. Only someone who'd studied her, as he'd been doing, would be able to recognize the hint of vulnerability that lurked in her eyes.

He had to give her credit; she might regret the things that had transpired between them in the past few days, yet only a cursory thought was given to them before she sat primly, ready for whatever task he needed completed. Those long shapely legs crossed and tucked to the side, pad and pen in hand, she exuded confidence and complete composure to the naked eye. But Jonah knew that self-assurance was nothing more than a façade that she put on display.

She had to be uncomfortable being stared at, but, like yesterday, his passion for her built like a pressure cooker and his eyes never wavered. And, to Jonah, this was even worse than yesterday. He wanted Camelot in his bed, that was a definite, but he felt a shift somewhere down deep as he watched her valiant battle for control over her own actions, while remaining aloof and unaffected by him. She was a fighter, and while everyone else was oblivious to her inner struggle, Jonah saw it clear as day, and his heart opened up just enough for her to slip inside. He cared about her and found himself wanting to be her champion. But unless she trusted him, he didn't stand a chance.

She raised one brow in question and prompted, "You wanted to see me Mr. McCauley?"

Jonah stiffened at the formal address. "We're in private, Camelot."

She flinched and slid her gaze away from his direct one.

"Remember what I said." He waited while she mentally pulled herself together and looked at him again. His eyes fixed on her. "Now try again," he ordered, his voice gravelly and barely above a whisper.

Jonah knew he wasn't playing fair, speaking seductively, but they had to get past this awkward "morning after" stage. "Camelot?"

"Jonah."

"Better."

She cleared her throat quietly, sitting straighter in her chair. The gesture only fueled his need. She struggled to remain composed, detached, and Jonah only wanted to tear down those walls she'd built up.

"This is wrong, Jonah. You know it as well as I do. No, wait." Camelot held up a hand when he opened his mouth, as much to ward him off as to stop him from interrupting. "What happened on the phone last night was . . ."

"Amazing? Incredible?"

She fought that grin for everything she was worth, but it still broke through. "I don't know about incredible . . ."

"Speak for yourself, darlin'," he countered, glad that they were finally engaging in conversation, but annoyed that she tried to pretend she hadn't been as shaken as he was. He knew different. Watching her hit her climax this morning with his name on her lips was all the proof he needed, but damn! He couldn't tell her *how* he knew.

He told her what he did know. "Your sweet innocent words coupled with my wicked imagination, and we have a formula for a pretty hot conversation, honey." He grinned when Camelot bit her lip and shrugged, conceding the point. It *was* incredible.

Jonah pressed his advantage. He went around the desk and half sat on the edge of it, inches from her chair. Her nervous energy was like a living thing in the room and her subtle scent teased and tested his limits of control.

Camelot's eyes traveled up his leg as it swung casually

back and forth. Her gaze settled on his lap, her eyes bright with immediate sexual hunger. Jonah's reaction was predictable; his cock swelled shamelessly under her blatant perusal.

Good! he thought a little sadistically. Let her see how hard he became from just a look.

Camelot bounded out of the chair, intending to bolt, but Jonah clamped his hand around her wrist before she could even take a step. He tugged gently, pulling her closer. When she was directly in front of him, Jonah loosened his grip, assuring her that he wouldn't stop her if she really wanted to go.

She trembled slightly, but he felt a burst of pride when she fought the impulse to flee and stood her ground. He knew he was a bastard for rushing her, but there was no way in hell he was going to be able to think clearly until they'd ironed some things out.

No wonder he'd avoided her these last months. She distracted him. That alone was an understatement. He'd been given only a glimpse of the woman in front of him, but he felt a clawing need to learn every facet of her.

And he hated to admit it, but it stung that she was able to work despite everything. He envied her fortitude. He'd never felt this wrecked over a woman. He didn't particularly like his unsettled emotions, but it just confirmed what he'd already figured out: Camelot was different from any woman he'd ever known. Special.

"Look, let's do this out of the office, all right? This isn't about work, Camelot. Your job is yours for as long as you want it, I promise. You know you're the best." She winced and lowered her head. He knew she was remembering her indiscretions right here in his office earlier today, and he wanted to soothe her, but he couldn't. Every minute he spent with her brought him closer to jeopardizing what she was trying so valiantly to protect: her reputation.

When the time was right, he'd give her the kind of pleasure she deserved. He'd carry her to the very edge, and he'd delight in her demands that he end his teasing. When he was good and ready, he'd bury himself deep inside her, taking her to heights she'd only ever dreamed of, only he'd make it better; he'd be holding her when she screamed his name and then fluttered back to earth, spent and sated.

Get a grip, McCauley! He swallowed hard and suppressed a shudder.

He still sat casually propped on the desk, but she stood so close, he was sinking fast. The door was unlocked, and he couldn't care less. Not when every pull of air made him dizzy with her spicy perfume and another, more potent scent that he registered as arousal.

His gaze dropped to her luscious throat. He had to taste her. Just one tiny sample to tide him over.

Jonah's hand shook as he drew that gorgeous red hair over her shoulder. He leaned forward, closing over the wildly beating pulse at her throat, and his tongue flicked at her warm, silky skin. Jonah's eyes rolled back and finally drifted shut in ecstasy as he groaned, gently suckling at her flesh.

"Ahhhh, Jonah . . ." Her high-pitched cry was music to his ears.

He dragged her against him, wedging her in the cradle of his hips. She dug her nails into his thigh as she tilted her head and gave him better access to her sensitive throat.

"Mmmmm, oh my God, you're delicious, Camelot," he murmured against her skin. "I ached for this last night. I knew you'd taste so good."

Nipping at her chin and along her jaw, he elicited shivers and gasps until she just couldn't stand it anymore. She blindly tipped her face to him, seeking his kiss.

She was ready for his mouth when Jonah growled savagely, covering hers, and he swallowed her whimper when his tongue plunged inside, seeking hers.

She met his frenzy with a force of her own, sucking

wildly and changing angles, getting as close as possible. It was exactly how he'd pictured their first kiss: needy, hungry, ferocious.

Jonah slid off the desk, pulling her completely flush with his body. Hours and hours of wanting her and denying himself took its toll; he was as obsessed with touching her as she was with him.

He cupped her rounded cheeks and rocked her against him in a steady rhythm. The only sounds in the room were fervid sighs, and his lips tore from hers to whisper a reverent "Jesus" when her hand snaked between them and closed over the hard ridge in his trousers.

She stroked him with an eagerness that made Jonah desperate to feel her fingers close around him without the barrier of clothing.

He cupped her breast, palming the tight nipple and kneading the mound. He grinned wickedly as she arched her back, her breath hitching against his lips.

He hissed his approval as her fingers contracted on his rigid cock, gripping him hard through the material. Jonah fought the urge to drop his head and suckle at her breast, blouse and all, just to feel more of her response to their reckless coupling. But he couldn't stop kissing her. She tasted so rich, so exotic, and he knew he'd never tire of it.

In the far corner of his mind, Jonah's annoying inner voice reminded him that he had to get control of things before they went too far, too fast. He was walking through a minefield of emotions with her. He wanted her trust, and this wasn't the smartest way to go about it.

But her touch felt so damn good that he let her hand tighten and squeeze him for a second longer, then he dragged his lips from her tempting mouth. "We have to stop, Camelot. We have to stop," he rasped, burying his face in her neck and halting her movements on his throbbing erection. His other hand reluctantly slid away from her breast and rested on her rib cage, keeping her close enough to still breathe in her scent.

Jonah was wild for her, but he forced himself to obey his own command. They'd barely touched one another, and just that easily she'd brought him so close to the edge. He pulled her hand away from his hard cock, and gently set her back from him. Her face was flushed with heightened color and her breath came in little puffs of air through her kiss-swollen lips. Jonah nearly hauled her back in his arms, the passion in her eyes burned so bright. It excited him that she was as aroused as he was. He groaned and kissed the palm of her hand, which had been stroking him so exquisitely.

He understood what he did to her. She wanted him bad, and Jonah was glad for that, at least, but his ego demanded it be of her own free will. Was it merely her passions that ruled her? he wondered. He hoped not. He wanted her to be sure of what she was getting into.

"Camelot," he murmured, the effects of their lovemaking still evident in his rough voice. "Before we go any further, I need to know what you want. Your job is safe, but there are consequences to getting involved with me, sweetheart."

He imagined the wheels turning in her head. She bit her lip, and he adored it. Still, his gut twisted for giving her an out. She was actually considering whether she should embrace those passions or reject them.

Jonah nearly took away her options altogether. She was pretty far gone; a few sinful thoughts voiced out loud, maybe a kiss or two more, and he knew she'd be putty in his hands, she'd agree to whatever he wanted.

But coercion wasn't his style. She had to be willing, or he walked away. He'd never taken a woman against her will, by force or persuasion, and he wasn't about to start now, especially not with Camelot. Now that he'd allowed himself to put his rigid rules on the back burner to see where this led, he'd accept nothing less than her absolute, enthusiastic consent.

It seemed like hours when only a minute had passed, but God, it was well worth the wait.

"What I *want,* Jonah, is to be able to be in the same room with you, or do my job typing your dictation, and not feel compelled to ease the ache of arousal I feel every time I hear your voice, smell your cologne, or set eyes on you. I can't think past the point of my next orgasm."

He didn't move, except possibly for his jaw, which dropped to the floor. He couldn't. He was frozen in some place where he'd shatter if he moved.

She didn't realize what she'd said until she glanced at him. He couldn't even help her out. Jonah was sure he'd swallowed his tongue. Or was it the sudden dryness in his mouth that made it stick to the roof like glue?

He might've laughed when her confession finally dawned on her and she slapped her hand over her mouth in mortification, her eyes going round as saucers.

Yes, it might've been laughable if he just hadn't had the wind knocked right out of him.

She muttered behind her hand, "Oh, Jonah, I'm sorry. I didn't mean to spring it on you like that. I—"

"No!" he growled harshly when her other hand reached out to him.

Camelot snatched her hand back, startled.

Jonah softened his tone. "Please don't touch me, sweetheart. Good God, woman! Do you have any idea what door you just opened?" Jonah asked derisively, trying without a lot of success to ignore the way certain body parts came to attention and struggled to stand proud to serve.

He grinned painfully. "One touch, honey, and I swear I'll recite the Gettysburg Address if it means you won't object when I throw you across my desk."

Her brows rose in surprise and she flushed from her neck

up, but he just knew she was hiding a snicker behind that hand.

"You like it now that the shoe's on the other foot, don't ya, darlin'?"

Camelot shook her head rapidly in denial, but the mischief in her too bright eyes belied her sincerity. He thought he heard a giggle, too.

Well, I'll be damned, Jonah thought. He was extremely uncomfortable at the moment, his erection growing like a stalk in his trousers, the lust he'd tamped down on, smoldering, ready to ignite, but he was thrilled that she was able to laugh, even if it was at his expense. That deer-in-the-headlights look had disappeared and it pleased him more than he could've hoped.

"What we need to do," he said with a little more surety and self-control, ignoring his desire and getting serious, "is see where we go from here and—"

Camelot dropped her hand and burst out laughing, but it was out of place now. Jonah mentally braced himself. The other shoe was about to drop. He could feel it.

"Go? Go where, Jonah? Until last night you didn't even know my *first name!*" She threw her arms up. This wasn't laughter he was seeing, it was a woman's hysteria. Her eyes shone bright with unshed tears, and her smile twisted up. "Oh, Mr. McCauley, you have no *idea* just how far I've gone already!"

Jonah clamped his arms around her again, only this time his heart ached, and sexual need was far from his mind. "Stop this, Cam. It's all right. We'll work this out together. Aw, please don't cry, honey." Jonah got nervous when women cried, but Camelot had finally reached the end of her rope; he figured she was entitled. He wanted to tell her everything would be fine, but he wasn't so sure about that himself. He wouldn't promise her something that he might not be able to give her: peace.

She calmed as he held her, taking deep breaths. Jonah could tell from her body softening, and the way she curled into him, nuzzling him, that the very things that worried her were beginning to affect her. How was he supposed to get things on an even keel if she couldn't hear his voice, be near him, or see him without getting uncontrollably aroused?

The craziest idea formed in his head. Could he? *Should* he? What if he only made things worse? Or even worse yet, what if his plan worked, and he "cured" her of not only the obsession, but the attraction, as well? Jonah knew that last projection was overkill, but it deserved consideration.

Jonah held her close and understood very well the need that gnawed at her. He felt it, too. But someway, somehow he'd find a solution to what was quickly consuming them both. For the first time ever, Jonah wanted more than just one night of passion, appeasing a physical need. He had to beat back his own lust for the greater good of eventually having Camelot trust in him.

They were meant for more than just sex; Jonah was positive of it. He'd always trusted his instincts, and he wouldn't start doubting them now. He'd deal with his blatant disregard for company policy later. Jonah was going to give his personal life top priority and try and help this woman who obviously needed him on a physical level, but he sensed on an emotional one, as well. God knew, he was beginning to need her.

He nudged her back until he could look down at her face. Tears clung to her pretty lashes and her sweet lips pouted. Jonah took her hands in his and stared down at them. Not just to avoid that lost look on her face; she was in the middle of a personal crisis, and he didn't want her to see that his thoughts of how to help her were keeping him aroused.

He fought the hunger that built inside him. She desperately needed the comfort he offered. Camelot was a strong, confident woman despite the few times he'd been privy to her vulnerability. And those rare times were wreaking havoc on her world. But by his words or deeds, she'd let him in enough for him to glimpse it, despite the way she reacted in his presence. The importance of that wasn't lost on him.

Jonah was selfishly relieved, knowing it wasn't him personally that made her keep her distance, but her own conduct when she was near him. He should have felt guilty for what he was about to do, but he didn't. Not when, if it worked, she'd have possession of herself again, and be able to make fair and candid decisions without drowning in her own arousal.

He grinned down at her. "Okay now?"

Camelot lowered her head and nodded, embarrassed again.

Jonah hated that look, but he remembered what she'd done here earlier. Thank God no one else knew. He'd remind Barb that the security cameras were secret, and the less people who knew about them, the less chance there was for them to be tampered with. Jonah would be happy if Camelot never discovered their existence in his office. But sooner or later, he'd have to come clean about seeing her. He just preferred later. He didn't kid himself, either. Secretaries were a dime a dozen in this town, but her skills were amazing and her contributions were on an executive level. One didn't get that way in this business without being savvy and taking some bold chances. He knew that when this obstacle was out of the way, she'd be back to her former self, a cunning businesswoman. When he told her about that tape, and his voyeurism, she was going to be furious with him, but looking at her now, he didn't care. He'd take her anger over humiliation and shame any day.

"Let me see you tonight," he said. If he hadn't known

what he did, her knee-jerk reactions might have been enough to give him a complex. She looked at him like he was nuts.

He squeezed her hands, explaining, "This isn't something that we can't help each other with. And you're right. I didn't know your first name until last night, but you've been on my mind for weeks. We *have* to discuss this, Camelot. I think we both know that it's something that neither of us can overlook anymore."

Camelot's eyes met his, and she nodded.

Jonah knew he had her.

Chapter Five

Camelot rushed down from the loft, hastily knotting her braid, when there was a knock at the door.

She was queasy with a mix of excitement and dread.

She'd agreed to meet Jonah when they got off work. He might not be as bad off as she was, but she felt a little less solitary when he acknowledged that he was having problems with this, too.

He'd suggested dinner at a nice restaurant, but she quickly nixed that; with the chaos of the last twenty-four hours, Camelot didn't trust herself in any setting with him other than a private one.

She invited him to her apartment instead, which brought up another anxiety of keeping her hands to herself until they could figure out what to do. At least she wouldn't make a fool of herself in public.

Then he told her to go on home after lunch. "Cam," he said, annoyed when she hemmed and hawed, "I've been thinking about nothing but last night, and of you here—"

She was sure he was about to say something else, but he stopped himself just in time. He raked his hand through his hair, something she'd noticed he did when he was agitated.

"And, well . . . you distract me, and I will be all day, knowing that you're right downstairs. I can't have this on my mind and deal with clients at the same time. We need to be alone, Camelot." He lifted her chin. "Can you honestly tell me you'll be able to work—ah God, Camelot!"

Jonah stepped back from her, and put his hands out. "Look at you! Your eyes are glassy, and you're all flushed! You're obviously aroused, and I've done nothing but talk. Anyone can walk in here, and even if I lock that door, I do *not* want to be interrupted for this."

The sharpness in his voice and his exasperation had been enough to douse the licking flames, but the embers still burned. Camelot pulled herself together as best she could.

She'd still felt like squirming, standing so close to him, but she blew out a gust of air, giving herself a mental shake. "You're right, of course, Mr. McCauley. We can't have this conversation here in the office." She'd focused, once again the consummate professional, but she couldn't extinguish the arousal that lurked in the depths of her eyes.

"Right. This is a place of business, and we'll conduct ourselves accordingly here in the office."

It had been all Camelot could do not to whimper. Oh, if he only knew how unprofessional she'd been earlier. Right behind her in the corner, no less!

She'd backed away, turned, and threw him a blind wave as she left his office. But no matter what they decided, discussed, or hammered out, Camelot was going to break the cardinal rule she'd made for herself after her last disastrous relationship. She was going to mix business with pleasure. And after that incredible kiss they'd shared, she was looking forward to taking charge of her life and, whether Jonah knew it or not, making her fantasies a reality.

The knock at her front door came again, and Camelot went to meet her fate.

Damn, she looks so good, Jonah thought when the door swung open and she stood staring back at him. Tendrils of her fiery red hair spilled out of her loose French braid; her eyes were that bluish purple, but they shone, and she was flushed.

Had she been rushing around before he arrived? He bit the inside of his cheek, remembering what had made that sheen of moisture form on her upper lip just this morning. He swallowed a groan.

Jonah didn't think either one of them were going to be able to govern their body's actions too much tonight, except to answer pleas and groans of need. But she was becoming too important to him to blindly reach out and kiss her, taking away her choices. They'd never talk if he so much as touched her now. But Jonah couldn't stop his eyes from appreciating the view.

Bad idea, McCauley.

His gaze began its descent along her tender throat, imagining kissing her there, getting drunk on her unique scent of flowers and spice.

Her blouse was silky and delicate enough to glimpse the lace of her bra through it, the hard points of her nipples pressed against the barriers.

Oh Jesus. Jonah wondered if she'd ever seen a grown man cry. Looking at her was like sneaking a peek at the presents under the tree on Christmas morning, but having to wait for the go-ahead to dive into them. She was a gift that he was dying to tear the wrapping from, so he could open her up to enjoy.

Her waist was tapered and slender. He'd only seen it once before. She always wore jackets that covered her elegant form at work. He stopped himself where her skirt began. If he went even a centimeter lower, he knew he'd see the curve of her hips, all his noble intentions would vanish, and he'd start undressing her right there in her doorway.

God, why am I torturing myself? he wondered, waiting for his inner voice to counter. Thankfully, it was silent.

"Jonah," Camelot chided, her index finger tickling under his chin until his eyes met hers, "Yeah, hi." Her lips curved in amusement, but he could tell she hadn't let his moment of distraction pass without checking him out, either.

He chuckled, whistling low as he tilted his head, his gaze sweeping over her again. "Oh, we definitely have a problem here," he declared matter-of-factly.

"*We* do?"

"Oh yeah, 'we.' In case you haven't noticed, honey, I'm hard already and you haven't even invited me in yet."

Her brows rose in surprise, but Jonah knew that she was well aware of his state of arousal. It was his bluntness that caught her off guard and made her flustered.

She smiled, pulling the door open wide. "Well then, won't you come—"

His own brow shot up.

"*In!* In . . . Won't you come in?"

That was a Freudian slip if ever he'd heard one, but he was still regaining his equilibrium from the full engaging smile she shot him before rolling her eyes and looking away. His knees nearly buckled. *She's so beautiful*, he thought. If it were up to him, she'd smile all the time. He was hoping she'd let him give that a try.

He'd changed at the office, but he brought his briefcase with him. Now that he had that tape, he wasn't letting it out of his possession until it was tucked away in his safe at home. Her shoes were in there too, but he'd give them to her later. No way was he going to let her see that tape. He set the attaché by the door as he stepped inside, and took a good look at her personal space.

The left side of the studio apartment held her living area and computer station. The room was light, airy, and the furniture displayed a tasteful combination of prints and stripes. *Eclectic*, he thought.

To his right, the butcher-block island served the practical functions of counter and cupboard space, and it enclosed a tiny kitchen. There were barstools around it, making it a place for informal conversation. Straight ahead of him, his eyes followed the spiral staircase up and around until they settled on the bed in the open loft. "Ah," he said aloud.

"Jonah," Camelot called, snapping her fingers in front of his face.

Now that he'd decided on a plan, it rankled that Camelot seemed more in control of herself tonight. They were on her turf, he guessed. But Jonah wondered how the tables had turned on him. He shot her a chagrined look, but he wasn't really sorry.

She smiled knowingly. "Come sit at the counter while I work on dinner," she said over her shoulder, heading to the kitchenette.

As the distance widened between them, Jonah admired her form in her long skirt, her pretty bare feet peeking out from underneath it as she walked. *Even her feet are adorable,* he thought. *Shit!* He raised his eyes, silently mouthed, *Give me strength.* Halfheartedly making the sign of the cross, he followed behind her.

He cleared his throat. "You cooked dinner?"

Good opening, McCauley. You moron, his inner voice mocked, and it was damned annoying.

"Well, we both have to eat, and I wasn't sure how long your meetings would run today. I stopped by the grocer on the way home. We couldn't go out to eat, for obvious reasons, of course, and takeout didn't really hold any appeal."

Jonah chuckled. *Obvious reasons is right!*

"Now, I'm no chef, but I can hold my own," she explained. Then she whirled around, alarmed. "Tell me you eat red meat. I made pot roast."

Jonah grinned, about to tell her that he loved homemade pot roast, but the words wouldn't come. He seemed transfixed by her teeth sinking into the soft flesh as she worried her lip.

"Oh, Christ," he muttered under his breath, but she heard.

"Jonah," she scolded, shifting her stance. "This is a lot

of fun, watching you wig out a little for a change, but you have to stop it. This is serious. We have to discuss our . . . problem. So unless you stop looking at me like *I'm* dinner, I'll blindfold you until we at least sit down to the meal."

Her finger pointed at him in warning made him grin. He raised a brow lasciviously, like the idea had merit. But then he grabbed her finger, and just that gesture was enough to make her gasp. He threw a wrench in her plan, asking, "Tell me, sweetheart. How can I talk? How will *you* control *your* urges?"

He had her there, he thought. He loved how expressive her face was as she worked things out in her head.

She pulled her finger from his grip, and turned back into the kitchen. "I'll work on my neurosis, you work on yours, Counselor," she replied flippantly over her shoulder. "I just can't believe that less than a day ago, I was avoiding you like you had a disease or something, and tonight you're here to help me figure out how I can keep my job without doing something very stupid like having sex with you on your desk." She shook her head and chuckled.

Or something like what she'd done alone in his office, he thought. Jonah cringed behind her, knowing how mortified she'd be if she knew that she'd had an audience this morning. He was glad her back was to him, or she might have read it in his eyes.

He pushed the achingly vivid image aside. "You'll keep your job, Camelot, no matter what. But I can't get you off my mind, and after today, I know it's the same for you. But one problem is that I'm your boss, and that has so many strings attached, we're bound to get ourselves in a tangle."

Jonah waited until she turned her head to look at him. "I don't know why all this started with you and me." He waved his hand, then curled it into a fist, pounding it on the counter to stress his point. "But I'd be a fool to let it end because of a technicality." He was determined to pursue this—whatever it was—with her. The policy he'd enforced up until now be damned.

Camelot grinned at his legal term for "these are my rules we're about to break." And his vehemence sent a tingle up her spine. It was a new side of him that she was seeing. She liked it more than she should.

She'd had lots of time this afternoon to think about what an affair would mean in the scheme of things, and she wasn't thrilled with the slant it took. She'd kept so many secrets these past few months; having to keep one more because of this didn't sit well with her at all.

In the amazingly short time they'd known each other, Camelot had felt a connection stronger than even the arousal that wouldn't let her loose. Jonah was a good man; she'd learned that shortly after being hired. He did charity work, made anonymous contributions, and just this afternoon he could've taken advantage of her, but he hadn't. No matter what, Jonah was letting her set the pace, and she found that as stimulating and arousing as any physical attribute. She couldn't jeopardize his career, or her own, for that matter, when he'd been so honest with her.

He did look delicious, though. She couldn't dismiss that out of hand. He wore a soft crewneck sweater, sleeves tugged up his powerful forearms, and his jeans were faded and threadbare at the rivets and pockets. They hugged his thighs and were tight, stretched over his fly.

She wanted to resent Jonah for making her less confident than she'd ever been, but when she saw his reaction to her and his own lack of complete control to stop it, she felt a kinship to him that was growing in leaps and bounds. She wasn't alone in this thing. In the broad scope, Camelot knew it would be easier if the object of her obsession wasn't just as stricken, but luck wasn't something she had an abundance of. They'd deal with it together. And maybe she'd discover a strength she'd been lacking lately. Either way, Camelot liked that Jonah was willing to do whatever it took to keep her job safe. He wasn't privy to her thoughts, didn't know that she hoped they'd end up in bed by the end of the evening, but he was here anyway.

She could feel his gaze rolling over her skin and seeping into her pores. "You're staring, you know."

He stood looking at her as if he hadn't a care in the world, but his muscles were coiled tight, and his efforts to draw steadying breaths revealed that pantherlike quality about him again. Ready to lunge, but holding back until the moment was right. She shouldn't feel safe right now, but she did.

"I know. You make me want things, and I'm trying not to push."

She chuckled. "You remind me of *The Horse Whisperer,* Jonah. Calming the spooked filly." Her smile faltered a little. An accurate description, but not one she liked very much. She didn't like having to be soothed.

"Is it working?" he asked huskily.

"That still remains to be seen, I'm afraid. But I'm glad to have you here. I feel more grounded than I have in weeks. A little edgy maybe, but I've managed to keep my hands to myself so far. That's a good sign."

"Speak for yourself." He grinned, giving her that "I'm a man" look. Then his smile slid off his face. "I do hope it's more than physical, though."

His composure is slipping, she thought. "Why don't you have a seat and we'll take this one step at a time, okay?"

He grudgingly nodded and sat down on a stool at the island. She needed a little time before committing to anything other than the obvious. He instinctively understood her reluctance, and her belly fluttered, knowing that what he wanted, what he could easily have, he wasn't going to take without her permission. *God, he's perfect!* she thought.

The counter separated them, and she took a deep breath. His voice, his presence, even his scent surrounded her. He looked so good casually propped on that stool that her fingers actually itched to reach out and touch. But that wouldn't be smart, especially since she'd managed to hold him off thus far. That fleeting contact wouldn't be fair if he wasn't allowed to reciprocate.

She wanted to throw caution to the wind and let go of every inhibition, but she'd done that once and had her spirit trampled on. Camelot knew that what she was feeling for Jonah was different, and worlds apart from what she'd been through before, but it didn't make her any less guarded. She told him with her resolute expression that she wouldn't elaborate, but she compromised, saying, "It's more, Jonah."

Camelot's eyes slid away from his relieved but steady stare. He was too close. She wasn't ready for him to learn every secret.

Her eyes fell upon the box she'd left on the edge of the counter. If horror had a face, Camelot was sure hers was it.

When she was at the market earlier this afternoon, she'd passed the pharmaceuticals and honed in on the assortment of condoms on display. She'd forced herself to concentrate on getting the fixings for dinner, but her mind kept going back to the prophylactics. She'd worried her lip raw while she battled with indecision as she pushed her cart up and down each aisle.

Would she look like a slut if she bought them and had them ready? Or would he be grateful that she cared about her own safety with a virtual stranger she was about to go to bed with?

In the end, she'd grabbed the first box within reach and threw it in her cart. *There, decision made*, she'd reasoned. She'd planned to put them in her nightstand by her bed; he'd never know if he came prepared, and she'd cross that bridge when she came to it if he didn't have anything with him. Hell, the whole night might turn into a disaster, and the point would be moot. But she highly doubted that last thought.

When she'd gotten home, she'd tossed the box on the island as she unpacked the rest of the groceries, intending to take it upstairs when she changed clothes. But not knowing what time Jonah would arrive, she'd hurried up to the loft to take a quick shower and forgot that she'd left the condoms on the counter. Now she just stared at them, unable to move and snatch it up, out of sight.

As if in slow motion, Jonah's hand entered her line of vision, reaching across the countertop. Her eyes followed the box back as he lifted it to his face, reading the label.

" 'Extra ribbed for more sensitivity and pleasure.' Hmmmm, his or hers, do you think?" He grinned and cocked his head at her, raising a brow.

Camelot's face went hot; she didn't want to look at him. Talk about mortifying!

"Oh, come on, honey, I was kidding." He tipped his finger under her chin, just as she'd done a few minutes ago to him, and made her meet his eyes. "I'm glad you got these. Not only does it take the guesswork out of tonight's outcome, but I feel a lot better that you care enough about my health to make sure I'm protected."

She gave him a wobbly smile, glad that if she had to be obsessed, it was with such a nice, funny man. He broke the tension and charmed her right out of her embarrassment. She relaxed, glad that he wasn't making fun of her, but enjoying her.

Jonah breathed a sigh of relief when she grinned shyly. It wrenched his heart when she was sad or upset. Teasing her put her at ease quicker than anything could. He tilted his head, saying, "I *am* hungry, though, so you just keep your hands to yourself until we're finished with dinner, lady."

Her giggles were like bubbles that tumbled up from her throat, sounding so sweet in the quiet of the apartment. Jonah felt himself going under. Everything she did made him want her, made him desperate to see her smile, laugh, or moan in pleasure. He hoped dinner would be ready soon, or he'd end up making a meal out of her. "Feed me, woman, and I may even help with the dishes." He leaned back on the stool and crossed his arms over his chest, trying to sound serious, but he was having too much fun for the mischief not to show through.

She laughed outright, shaking her head and saying provocatively, "Forget the dishes. If I feed you, you'll help me with a hell of a lot more than household chores, boss man." Then she gasped and clamped her hand over her mouth like she'd done earlier, surprised at herself again.

Jonah's foot slipped off the rung of the stool and hit the floor with a thud. He wasn't prepared for that one, but passion was like a storm as it churned and pumped the blood through his body.

"Dinner. Go. Now." He pointed across the room to the oven and closed his eyes when she scrambled to do just that, not daring to push him another step. He wanted to take her right there against the counter! Comments like that were going to get her in trouble if she didn't watch it. She was an enigma, throwing him and herself off balance every time she opened her mouth. But Lord, he was enjoying the contrasts.

When he was sure he wouldn't beg her to tell him what help she had in mind, he steered the conversation away from condoms and sex, hoping to focus on something other than the erection that had swelled to the point of pain in his jeans.

"So, tell me about yourself, Camelot. Like, how did you get your name?" He'd wanted to ask before because he was so intrigued by it. How he'd forgotten it, he couldn't fathom, but Jonah knew that for the rest of his life he'd never forget how his memory had been jarred. And they needed a distraction from the extra-ribbed condoms, *which he might take offense to if he thought about it*. He figured asking a question was as good a distraction as any.

Of course, the memory of their name game from last night came flooding back to him, but he forced himself not to look up at her loft and that bed, with its comforter hanging off it, unmade, perfect for tumbling into.

Focus, McCauley!

Her face was in profile and she grinned at his question. Probably because she'd been counting the minutes it took for him to ask, knowing he would. He'd bet everyone did.

She sliced the French bread that had been baking on the rack next the pot roast in the oven. The steam rose and heated her face as it filled the room with the warm, delicious aroma. Jonah loved these sights and smells of her home. He didn't know why he was so comfortable with her here in her studio, but looking at her, barefoot and flushed in the heat of the kitchen, preparing the meal, felt so natural to him. He'd return the favor and make her a scrumptious meal one night soon, just so he could turn and see her sitting in his place, making herself at home in his surroundings.

"My father was a workaholic. It's actually what killed him. But years before I was born, when my parents were struggling, starting out, Dad was much worse. In 1960, when *Camelot* was running on Broadway with Richard Burton, Mother made Dad take his week's vacation, and they went into the city to see the show. They did all kinds of things that young couples do on a budget, but she'd saved for weeks to get tickets for that performance.

"When I came along many years later, Dad was so busy with work that Mother wanted to remind him of what was important—time spent with family. So she named me Camelot, remembering that amazing week they'd spent together. It was the only vacation he ever took, as a matter of fact. When Dad would get home, he always found time to read to me or dance with me in the living room while Mother made dinner. But by the time I was old enough to know that he worked too hard, the damage had already been done."

Jonah could see that she was lost in memory, and though it wasn't all pleasant, she smiled faintly. He was at least glad that she knew she was loved. But like his own family, work seemed to be more important than anything, even taking time off to be with the children. And it also told him why she was on the low end of the totem pole as a secretary, when she had the potential to be taking home a six-figure salary; she wasn't going to make the same mistakes, pushing and working herself to death like her father did. He admired her all the more for not selling out.

She went on. "That play brought happy memories of the week they'd spent together. Mother said that naming me Camelot was her gift to me, just as I was to them."

She talked while she got the roast out and sliced it onto plates. Then she started on the salad. Her back was to him, but he could hear her voice catch every now and then. He wanted to go to her, comfort her, and tell her what an amazing woman he thought she was, but he knew one touch and the sexual tension would be back. Right now, Jonah felt cozy sitting here with her. He liked that she seemed much more comfortable around him now, too. Her spine still stiffened when he spoke, but she fought the effect.

So many things she did were aimed at making him feel like he belonged there. In the midst of her story, she'd brought the bottle of wine over to him and handed him a corkscrew before turning back to her own tasks. Anyone peeking in on them would think they were a couple that did this every night. Jonah felt the burning in his gut, and a lump forming in his throat. Despite the painful memories his mind recalled of his family never having time to eat dinner together, he savored the rightness of it with Camelot.

"Where is your mother now?" he asked, changing the subject, and banishing his bitter memories.

"She's in Rose Grove."

"But isn't that . . . ?"

"Yes, it's the cemetery. She's buried next to Dad there.

She had cancer, but didn't tell anyone. When Dad died, she didn't want to frighten me, knowing I was going to be orphaned very soon. She thought she'd have a bit of time to prepare me for it, but it turns out the cancer was much more extensive than the doctors first thought. She died about four months after Dad passed away, but I was frightened of being alone almost from the moment Dad died."

Jonah cocked his head, questioningly. "If she didn't tell you she was sick, why were you afraid?"

"At the burial service, Mother knelt at the gravesite and touched her hand to the casket, then leaned in to kiss it. She whispered, 'I'll be joining you soon, darling. Look for me and bring me home.' I was only nine, but I knew what that meant. She was going to die, too. She didn't know I was standing right behind her."

As Camelot recounted that awful day, the fear and sorrow that she remembered so vividly were with her again. Her bitterness was clear, too; she chopped the hell out of the lettuce in front of her. Her shoulders slumped and her head bowed, trying hard not to show how much that one betrayal still hurt.

Then Jonah was there.

Gently, he took the knife from her hand, laid it on the butcher block, and slipped his arms around her from behind. But she turned in his embrace, needing the contact, and buried her face in his neck as she wept the tears he suspected she'd never shed before now. No, she was strong, and somehow he knew she'd been strong then, too. She'd held it all in, and never let her mother see her fear. He was sure of it.

He absorbed her pain and let his silence console her. They rocked back and forth, but his insides churned in anger that what her mother thought was a private moment shattered the world for a little girl not yet ten years old. God, she tugged at his heart!

Neither spoke. There was no need. They just held on to each other and swayed gently. Her arms came up his back and clung, her fists curled into the sweater.

His hands made circles on her back, keeping her enveloped in the warmth of his body. His cheek rested on her hair, and he found a contentment that he'd never felt with anyone.

Every reason for not pursuing a relationship with her was forgotten. She needed him and Jonah found that in giving nothing but the solace she craved, his soul was soothed, as well.

He'd grown up in a house packed with kids, four older brothers and three younger sisters. But with only two parents who worked to feed them all, time was like a tapestry, intricately woven. Too many school activities, schedules, and projects kept Jonah from getting quality time. His parents saw them as the Children, rather than individuals. He was the middle child, and lost in the shuffle too many times to count. Jonah was smart enough to know that it was the reason behind avoiding serious relationships. Loneliness didn't always mean being alone. His heart squeezed; he felt the old hurt like a fresh wound.

He'd learned to be independent, to count on no one but himself. But that was before he met this woman who had her own demons to conquer. In less than a day, he'd determined that he wanted to be the one she turned to in a crisis. His problems were nothing when compared to hers, but with every minute in her company, he needed her more and more. If he believed in things like karma or fate, he imagined that Camelot was his soul mate. But yesterday he didn't believe in telepathy, either, and then that elevator ride had proved him wrong. He was beginning to believe anything was possible if Camelot was by his side.

The crook of his shoulder was wet with her tears, and she hiccupped as she calmed. Jonah felt a pang of guilt. Comforting her felt so damned good.

"Shhhhh, baby. I'm sorry. I didn't mean to bring up such a painful memory for you."

She pulled away, and her tear-streaked, puffy face looked beautiful to him. There was wonder in her eyes. "What, honey?" he said.

"I've never told anyone that before."

He shrugged, but she gripped his arms.

"Jonah, you don't understand," she said vehemently. "I've *never* told anyone that. Not my grandmother, who I lived with after they both died. Not Kat. No one. Why you? And why now?"

He chuckled, pulling her back in his arms. He cupped the back of her head and settled it on his chest, keeping it there. "Because this relationship is going to take trust on both our parts, and somehow your heart is telling you that I won't betray you." At least, that's what he *hoped* her heart was saying.

Camelot sighed, not commenting either way, but she breathed through the loose knit of his sweater, heating his skin instantly. Jonah ignored the signs of arousal, barely. *She needs comfort right now, not seduction*, he repeated over and over to himself, even as her breath continued to tease and stir the chest hairs that mingled with the wool and rayon.

What Jonah forgot was that Camelot's obsession with him was even worse than his affliction to her. She'd been contained and, for the most part, in control since he'd arrived. He wanted to console her, but all he was managing to do was incite a riot on her senses.

She nuzzled his chest, her hot breath fanning his male nipple and making it hard. Her openmouthed kisses on his sweater were more than he could stand, and he brought both hands to her head, tangling in her fiery red hair.

He tipped her face up to him to look in her eyes. They were sharp with raw desire. His conscience did battle. She was a victim of her own lust. This wasn't the Camelot he'd gotten to know in the last half hour. She wasn't a vixen or a woman who played the games he'd played with numerous women over the years.

She was innocent—at least in her attraction to him, she was. If he gave into her pleading eyes, wouldn't that be a violation of the trust he'd just declared he wouldn't betray?

He'd never been involved with any woman for more than a night or two, but with this slip of a woman, who drove him to break rules and risk his own integrity, he saw his future, corny as it seemed. Jonah had intended to follow her lead in this, go at her pace, but she wasn't thinking rationally, and he was on the brink of doing something really, really stupid—like taking her when she was so vulnerable after a moment that was an epiphany.

Either way he chose, he was going to hurt, Jonah knew. He took the high road, praying he was doing the right thing. "Okay, baby, time out," he said, moving back from her.

"Huh?" Her face contorted with doubt and rejection.

He felt like an ass. Attempting some damage control, he said, "Now, don't go getting all riled on me, honey," he said, squeezing her shoulders. Even her confusion tempted him nearly beyond his noble intentions. "I just think we should slow down a little." Did he just say that?

She looked at him like he'd lost his mind. Hell, he couldn't even believe it himself!

He tried again. "Sweetheart, you've just shared something with me that no one else knows about you, and it's special that I'm the one you chose, whether you meant to or not. I don't know why it matters so much, but it does," he said in defense.

She stared hard at him, not buying it, though it was the truth.

Her lips pursed in annoyance. "If you want to wait, Jonah, then do it for yourself. But if you think I'm vulnerable and need a little TLC, then let me share something *else* with you, Mr. McCauley."

He was really beginning to hate it when she called him that. She knew what buttons to push, and she sure as hell knew how to get him fired up. But this was what he'd come for, after all—wasn't it? To help her any way he could? If she needed to lash out and vent, then he was man enough to take whatever she dished out. He hoped.

"I love my job. It's easy for me. I make good money, I like the people I work with. And I happen to like my boss."

His eyebrows shot up.

She snickered. "Okay. I like him a lot. But if the things that happen when I'm around him, or when I hear his voice, don't stop, I'm going to have to quit or I'll get fired. I could get in a lot of trouble for the things I've done to scratch this itch Jonah, but so far those things have done nothing but make me want you more."

She turned away and began collecting silverware from the drawer. Loudly. She'd been blunt, and Jonah wondered why she felt the need to hide from his probing gaze now. She'd already been more honest than he'd ever been with a partner. What she said next had Jonah at once concerned and dangerously aroused.

"I want to have hot, wild, draining sex with you tonight, and maybe finally lay to rest these unsettling feelings that I have no control over. If I can get some of my self-control back, then just maybe I'll get some of my self-respect back as well."

His heart squeezed tight. He'd seen her face this morning after she'd finished printing up his report. She was ashamed of the things she'd done. Until now, he hadn't realized that it was turning her inside out every minute of the day.

She looked at him. "No one but me knows my secrets yet, Jonah, but my sex drive is ruling me lately, and I'm bound to get caught in my body's trap sooner or later. I'd rather try and defuse this bomb before I'm arrested and the firm suffers the fallout for my actions."

She maintained eye contact, barely. And he knew why.

Without calling a spade a spade, she'd agreed to have him over for the same reason he needed to be here: physical therapy.

He wondered if he should feel used right now, but she stared expectantly and Jonah swallowed hard. Being this woman's boy toy wouldn't be a bad thing, he thought. Only hours ago he'd come up with that very option, a plan to help her, but he thought he'd have to convince *her* that it was for her own good. Now she was the one laying her cards on the table.

She wasn't aware of the signals she was putting out right now, either. But he'd seen the signs all night, the flirtatious banter, the condoms, the dinner that was getting cold. Everything pointed to a night of unadulterated sex. But it was because of her shyness that he held back. When she was in control, she took careful steps, and only when her desires took over did she get surly with him. She needed a resolution, but Jonah was still able to see the whole picture, and it was more than what she had in mind.

"Okay," he said. "But let's get one thing straight. We help each other because, let's face it, I'm as caught up in this as you are. But if it works, and you can control the power of these . . . urges, then you don't banish me along with them."

He decided the only way for her to trust him was to be honest about his feelings, even if it put a halt to things now. "I want you for more than just one night, Camelot."

She smiled indulgently. "Somehow I don't think that's going to be a problem, Jonah." Her fingers grazed the hair on his forearm where the sweater ended, and the nothing touch made him crazy to take her in his arms and start.

God! How was he going to take this slow? He wanted to still be making love when the sun came up, but he didn't think they'd last as long as it took Leno to finish his monologue.

The pull was getting stronger and stronger. Wanting to make love all night was enticing, but he was anticipating the aftermath, and the comedown from the rush of passion, almost as much. He'd never wanted that with any woman before, had never had it, but as he gazed at her quivering lips, beckoning him, he decided that he was going to have that with her. But he refused to be rushed.

"Go sit down. I'll serve." He indicated a little table in the corner. The tension broken once again, it didn't do anything to slow down his racing heart.

Camelot brought the linen napkins, silverware, and their partially full wineglasses to the table while Jonah carried the salads and then their plates.

The only two chairs faced each other. She arranged his place across from her, but he moved the entire setting and pulled the chair around so that he sat catty-corner to her.

"I want to sit close to you," he said. Lifting her hand to his lips, he kissed the back of it. Camelot smiled and lowered her head, but he could tell she was pleased.

"So. How old are you, Camelot?"

"Twenty-nine."

"When was your last relationship?"

"Why?" She asked curiously.

Jonah hid a grin. She was such a suspicious little thing. With all that she'd been going through lately, he couldn't blame her, he supposed. "Because I want to know how gentle I'll have to be if it's been a while for you," he replied nonchalantly. He got the response he was looking for; she blushed prettily and ducked her head.

"It has been a while, Jonah."

Then she lowered her voice to barely above a whisper and said, "But I hope that won't stop you from doing all those things I mentioned."

His fork clattered onto the plate.

Jonah snapped, "That's it."

Chapter Six

Taking her hand and pulling her to her feet, he helped her maneuver from around the table, and then nearly dragged her across the room as he headed for the stairs.

"Jonah, wait. Slow down," she said, tugging on his hand.

He stopped short and looked back at her, worried that now he'd reached his limit, she was the one calling a halt.

"My legs are a little shaky, I'll fall if I rush."

Jonah laughed, smiling broadly before his head swooped down and captured her lips in a kiss meant to make her lose feeling altogether. She did go weak, but her arms wrapped around his neck, and she hung on for dear life.

He walked her backward until she was pressed between the wall and his obvious erection.

His lips sealed to hers, and their tongues tangled, tasting and teasing. He pressed so close to her, but it wasn't anywhere near as close as he needed to be. His hands caressed her hips, and her nails dug into his shoulders as he ground into her. No other woman had met his sexual appetites before. He knew that Camelot was going to be the one. Maybe hers would even surpass his.

Reluctantly, he dragged his mouth from hers, whispering gruffly, "Okay now?"

"Of course not!" She laughed breathlessly. "If you let go of me now, I'll sink to the floor like a stone."

He took his weight off her by backing up, and she began to do just that, but he bent down and scooped her up like a sack of potatoes onto his shoulder. He strode across the floor again, swiped his hand across the counter, and snagged the box of condoms off it as he went.

"Oh, you have got to be kidding! Jonah, put me down right now!" Camelot yelled around her laughter. Her hand smacked his butt playfully, but then she splayed it over one cheek, enjoying the feel of its flex as he walked.

"You'll get that right back, sweetheart, so I'd rethink your abuse of my poor body." He squeezed his arm tighter around her thighs and nipped at her hip, which grazed his cheek.

"Oh," she sighed, going slack.

We're gonna be so damn good, Jonah thought, grinning in anticipation. With a burst of energy, he took the curving stairs as if she weighed no more than a child.

When he reached the top, Jonah thought about tossing her on the bed and watching her bounce on the mattress before he joined her, but he was desperate to feel her pressed to him again.

He shrugged her off his shoulder and let her slide down the hard length of him until her toes landed on the tops of his shoes. He tossed the box of condoms on the bed and held her warm body to him. She was going to be his. Jonah had never looked forward to anything more.

Her arms encircled his neck again, and she tilted her head up for his kiss. He didn't disappoint her. Her fingers tangled in his hair and he cupped the back of her head. Their lips met again in another crushing kiss, and his hands skimmed down, clutching her hips, pulling her tight to him.

Her tongue darted into his mouth, searching and finding his own. Jonah wondered if he'd died and gone to heaven.

She was obviously a novice at being the aggressor, but what she lacked in experience, she made up for in enthusiasm. In the recesses of his mind, he whispered her name over and over again, like a mantra. *Camelot . . . Camelot.* She truly was an enchanting place to be.

Jonah didn't know if he could separate himself from her long enough to be able to look at her. But his cock weighed heavy and rigid in his jeans, and if he didn't free it soon, he was going to embarrass himself by coming right there, pressed against her belly. She drove him close to the edge every time her tongue delved into his mouth, or her breasts pressed hard against his chest, and especially when she undulated her hips against his thickening erection.

"Slower, baby. Slower," he managed to whisper when he could drag his lips from hers and bury his face at her throat.

"Next time," she murmured, and kissed the shell of his ear, nipping at the lobe.

Was she kidding? At the rate they were going, he wasn't sure he'd survive this *first* time, never mind the next one!

Unfastening the single button at the back of her blouse, Jonah pulled it free of the skirt. Her hands found their way under his sweater, causing him to shudder and suck in his breath at the feel of her fingers on his heated skin.

He lifted her blouse, craving the same contact. She took her hands off him and raised her arms over her head to be free of the garment, and he let the silk whisper to the floor.

God, she could stop a clock, he thought, eyes devouring her soft form.

She took a step forward, but he took two steps back. "No," he said, "let me look. This is what I missed last night on the phone, what I dreamed of in the elevator yesterday. I've been dying to see if my fantasies did you justice."

She stood there, a little self-conscious, but primed and ready for him. Her nipples were hard and pointed, confined in the lacy bra. Her hair was still bound in the braid and he ached to feel his fingers tangled in it, but Jonah knew that if he touched her, even in that small way, they'd be all over each other again, and his moment to admire would be gone.

Her belly was smooth, flat and tanned. He would kiss her navel and feel her gasp. Her hips flared out slightly, and Jonah imagined her straddling him, his hands steadying her there as she rode him hard until each shouted the other's name when they came.

And her legs. They were still obscured by the skirt she wore, but he'd seen them so many times in the tasteful, sexy short suits she wore to work that he knew they'd be perfect for wrapping around his waist as he drove her from one peak to the next. He was dying to see all of her.

She shifted her weight, placing her hands on both of her hips, and Jonah chuckled. He could tell she was unsure of herself, but her desire ruled her now, daring her to entice him, excite him.

"Well? Were your fantasies as good?"

"Not . . . even . . . close, babe," he whispered. "Not even close."

Her delighted, shy smile lit up her face; her eyes darkened and sparkled to a deep violet. Jonah's knees went weak. Her timidity in the face of her eagerness was like a drug, luring him to overdose on what she offered. He hooked his finger in her waistband and hauled her back into his arms.

"God, what you do to me," he said huskily, and lowered his head to the valley between her breasts.

"Is nothing compared to what you do to me, Jonah. Nothing." She sighed and wrapped her arms around his head.

Her confession finally drove him to his knees, literally. He knew what obsession was. It was Camelot, and he hoped he never found a cure. He loved being her obsession. He only hoped he could ease her hunger enough to get them through the day, but still make her wild for him at night. He couldn't lose her at the firm. He'd already promised that her job was safe, but if she did any more of those things that she'd done in his office this morning, life could get messy. Yet even with all the emotions rolling inside him, he knew they'd find a way.

His mouth opened, and his tongue snaked out to dip into her navel as he unzipped the skirt at her hip, easing it and her panties down her legs. Her skin was so warm and smooth; he loved the feel of its softness against his rough cheek.

Jonah turned his head, moved lower, and raked his teeth along her thigh, gently nipping the flesh. He groaned, feeling her legs quiver beneath his lusty mouth as his hands clasped her hips, holding her steady.

She moaned in pleasure and frustration. "Please, Jonah. Oh, please." She parted her legs, lifting one to rest on his shoulder, her fingers clutching at his hair.

He'd never heard a woman say his name quite like that, with a mixture of desperation and rapture.

He breathed in her musky scent, his face nuzzling through the soft curls to the slick place between her legs. His tongue flicked over the swollen flesh, tasting her sweetness as she gasped. Then he separated the soft folds with his fingers and his mouth covered her, suckling and savoring her, feasting on her.

She moaned and pressed closer.

He pushed two fingers into her heat, stroking her inner walls as his tongue lashed her exposed clitoris, driving her to the pinnacle. He gently nipped at the nubbin of flesh, and she cried out sharply, a high-pitched keening sound as she shuddered violently in his hold, tumbling over the edge in fulfillment.

Jonah enjoyed her for a moment more, giving as much pleasure as she could stand, then lifted his head, rolling his face back and forth on her belly as she still quivered with the force of her climax.

"Camelot..." he whispered against her warm skin, leashing his own hunger and keeping it at bay. This first time was for her.

When he knew he could stand it, he rose and cradled her in his arms. She trembled, and he grinned at how easy it had been to bring her to orgasm. *Oh, wait until I start talking!* he thought. *She'll be a wild thing.*

He chuckled. "Okay now?" he asked, repeating his question from earlier. She made him feel so damn good, he wanted to laugh and play with her and hear those sighs all night long. But he still had the nuisance of an aching, very hard erection wedged between them.

He felt her grin against his chest, and she nodded her head. "A little," she said, "but it's about to be so much better."

Her hand slid from his side to the front of his jeans. She curled her fingers around his throbbing erection.

Jonah groaned against her ear. "Oh yeah, baby. Squeeze me," his husky, unsteady voice encouraged her.

"I have to touch you, Jonah," she whispered impatiently, and let her hand tighten around him one last time. Then she skated it up and took the edge of his sweater in her fists, turning it inside out as she dragged it over his head.

Jonah didn't think he could get any hotter than he already was, but then her soft, lace-covered breasts came in contact with his chest, and she rubbed against him seductively. He was so wrong.

She tipped her head up and his lips crashed onto hers, his tongue tasting her passion, thrusting and withdrawing in a parody of what he would do to her soon. Both the mental image and the physical stimulation made him as impatient as she was.

His cock throbbed and strained against the fly of his jeans, and he lifted her closer. Her legs spread and snaked around him like a vine climbing a trellis; she ground her wet heat against the denim barrier that kept him from sliding into her. His arms spasmed as he cupped her soft bottom in his hands. He held her against his erection and she rocked, slowly driving him insane.

At the very brink, he dragged his mouth from hers. "Ah, babe, no more," he groaned, untangling her from him, and setting her back on her feet as he clumsily unfastened the row of buttons at his fly.

He kicked off his shoes as he pushed his clothes down, boxers and all, and cast them away, too. His socks followed until he was completely undressed in front of her. Her eyes ate him up and she licked her lips, then bit down on them. Jonah ached for what he knew she was thinking.

God! He'd never seen that kind of hunger in the eyes of a woman. She took his breath away.

Camelot licked her bottom lip and sucked it between her teeth, biting down hard. Jonah was a work of art, and she couldn't help but stare at what she considered to be a masterpiece. His sinewy arms connected to broad shoulders, the dark curly hair on his chest tapered to abs that were defined, but not pumped up. She knew he kept himself in shape with jogging, but he wasn't a slave to a fitness regimen. He didn't need to be; he was absolutely perfect the way he was.

Her hands absently unwound her braid. His fingers had been tangled in it a few minutes ago, and it had felt so good. His eyes turned dark as she shook her head and her hair became loose tendrils over her bare shoulders. Oh yes. She smiled. *He likes it free and flowing.*

She watched him as she reached behind her and unclipped her bra, dropping it to the floor with the rest of the clothes scattered all over her loft, but she didn't feel an ounce of embarrassment at her nudity anymore. The climax Jonah brought her to shattered the last vestiges of timidity she'd harbored. Enjoying the sight of his toned body was a delicious distraction, too.

He stared at her breasts; his eyes filled with a lust that reflected her own as she admired him. The nipples peaked under his possessive gaze and she felt that connection with this man all over again. How many times had she been unwillingly affected by just the thought of him? But this was real and she was *more* than willing to feel the effects of his aroused, hard body.

"Don't go speechless on me now, Jonah," she quipped, sliding her fingertips over his chest and hard stomach. He sucked in his breath and closed his eyes. The muscle in his jaw flexed, and Camelot smiled. *Oh, this is perfect*, she thought. *He's trying to stay in control.* But she wasn't going to let him hold anything back.

He opened his eyes again and raked them up and down her nude body, but his real scrutiny came when they settled on her face. His gaze locked with hers, and she felt more exposed than she had when he stared so hungrily at her form. *Now* she felt naked, but in a way that was sensual and erotic. She wanted to give herself over to Jonah as she'd done in her dreams. She knew he'd fulfill every fantasy.

He stepped up close, gently pushing her back on the bed and following her down. He held himself above her, his lips brushing her ear. She shivered as his breath stirred the wisps of hair surrounding the pink shell. "It's my voice that has the most effect on you, babe."

She sighed and whimpered.

"We need to do something drastic, and I've decided that you need an overdose of it. You'll get used to hearing it, and in time the problem will be solved."

Her nipples brushed against his chest, her breath little pants of air. She was getting caught up in him.

But she worried, too. "What happens if we only make things worse? What happens if, when I hear your voice, I lose what tiny grip I have left, Jonah? What then?" she asked uncertainly. The prospect of being even more addicted to his voice was at once tantalizing and unbearable.

And after what she'd done in his office this morning, she needed reassurance.

He petted her hair, murmuring in her ear, "Then you come to me, and I'll take care of you."

She laughed quietly at the absurdity of it. "Oh sure," she said against his cheek. "I'll just hop up on the table in a staff meeting, spread my legs, and say, 'Jonah, I need you now.' "

He growled, aroused by the visual, but her fear that she really might do it was an impossibility. He understood that they needed a plan better than that one.

She squirmed under him. His body was settled between her spread thighs, and she wanted to scream at him to test his theory. But he fought the temptation to try and kiss away her fears.

"Let's do this then," he said, waiting for her to hear his words and focus on what he was saying. She'd already begun to succumb to the feelings. "If this doesn't work, when you feel an urge to 'take a meeting' "—he grinned shamelessly as his arousal insistently nudged against her cleft—"go to my private quarters next to my office. Page me and wait. As soon as I can, I'll come to you."

Camelot just smiled. He was obviously joking. *Or was he?* Caught in his pointed stare, she got the feeling that if— no, *when* it happened—he'd be ready for her. He was going to fix her, one way or the other. He meant every word.

Then he distracted her, taking her hands and holding them next to her head. He was going to use his voice as a tool to learn her secrets, to wring every drop of pleasure he could from her. She struggled. Not in fear, but anticipation.

Her first lesson was about to begin.

"What do you think of when you hear my voice, Camelot?"

It was an exercise in self-control, not something she'd had much of in the past months. And he expected her to *think*, too?

"Tell me, babe."

"What?"

"Tell me what you think of."

"I think of sex, Jonah. I told you. Raw, hard, thrusting sex," she said viciously, like a caged animal being teased with food beyond the bars. She was starved for what he held just out of her reach. "Please, Jonah," she implored.

He smiled broadly and chuckled, though she felt his body react to her frustrated plea. His arousal pulsed at her cleft, and she writhed under him, her hips bucking against him as her eyes dared him to let go of his tight grip on control and end their play.

He turned it up a notch instead. "I heard *your* voice last night, darlin'," he said. "All excited and sexy, giving me clues to remember your name. You drove me wild because you knew what it was doing to me, didn't you?"

Her catchy breaths were loud in the room, and she shook her head in denial, but the mischievous look she couldn't hide made her a liar.

"Oh yes, sweetheart. You knew exactly what you were doing. Words like magical, forbidden love, enchantment— those things brought your face to my mind, your bright eyes, shining in excitement. The way your hair bounces around your shoulders and caresses your back. My hands shook when I imagined you teasing me with it. I envisioned you wrapping it around my cock, stroking me with the silky strands, splaying it over my stomach. Do you know what I was doing while *you* talked to *me*, Camelot?"

She nodded as he dipped his head to kiss her pouty lips, letting his grasp go slack. With a strength born of lust and need, Camelot pushed up hard, and then smiled wickedly at Jonah's surprised expression to find himself flat on his back.

She draped herself over his body, and Jonah closed his eyes, groaning when she brushed her thigh against his very hard erection. When he opened them, they blazed with the passion he barely held in check. It thrilled her that he was finally as close to the edge as she was. She felt the power of taking charge, but she was well aware that he could take it back at any moment.

She straddled him, nestling against his penis and wriggling her hips to settle it along her wet heat.

"My turn, Jonah?" she asked eagerly.

"Hah. I'm all yours, sweetheart. Do with me what you will," Jonah said, closing his eyes again and spreading his arms wide like a sacrifice.

Camelot's throaty laugh elicited a groan from him. "Now it's your turn to be tortured," she said playfully. He still awaited his own release, so it would be agony to let her have the lead. She wouldn't make it any easy for him, either. Payback was sweet.

She leaned down, close to his ear. "I wondered if I'd ever get a chance to touch." Her fingers flexed on the bunched muscles of his biceps; her teeth tugged at his earlobe. "Or the chance to taste," she whispered, and sat up again.

His eyes opened, burned into hers. "Oh yeah, baby. Taste me."

Camelot grinned at his intense, serious expression. He had that predatory look about him again. Only this time, it wouldn't be Jonah who would do the devouring. She leaned down and took his mouth with a wildness they were both feeling. Her kiss was carnal, primitive, savage.

Jonah's arms wrapped around her back, and her breasts were crushed between them, her nipples tickled by the springy hair. He rolled his hips, tempting her to take what throbbed against her sex. He brought his arms back down to his sides with reluctance. But this was her show for the moment. She was finally going to indulge her fantasies and have Jonah the way she'd been dreaming of. And he was going to let her. He *was* what fantasies were made of.

Her tongue boldly explored the warm inner cavern of his mouth. She tasted the wine they'd only sampled earlier, but she was intoxicated nonetheless. Her fingers dug into his shoulders and she swallowed his hungry groans. It excited her that such a sexy, virile man was hers to do with as she wished.

His eyes opened and fixed on her as she looked down at him, reminding her of that elevator ride again. He'd pinned her in place with nothing more than his piercing gaze a number of times, but it was more than that now. In his eyes, she saw a need that she would have given over to if she weren't already so turned on by the feel of his body under hers.

She leaned forward, pressing her lips at the pulse point on his throat. She grinned as her teeth nipped at him there, thrilled that his blood ran just as fast and furious as her own.

His delicious cologne mixed with his own masculine scent steamed off him like hot on asphalt as he lay there enduring her slow ministrations.

She didn't want to appear too eager to have him inside her when that was *exactly* what she wanted, but the months in which she'd pictured what he'd really look like made her determined to enjoy every inch of him. Her tongue snaked out and traced along his collarbone.

"Oh, honey, do that again." He sighed.

She repeated her teasing strokes on the other side, her hips grinding down against his arousal.

His hand gently grazed up and down her back, sweeping over one bare cheek and lightly squeezing before it came back up for another pass. His sweet strokes blurred her focus, but she didn't care. Nothing either one of them did to the other could be wrong. They were finally together, and in private. For that reason alone, everything was right.

Her last involvement had ended in disaster a year before. Her former boyfriend had been a fraud, a user, and he'd made her vulnerable, dependent on him. When she'd finally been able to break out of the destructive relationship, Camelot vowed never to let anyone have that much power over her again.

But fate had stepped in when she took her job at

McCauley, Parrish, and Hawke. Jonah was there, and he had a power that completely shadowed anything in her past. But his attraction was real, not contrived, and in his arms Camelot felt beautiful, sensual and ... free. He used the control she gave him to bring pleasure, never pain. And she'd do the same for him.

She wriggled down his body, her lips closing over one dark male nipple. If Jonah's groans were any indication, then he was definitely enjoying her teasing. His hands tangled in her hair and clenched tight with each pass of her soft tongue over the dark flesh, and his breath hissed out when she sucked at his skin. Camelot grinned against his chest, her low, deep chuckle rousing him out of his dazed rapture.

"I'm glad you find my predicament amusing, sweetheart. You're a wicked woman, Camelot."

"You think so?" she asked, tipping her head, although she knew she was being wicked, and loving it.

He played the wounded party. "Here I've been such a gentleman and given you an orgasm, and not once have I done a thing to help myself along."

Cam rolled her eyes, struggling to maintain her pitying look and not laugh out loud at him. He was a bad liar. He'd helped himself along quite a bit. Whose fault was it that he hadn't followed through when he had the chance?

He lifted his head off the pillow to look at her, like he was in grave pain. "I've left it up to you to make me come, and here you are, sprawled on top of my poor body, driving me out of my mind. There's only so much a man can take, darlin'. Have mercy!" he said, but he chuckled, and she knew that no matter what she did, he loved it, too. "Don't make me beg, Camelot."

Her belly vibrated with a throaty giggle. "I think you just did, Counselor," she teased.

The feel of her had Jonah groaning in delicious agony, dropping his back on the pillow. "Never mind, forget I said anything. Just ... ah, Christ, don't laugh."

"I'll take care of you, Jonah," she said indulgently.

Fast as lightning she slid down until she was lying between his spread thighs. Her hand closed over his thick sex, her mouth a hairsbreadth away from the throbbing, wet head of his penis.

He looked down his body to see. "Oh Jesus . . ." he whispered, and his fist pounded against the mattress. He caught his breath as she brought one of his many fantasies to life.

Camelot flipped her hair up and over her head, spreading it over his stomach as her mouth descended on his turgid cock.

His hips bucked of their own volition and he growled his pleasure when her lips closed over him. "Ah, God! Cam . . ." he breathed, swallowing hard.

Camelot waited until he'd calmed enough to take him deeper, but her tongue laved the tip, sending shock waves through his body. She wasn't sure, but she could have sworn she heard a very unmanly whimper come from him.

She lifted her eyes, tilted her head just a fraction, but her hair was so full she couldn't see anything through the veil she'd created with her tresses. She didn't have to see his face to know that he was in ecstasy, though. His erection throbbed in her hand, and she licked each pearl of moisture that formed immediately after every swipe of her tongue. He forced his hips to be still as she learned him, but she knew he wouldn't be able to stay that way for long.

She took him deeper into her mouth, enveloping him, but she realized that some of him just wasn't going to fit.

"Oh babe . . . God, yes! Take all that you can," he whispered hoarsely.

She felt his whole body shudder with arousal and rigorous restraint, a fine sheen of perspiration making his skin slick and glistening. His hand shook as he swept her hair out of the way so he could watch her bring him to the brink; then he twisted his fists in the sheet, determined not to harm a single hair on her head by tangling his fingers in it and pushing her farther down on him.

Camelot knew it was a stupid time to realize she was in love with Jonah; sex wasn't love, after all, but the way he battled every instinct to thrust into her warm mouth and seek satisfaction was the last gesture in a string of them that proved what a considerate and caring man, and lover, he was.

She grinned and lowered her head again, letting him feel only her tongue as it swirled over the velvety flesh. He groaned deep in his chest, and his head fell back on the pillow, rolling from side to side as he murmured nonsense. She had the upper hand and he was determined to let her keep it, but she knew it took a lot of trust and self-control on his part.

Camelot closed her eyes and let her lips just brush the tip of his penis, back and forth. She squeezed him in her fist and slowly stroked him.

Odd noises from above made her open her eyes again. She looked up and giggled, thrilled at the ridiculous picture he made.

Jonah's hands were shaking so badly, it took three tries before he was able to grab the box of condoms off the mattress. Just his luck—it was securely closed. Finally giving up, he tore one whole side off it, its contents flying all around him.

He sighed with relief as some of the foil packets fell out onto his chest. He reached for one, sweeping the others onto the spread, but Camelot was quicker and plucked it from his hand. He growled as he watched her teeth tear at the wrapper and her fingers pull the latex from its packaging. She held it poised over his aching cock.

"Let me," she whispered, rolling it down until it was secure, sheathing him.

"Like I'd stop you now," he said sarcastically, his husky laugh strained.

He again fought the urge to close his eyes and just let the incredible sensations wash over him, but the sight of her crawling over him, straddling his waist and positioning his sex at her opening, was just about the most erotic thing he'd ever seen. Her eyes were that dark purple color he'd learned signaled her arousal. They'd been that color in the elevator. Her lips were swollen from their shared kisses. She looked so beautiful with her hair in disarray from using it in their play. Jonah would bet a year's salary that it looked like that when she woke up in the morning. He stared into those stunning eyes, determined he'd be here come morning. Not because she'd fallen asleep and had forgotten to kick him to the curb, but because she wanted him to stay.

"Ready?" she whispered, poised over him, her eyes bright.

"You can ask that?" he half chuckled, half groaned. *Dumb question,* he thought. His eyes stayed locked with hers, showing her just how tenuous his control really was. "Ride me, babe."

She sank down and they both let out sighs of sweet satisfaction as he slid into her warm, tight passage. Her inner thighs flexed and widened; she was effectively impaled on him, and Jonah sucked air through his tightly clenched teeth, forcing his body still.

She grinned impishly at him. "Okay now?" she asked, and tilted her hips just a fraction.

"Damn, but you're incredible. Beautiful," he said, his fingertips brushing her cheeks, her lips kissing the tips softly.

She rocked back and forth; Jonah loved the sight of her astride him. She gave him more pleasure than he'd ever thought possible. *God, sex is so much better when you're in love.*

His breath rushed from his lungs, but for a different reason. *Where the hell did that come from?* It was true, but it was a damn strange time to realize it. And *mean* it.

What was even more profound was that no matter how amazing the feelings evoked by the act were, he still looked forward to that moment when she'd collapse back down onto his chest to catch her breath and he'd feel her heart pound in rhythm with his own.

She rocked and moved on him, and Jonah fought to keep the lust in him restrained, but he knew he couldn't take much more. He'd let her have her turn. But he was buried so deep, and she felt so damn good surrounding him, that his raging passion finally took over.

She leaned down to kiss his lips and Jonah took the lead once again. Wrapping an arm around her back, he reversed their positions until she lay under him and he pressed down into her.

"Your turn now?" she sighed, her face radiant.

"Oh yeah," he replied gutturally. "I'm sorry, baby, I can't wait."

Camelot laughed, and both of them gasped. "Don't be sorry, Jonah," she said. Then the smile slid off her face. "Don't ever be sorry."

Jonah got her meaning. Hoping she'd see what was in his heart, he said, "I'll never be sorry for you, Camelot."

He kissed her gently, then switched gears and braced one arm by her head. He lifted his weight slightly and hooked one of her legs over his hip. "Hang on," he said, and began the slow, sensual climb again where they didn't have to think at all. Only feel.

He cherished every labored breath, every catch or cutoff whimper as his thrusts became harder and more frantic. Pleasure wrestled to break free and crash over him, but Jonah tamped it down as long as he could, determined that this time they'd find their release together.

She met his hard thrusts, nails digging into his biceps, and her neck strained with a scream he needed to hear. "That's it, baby. Let go. Come for me," he coaxed, and allowed his voice to be the catalyst in their lovemaking. She was so beautiful in her passion that words were a natural part of the whole experience with her.

"Ah, God. Jonah!" She shouted loud enough to wake the dead, but there was nothing as sweet as Camelot screaming his name when she came. It triggered his own climax. He buried himself deep one last time and let himself feel the pleasure of her surrounding him. His body shuddered but he held still above her, watching her as her warm passage gripped him tight and his cock pulsed inside her.

Her ragged whispers were like echoes down a canyon, repeating his name until she went limp and quieted.

"This is how you looked in my office this morning. God, you were beautiful then, too. Thank God I put that tape in my briefcase. No one but me should ever see you climax," he whispered lazily, the last of his own tremors ebbing away, his voice creating little aftershocks in her.

Week as a newborn pup, Jonah mustered enough energy to slip out of her and roll away, disposing of the condom in the wastebasket. He switched off the light, pulling her to him in the darkness. Spooning her, he draped his arm over her, cupping her breast. Neither of them were going anywhere tonight.

Jonah's lips tilted up sleepily. This was what he'd wanted so badly with Camelot. Not the sex, though he couldn't remember ever enjoying a woman more. Not the need that had held them in its grip. It was the aftermath of the passion, the repletion that made him content, gave them peace. He closed his eyes and slept soundly for the first time in a long, long time.

He awoke hours later with a sense of foreboding. His hand stretched across the mattress. Empty. Crawling to the end of the bed, Jonah stumbled around the comforter on the floor and looked down over the banister of the loft, into the living room.

Shit!

His briefcase was open on the coffee table, and Camelot's

shoes were still inside, but the security camera tape was missing.

How had she—?

Thank God I put that tape in my briefcase. No one but me should ever see you climax . . .

Jonah closed his eyes, slumping against the rail. He felt sick. Last night in his satiation, he'd mentioned her climax in his office. *"Dammit!"* he cursed under his breath.

"Come on down, Jonah," she said too brightly from somewhere below, but her voice was laced with warning. She was pissed, and he knew it. *You're dead, McCauley.*

"I've already seen the show, but I can rewind it if you'd like."

Jonah cursed again quietly, turned and snatched up his jeans, sliding them up over his hips. He took the time to button them as he tried to figure out what to say to her. He was still clueless by the time he hit the bottom step.

The television was tucked under the overhang of the loft, and he turned to her as she stood by it, her eyes hard and accusing. There was a glimmer of hope that she was wrong, but she held the incriminating evidence in her hand.

"Talk to me."

How ironic is that? he thought.

"There's a security camera in each of the executive offices. I had them installed when we fell victim to spying and theft last year, but only the partners and their assistants know about them. You should have been told, being in that circle, but you don't work upstairs. How could I know that you'd—"

"Oh, that's rich, Jonah," she said bitterly. "I know what *I* did wrong. But I want you to admit *your* indiscretion."

He approached her. "I kept the tape to protect you."

She shook her head, her eyes bewildered and stormy before her gaze dropped away, afraid to believe him when he'd watched her and not mentioned it yesterday.

He gripped her shoulders, stroking gently. "Cam, I don't

know how to make up for watching you like I did. I'd do anything to take away your shame of it, but I'll be honest and tell you I'm not sorry for being privy to that scene."

Her head popped up in surprise. Jonah tipped his head close, his voice like whiskey, searing and rough in its tone but soothing her with its potency. Remembering her there in his office made him feverish. "You're beautiful in your passion, babe. I know you couldn't control yourself and I'm sorry that upsets you so much. But a man would give his eyeteeth to see the woman he desires pleasuring herself when it's him she's thinking of. It was wrong because you didn't know I was watching, but I'm just a man, Camelot. I'm human. And you were fulfilling *my* fantasy."

Oh yes, she was listening, he concluded. The tip of her tongue darted out and left her lips glistening. He groaned and clutched her shoulders tighter. He ached to capture that teasing tongue, to lure it into his mouth and taste her sweetness again. But he wanted her forgiveness more.

His hands slid up and cupped her throat. "Tell me how to make this right between us, honey." Jonah didn't care that it sounded like a plea.

Her eyes were focused on his mouth. Then, slowly, they raised and met his gaze.

He shuddered at what lurked in their depths. The anger and shame were gone, and in their place was an eroticism he'd only ever experienced with her. His cock grew hard and heavy and increasingly uncomfortable in his jeans.

Her voice was sultry but skeptical. "You'll really do anything to make it up to me?" she asked.

His erection throbbed painfully as he imagined the possibilities. "Anything you want," he croaked.

Camelot moved out of his reach and sat down on the sofa. Her thin silk robe parted slightly at the waist as one incredibly sexy leg crossed over the other. Laying the tape beside her, a reminder of his transgression, she wriggled down into the lushness of the cushions and folded her arms under her breasts. The nipples peaked and the shadow of the dark areolas made Jonah silently vow to keep his promise of "anything."

"All right then," she said. "I want to watch you."

"Watch me?"

"Uh-huh. Just like you watched me."

"But I'll know you're here. It's different."

"The only difference is that I won't be *spying* on you."

Ouch! That stung.

But she'd turned the tables on him, seeking vindication. She ruled her passions now; they didn't rule her. He loved it! His plan had worked, and from the looks of it, her attraction was still as strong as before.

He was so relieved. And the punishment fit the crime, he supposed. *Hah! Punishment?*

Grinning smugly, he said, "I should warn you, babe. Men aren't like women. We don't feel embarrassed. We just live the excitement." It was a half-truth. Envisioning *Camelot* watching him as he stroked his cock was what excited him. He'd never do this for anyone but her.

"Show me then," she whispered huskily.

Jonah knew better than to mention that this was supposed to be payback. He'd been forgiven. That was good enough for him. She knew he'd brought that tape home to protect her privacy. But this wasn't even about the tape now. It was about trust. She'd given hers by letting him explain, and she was satisfied. Now she wanted his in return. He was getting a second chance. Masturbation was an especially personal thing, he knew. A lover needed a wealth of trust for such an act. Jonah was going to give her every bit he had.

Her breath came fast and the pulse in her throat pumped a staccato beat. Her crossed leg rubbed up and down along the length of the other, creating a friction that he'd bet was an attempt to appease an ache at the juncture of her thighs. He ached just watching her.

"I'll do this, Camelot, but on one condition," he growled, hardly believing he was able to form a coherent thought, he was so tied in knots.

"Name it."

"Don't close your eyes. Or even look away. I want you to be as caught up as I was."

"Oh, Jonah," Camelot murmured throatily, seductively. "It's true that I'm embarrassed that you watched me without my knowledge, but I'd be crazy to look away if I can see you do it for me willingly." She lowered her arms and leaned forward, her fingers biting into the edge of the cushion. "I want you to imagine my hands on you, feeding your hunger."

His jaw clenched and endured her verbal torture. *This* was his punishment.

"When I was there in your office, that's what I thought of. In my mind, it was your hands on me, your mouth taking me to that edge and pushing me over it." She wet her lips again with her tongue. "I said your name when I climaxed. Did you see that part?"

The memory washed over him and he nodded stupidly. His throat was so dry now he couldn't have uttered a word to save his life.

"Say my name when you get there, Jonah," she commanded throatily, her voice wrapping around him and touching off every nerve ending until he burned.

Off came his jeans, and he dropped into the armchair across from her. His hand shook as he wrapped it around his pulsating length; she grinned. Jonah wanted to laugh. She thought her scrutiny was making him self-conscious, when in fact he was shaking because he was so aroused and already so far gone that he was going to embarrass himself. He was going to come quicker than he ever had, she excited him that much.

The plum-shaped head of his erection pearled with fluid

and his thumb swiped at it, lubricating the steely hard shaft. He watched as she slipped off the sofa and crawled to him, her eyes never leaving his cock as his hand slid from base to tip and back down again, his grip tight and squeezing.

She's too close, he thought. He could feel her warm breath fanning his heated flesh. Jonah growled low, his orgasm fast approaching, and then her hand joined his, sliding and stroking up and down the hard length of him. The intimacy of it tipped the scales.

Jonah roared her name as he stiffened and exploded, but it was muffled as Camelot reared up and covered his mouth with her own. She swallowed his groans of satisfaction and shared his passion. *Yes!* he thought. *This is how it should be. Together.*

Her lips softened as their joined hands milked his essence from him until he slumped back into the chair, spent.

Jonah looked up at her as she leaned over the arm. "I love you, Camelot."

Her eyes were bright, a deep violet hue of excitement, happiness. "I know. I love you, too," she said, kissing him gently again and dropping her hand away from him. "I thought I fell in love with you when we were in bed and you held back so I could play, when you risked me losing my attraction along with the obsession. But really, I knew when we were in the kitchen. You told me that my heart could trust you and you were right. Thank you for keeping my secrets, Jonah."

He dragged her over the arm of the chair, carefully settling her onto his lap. "Marry me."

She giggled. "Well, it wouldn't be the wildest thing I've done lately."

Jonah smiled, glad that she was comfortable in her own skin again. "Say it for me, Camelot," he demanded selfishly.

"Yes, I'll marry you, Jonah."

"Mmmmm," he groaned, nuzzling her throat, so happy

that whatever twist of fate brought them together, he'd come to his senses before it was too late. He didn't want to think about how close he'd come to losing her.

A pounding at the door startled them both.

"I know you're in there, Jonah McCauley, you bastard! You've got some explaining to do! For two years I've abided by your damned rules!"

"That's Kat!" Camelot said, and started to scramble off Jonah's lap, but he held her firm.

"No! Wait, sweetheart. She'll skin me alive if you let her in here."

"Whatever for?" Camelot had a sneaking suspicion it had something to do with her.

"Because Kat Murphy is in love with Sam Parrish. *Her* boss."

Camelot almost laughed. Kat *would* have understood what she'd been going through! But it still didn't explain why she was pounding on Camelot's door so early in the morning. "So?" she prompted.

Jonah snuggled back down in the chair, cradling Camelot in his arms, kissing her long and deep and obviously not planning on opening the door anytime soon.

His eyes squinted mischievously. "It's obvious that you didn't read the company policy that prohibits the partners from dating any of the employees."

She look at him sideways. "Well, it's a good thing I'm so sure you're going to amend that policy, or I might have to open that door and let her at you."

"Yeah, it *is* a good thing then, huh?" Jonah chuckled, and kissed her again.

CABIN FEVER

LuAnn McLane

To Lori Foster for helping to make
my "wildest dreams" come true.

And to my family for their love and support,
especially my parents,
who always believed I could do this.
I love you!

Chapter One

Rachel Manning sat down at her desk and felt a familiar tug of guilt. She shrugged it off, turned on the computer monitor and watched it come to life, shedding light into the dark room. *This is wicked*, her inner voice warned. She paused, but then lifted her chin a notch and placed her fingertips on the keyboard. She brought up her story and read through the first few paragraphs.

Her hands came up to her cheeks.

Oh God, did I really write that? Rachel read the next paragraph and swallowed. Her cheeks suddenly felt warm beneath her cool hands. "That's so naughty," she whispered, but scrolled to the next page with wide eyes and a thudding heart. "So . . . sexy." She bit her lip to keep from grinning, but didn't succeed.

"And so much fun."

Rachel lit the scented candle on her desk and took a sip of her white wine—another forbidden fruit that she was learning to love. With a soft sigh, she pulled the clip from her chestnut hair and let the unruly waves tumble to her shoulders and caress the silk of her red pajamas, an indulgence worn only when she came to her cabin.

She turned on some soft sultry music, heavy on the saxophone, then let her eyes flutter shut, and her imagination run wild. Rachel inhaled deeply, allowing the scent of vanilla and spices to fill her head. She swayed slightly to the music, swirled the wine in her long-stemmed glass, and then took a sip. Slowly her inhibitions slipped away, and her fingers began to move over the keyboard.

The safe little existence of Rachel Manning, author of inspirational novels for teen girls, faded as the sexy, secret world of her pseudonym, Jade Johnson, writer of erotica for women, sprang to life on the computer screen.

Rachel had stumbled upon the Web site for women, GirlsNightOut.com, by accident one night about a year ago, just after she had bought her cabin hideaway in the remote woods of eastern Kentucky. It had simply popped up on her screen in all its glory, with vivid, steamy stories. She had only read a few words—just out of curiosity—then a paragraph. Before the night was over, Rachel had devoured an entire novella and had come back for more.

But only on the weekends. Only when she came to her cabin in the woods, let her hair down, and entered the forbidden fantasy world of bold, sexy women who knew what they wanted from a man.

And got it. In the most unusual places, with handsome, hard-bodied hunks who knew how to please a woman. And if they didn't? Well, the daring heroines of GirlsNightOut.com would show them how. And then some.

When the Web site offered a contest for readers to submit their own fantasies, the writer in Rachel gave it a whirl. The story flowed from Rachel as if she were born to write erotica. She won the contest and Jade Johnson now had a loyal following of fans. The publisher had begged Rachel to write more, and offered her a respectable sum of money to do so. If she'd had the nerve, she would have called her agent, Jake Nichols, and let him negotiate the deal.

But she hadn't. Jade Johnson was a closely guarded secret. Rachel had told no one, not even her brother Michael, her best friend with whom she always shared everything. Rachel grinned. Michael would get a kick out of this.

Her parents would not. Her father was a Methodist minister and her mother taught third-graders at a private Christian school. Dr. James Manning and his prim wife Sarah would be mortified, scandalized, and highly disappointed. Rachel could *never* let them find out.

She had always been the good preacher's daughter. Michael had been, and still was, the rebellious one. While Rachel had always tried to live up to her father's strict standards, Michael tried harder not to. They had both succeeded.

Until now. Rachel took a deep breath as another wave of guilt washed over her. She shook her head and gave herself a pep talk, something she had been doing since childhood whenever she was lacking in courage.

"This is harmless, Rachel," she told herself firmly.

You're promoting promiscuous sex, argued her conscience, perched like a bobble-head of her mother on her shoulder.

Rachel shrugged, trying to shake her off. "It's only fantasy. Women need this." She determinedly typed another sentence. *I need this.*

Your father would not approve, the voice warned. God, it even *sounded* like the stern voice of her mother.

"My father will never know. No one will."

If this gets out, your career writing inspirational fiction could be ruined.

Ouch. Rachel's fingers paused on the keyboard and a clenched fist came up to her chest. "No one will *ever* know," she repeated firmly. "Go away," she said to the pesky voice. "I'll whistle if I need you."

Rachel took another sip of wine and reread her last paragraph. She chuckled as she fanned her cheeks. Who would ever have thought that *she* of all people could write so well, about something she had never experienced? Scorching hot glorious sex. Wild and uninhibited.

Her stories were popular because her heroines were smart, bold, and in control. The plot usually involved the heroine taking a gorgeous, arrogant, alpha male down a notch or two, giving them a taste of their own love-'em-and-leave-'em medicine. And then had them begging for more.

Rachel's latest adventure involved a blond bombshell named simply Sasha. Who needed a last name when you had a sexy name like Sasha? Six feet tall with endless legs, torpedo breasts (her own, of course), and a slight Ukrainian accent, Sasha brought men to their knees.

Rachel grinned. Sasha had just spotted her latest prey across the crowded room of the party. "Yes!" Rachel said, and laughed out loud. "I finally have my new title." She hated working without a title. "Man Eater"—perfect!" She chuckled again and dove headfirst into the steamy story. This was just too much fun to *ever* consider quitting.

"Oh my," Rachel said as the story played like a movie in her head. Her fingers could barely keep up with her vivid imagination while the scene unfolded on the computer screen.

Sasha spotted him at the bar, sipping a martini while flirting with the bartender. He had come on to every woman in the room, but every time he had tried to catch her eye, Sasha had retreated to a far corner and watched him. Her blue eyes narrowed when he approached Nina, a very married friend of Sasha's who had sucked down too many vodka tonics. He angled his dark head at Nina and whispered something in her ear. She gazed up at him like he was Godiva chocolate and she wanted to devour every inch of him.

Sasha tossed down the last of her vodka and headed across the room before Nina did something stupid that would ruin her marriage. All for some arrogant ass who liked to toy with women and then toss them away.

Sasha caught his eye, lingering long enough to give him the message, and then walked out the door of the bar and into the lobby of the elegant hotel. He was following her. She could feel the heat of his gaze. Sasha paused, bent over, and adjusted the slim strap of her sandal, giving him a long look at her legs and a peek at her thong.

She stepped into the vacant elevator and turned slowly around, knowing he would be there. The doors closed with a soft whoosh, leaving them in dim light with soft music. He stepped close and smiled, sure of himself, flashing even white teeth in his tan, chiseled face. Broad-shouldered, slim-hipped, he wore the Armani suit with casual ease.

"Who are you, beautiful lady?" His voice was deep and husky with a hungry edge.

"I am Sasha. Who are you, arrogant man?"

He laughed and pushed the button for the door to the elevator to remain closed. "Dominick Garrison."

"Ah, yes, you play American football." She toyed with the slim gold chain around her neck, then let it fall into the deep vee of her silk blouse. She watched him swallow and suppressed a smile.

"You like football?" He brushed his hand through his short-cropped black hair, making sure she saw the flash of his heavy Superbowl ring.

Sasha arched one elegant eyebrow. "I like . . . how you say . . . contact sports."

He moved closer, crowding her against the mirrored wall of the elevator. When he dipped his head, Sasha let him get just a taste of her lips, then gave him a hard shove.

"You go, girl!" Rachel grinned, nibbling on her bottom lip. "Oh, how I'd love to be you for just a day." She poured more wine from the slim blue bottle into her glass and took a sip. A sudden pinging against the windowpane caught her attention. There was the ice storm the weatherman had predicted.

Rachel shrugged. *Who cares,* she thought, and returned her gaze to the glowing screen. A fire crackled in the stone hearth and she had enough food to outlast even the worst weather. Wind whipped against the cabin, drawing her attention once again. Already, a thin film of ice covered the window, making the bending tree limbs look blurry. Rachel shivered despite the warmth of the cabin, but returned her attention to Sasha and the man she was about to devour.

Sasha gave him a toss of her head. "Let me make one thing clear, Mr. Football. I make the moves. I am in control."

He grinned at her, but she noticed a little of the cockiness was gone. But not the desire. The doors to the elevator opened an inch and she slammed her hand against the button. She crooked a red-tipped finger at him and he was on her in an instant, but she shook her head, holding him off with one hand. "You forget too soon. I am in control. I do the touching."

She was aroused now, too, making her accent thicker, her voice huskier. This was the hard part, Sasha thought. Bringing him to the point of exploding . . . but then leaving him that way.

Leaving herself that way.

She took a deep breath, inhaling the spice of his cologne with the underlying hint of sexy male. Her eyes fluttered shut and she felt his warm hands cup her breasts, but she brushed them away. "Stand very still and close your eyes. I will do the touching."

Sasha smiled when he obeyed. In her stiletto heels,

she was almost at eye level with him. Leaning close, she let the tip of her tongue slide lightly over the sleek softness of his bottom lip. He groaned and opened his mouth, but she let her tongue trail up the rough stubble of his cheek to his ear, where she nibbled and sucked.

"Let me touch you," he growled.

Sasha laughed deep in her throat. "Not yet . . . no, keep your eyes shut, or I will stop." Her mouth found a sensitive spot on his neck and moved to the hollow of his throat while she unbuttoned his shirt. Her fingertips grazed over his chest then down to his abdomen, making his muscles quiver.

She cupped the hard heat between his legs and seared his mouth with a deep, hot kiss at the same time. With her other hand, she unbuttoned—

A loud banging penetrated Rachel's racing thoughts. She paused and frowned. There it was again. Rachel suddenly realized that someone was at her front door. She stood up, but swayed slightly and had to find her balance by grabbing onto the back of her chair.

"Whoa." She put a hand to her forehead and realized she had worked through dinner and consumed a little too much wine. After taking a deep breath, she headed across the room to the front door. A quick peek through the lace curtain revealed a set of wide shoulders, dark hair. Rachel smiled, but then wondered why Michael would have braved such nasty weather for a visit.

She swung open the door, letting in a blast of cold, damp air. She grabbed his wet hand and hauled him inside. "What are you doing out in this mess?" Shivering, she pushed the door shut, turned, and yanked the chain on the lamp next to the couch, casting a soft glow in the dark room.

"Damned if I know," he growled, and shoved dark dripping hair out of his eyes.

Rachel's gaze widened at the tall figure looming before her. "You're not Michael!" She backed up and bumped against the edge of the couch, groping for a weapon. She grabbed a pillow and threw it at him. It bounced off of his head and landed in the puddle that was forming at his feet.

"Whoa, wait a minute!" Jake Nichols blinked in confusion at the wide-eyed woman dressed in clingy red pajamas. This didn't look like the Rachel Manning pictured on the back cover of her books. He had met her in person only once, and he remembered a shy, rather prim young woman. Another pillow hit him in the face and he realized she was looking for a more substantial weapon. She found it.

"Calm down, I'm not going to—ouch!" A candle hit him in the forehead and she hoisted the candlestick over her head. "What the hell?" He was on her in three long strides. She squealed and swung at him. Jake caught the candlestick just before it hit him in the chin, and they both tumbled onto the couch.

She struggled wildly beneath him, bucking her hips and pounding at his chest. Jake pushed up with one hand. "Would you just stop and listen—ouch!" She caught him on the nose with one small fist. Jake grabbed her hands with one of his and pinned them above her head.

"Dammit, listen, you little hellcat!" Wide green eyes gazed up at him, full of fear. She made a sound deep in her throat, a cross between a frightened scream and an angry hiss. A riot of deep brown curls framed her flushed face and spilled over the leather cushion. She strained against him.

"I'm not going to hurt you," he said softly. "I'm looking for Rachel Manning. I must have the wrong cabin."

She stopped struggling, blinked up at him, and opened her mouth as if to tell him something, then hesitated. "Who are you?" she asked with a curious, less frightened look.

"I'm her agent, Jake Nichols."

Chapter Two

Her eyebrows lifted and she shifted under him, making his body react to the sudden realization that he had a beautiful woman pinned beneath him. A drop of water fell from his wet hair and dripped onto her mouth.

Her tongue darted out and she licked it away. When it happened again, Jake didn't think, he simply reacted, and licked it away himself. God, her lips were soft. She gasped, giving his tongue access to her mouth. She tasted sweet, like warm wine and woman. Needing another taste, he kissed her again.

At first her body stiffened and he realized he still had her hands trapped above her head. She made a noise in the back of her throat and he wasn't sure if it was a protest or surrender. God, this was like some wild erotic fantasy coming to life in his arms—so unexpected, yet *irresistible*. She was quite simply the most seductively sexy sight he had ever seen, and yet there was something vulnerable in the soft set of her mouth. He let go of her hands, telling himself if she pushed him away, he would stop. Gazing down at her, he waited, holding his breath, and then dipped his head toward her to kiss her.

She splayed her hands on his chest. "I—I don't think we should be doing this."

"Then don't think. Just feel."

"But—"

He silenced her with a tender kiss and then pulled back to gaze down at her. "I came here by mistake. This was fate." God, that sounded like a cheesy line, but he, at least at the moment, believed it.

"It wasn't by mistake," she murmured. "I'm—"

"You're irresistible. Now, let me kiss you."

She hesitated, but then, with a breathy moan, she delved her hands into his dripping hair and opened her mouth for more. Desire slammed through Jake. This was incredible. *She* was incredible. His body throbbed . . . ached. He trembled with need and wanted her with a passion that took him by surprise. She was a complete stranger, yet it didn't feel that way, but somehow managed to feel . . . *right*. Looking down at her, he wondered if she felt the same way.

Oh, she did.

Rachel was cold and on fire at the same time. She shivered from his wet clothes that seeped into her own, but also from the heat of desire coiling in the pit of her stomach and spiraling out of control. She watched, fascinated, as he pushed up, one knee on the couch and one leg braced on the floor. With one fluid movement, he pulled his sweater over his head and tossed it to the floor.

The light from the fire flickered over his bare chest, casting a golden glow over his damp skin. He raised one hand to slick back his dark wet hair, causing a ripple of lean muscle. Piercing blue eyes dilated with desire and held her captive. He traced one long finger over her lips, down her neck, and then slowly opened her buttons while his gaze remained on her face.

Rachel shivered. She shouldn't let him do this, but was powerless to stop him.

"You're cold." His voice was low, seductive. She swallowed and nodded. "You're wet," he continued. "So am I.

We should get out of these clothes." She nodded again, knowing in some faraway place in her mind that she should stop him, but she could only watch while he stood, unzipped his jeans, and peeled them off with his back to her. He stood there for a long moment, motionless, making Rachel's pulse race.

Firelight flickered and danced, casting shadows on the rough-hewn walls. A heady mixture of scented candles and smoke filled the room while sultry music crooned in the background. Through heavy-lidded eyes Rachel admired the wide set of his shoulders, tapered waist, and muscled butt, clearly defined in the clinging cotton of his boxers. "Turn around," she coaxed softly, needing to see him.

Swallowing, she watched as his fingers clenched into fists as if at war with himself. "You said that this was fate, Jake," she reminded him—and convinced herself.

He slowly turned around, clad only in damp, white cotton boxers. And, heaven help her, he was . . . *aroused*. "Oh my."

"You seem surprised." His deep voice was laced with humor.

Feeling heat in her cheeks, she quickly averted her gaze, but couldn't resist another peek through her lashes. The light from the fire flickered and teased the golden skin of his chest, lightly furred with dark hair. Her breath caught in her throat. My God, this was too much! She blinked, trying to clear her head. She had to end this before they . . . God . . . before they *made love*.

"We . . ." she began, but forgot what she was about to say when he reached up and threaded his fingers through his damp hair, causing a delicious ripple of muscle. Fascinated, Rachel pushed up to a sitting position on the couch, causing her unbuttoned shirt to gape but not fully expose her breasts. She had to see the rest of him. Totally naked, bathed in the light of the fire.

"Come closer," she whispered. With trembling hands that seemed to have a life of their own, she reached up and eased his underwear over his lean hips and down his thighs.

Rachel gasped. His penis thrust forward, proudly erect, just inches from her mouth. If she leaned over just slightly, she could touch it, stroke it.

Rachel looked up at him. His nostrils flared like he was fighting for breath. A muscle jumped in his jaw and his gaze locked with hers. There was no arrogance, no pleading in his eyes. Just raw need.

He needed *her*. No man had ever needed her, wanted her like this. She felt powerful. Beautiful. And she wanted desperately to please him. Rachel felt a hot wave of longing rush through her veins like she was burning up with a fever. She moved slowly, unsure of what to do. This was like a dream. Her wildest written fantasy coming vividly to life.

He inhaled sharply when she shyly cupped him, reveling in the weight, the softness. Rachel moved her hand lightly up the hard length of him and watched his eyelids flutter shut and his head fall back. He felt like velvet over steel. Her heart pounded and she wished she had the nerve to take him into her mouth.

"Your name." His voice was a strained growl. He put one finger under her chin and brushed her hair back from her face. "I want . . . I need to know your name."

Rachel's heart pounded harder as reality threatened to invade her fantasy. She tried to think clearly, but blood pounded in her ears and the wine flowed through her veins. Who was she? Not Rachel. Rachel had never, would never, do *this*.

"Jade," she whispered—her secret pseudonym. He moaned and threaded his fingers into her hair, pulling her closer. She reveled in the scent of him, the feel of him— clean soap, smooth skin. Raw power.

But then he abruptly stepped back. "No." The word was a ragged croak torn from deep within.

Rachel's heart sank. She was doing something wrong. She wasn't pleasing him. "Tell me what to do, Jake. Tell me what you want."

God, that was almost his undoing. She looked so lost, so eager . . . so innocent? She gazed up at him with luminous green eyes, mouth swollen from his kisses, while poised between his legs. Her small hands rested against his thighs and strands of her chestnut curls clung to his damp skin.

She was every man's dream, a heady mix of sex and innocence. Eager to please, wanting to give, bold and shy at the same time. No, she was *his* dream, and about to become his reality.

He didn't want to come in her mouth—well, okay, he *did*. But he wanted her lying beneath him even more. Crying out his name.

"I want you. All of you." He bent over, scooped her up in his arms, and carried her over to the warmth of the fireplace. Gently, he laid her down on the soft lamb's wool rug. His breath caught in his throat.

She was exquisite. Her hair framed her face and fanned out in dark contrast to the cream-colored rug. The unbuttoned red silk pajamas fell away from her body, revealing smooth skin bathed in the glow of the fire.

"God, you're beautiful." He reached down with trembling hands and tugged at the waist of her pajama pants. She lifted her hips to help him and he tugged the damp silk off and tossed it across the room.

She wore only the red top, open for him. He reached down and brushed his fingers between her breasts, over her belly, lightly grazing her mound. She quivered and her fingers dug into the rug. It was killing him, but he teased her a moment longer, wanting her to be wild for him.

Jake eased one knee between her thighs, parting her legs. He heard her breath catch when he leaned down to kiss her, and he hesitated. He looked into those green eyes and caught a flicker of uncertainty.

With a low curse, he pulled back. This was insane. With another oath, he pushed up and turned his back on her, breathing like he had run a marathon. His heart pounded, his penis throbbed.

"D-don't you want me?"

Jake whipped his head around to look at her. She looked hurt, like she was being rejected. Tears swam in her eyes and one slid down her cheek. Jake felt something constrict in his chest and he leaned over and kissed her tenderly.

Her lips clung to his and she sighed his name. "I want you. Don't let this end now."

Her soft, pleading voice almost pushed him over the edge. He wondered briefly if some Kentucky backwoodsman was going to show up and shoot his dick off, but he didn't care. He would just have to die dickless but happy.

Jake reached for his jeans and fished out his wallet, praying he had a condom. *Yes!* He ripped open the packet with his teeth and slid it on. He was desperately, painfully hard when he turned back to her. He wanted to kiss her, to lick her everywhere and then sink his—

"Aw, damn." Jake spotted an almost empty wine bottle on a table next to her computer. So she had been drinking. Damn, damn, *damn!* He sighed as he ran an impatient hand through his wet hair. He knew sometimes he could be a real jackass, but taking advantage of a vulnerable tipsy woman wasn't something he could bring himself to do. Well, hell. He knew this was too good to be true.

"Jade?"

"Hmm?" She looked up at him with heavy-lidded eyes.

"Have you been drinking?"

She pursed her beautiful lips and held up her thumb and forefinger. "Just a teensy bit."

He forced the next words though his lips. "Baby, I don't think we should do this."

"You came to me on the edge of the wind and the rain.

This was meant to be. Love me, Jake. Tomorrow will come soon enough. Give me tonight."

Jake swallowed a groan. Damn, but the woman had a way with words.

The cynical side of Jake reasoned that she had a damned good point. He had meant to find Rachel Manning and had somehow ended up here. Fate? Perhaps this was "meant to be," as she so eloquently put it. Who was he to thwart fate?

Chapter Three

Give me tonight. Usually Jake didn't go for that kind of syrupy crap, preferring good sex to be just that, and nothing more. Normally, he would have some sort of smart-ass comment to make things real. But her soft-spoken words moved something deep within him. Cynical Jake Nichols, shaken to the core by three simple words—*Give me tonight.* With a huge effort, he pushed himself up on wobbly arms and gazed down at her. Maybe she was fucking with him. Her lips trembled as she smiled, sighed—and her eyelids fluttered shut. He watched her for a few long torturous moments while contemplating what to do.

"Jade?"

Her lips were parted, and her breathing was soft and even. Shit, she was sleeping. Jake tried to kiss her awake. She stirred and mumbled something but her eyes remained shut. With a groan, he pushed away from her and flopped onto his back.

For a long moment he simply lay there, slightly stunned. Finally, he pushed up to a sitting position, shook his head, and grinned in wonder at the woman lying on the rug.

Jake smoothed the mass of dark curls from her face and traced his finger along her swollen bottom lip. He gently pulled the red silk closed to cover her naked body and slowly began fastening the buttons. She was small but lush, with high firm breasts, a smooth belly tapering to a tiny waist, and nicely rounded hips. The pajama top only came to the top of her thighs, and he let his fingers trail lightly over the damp nest of curls before closing the last button.

Jake pushed up from the soft rug and looked around for something to cover her with. His legs were like rubber and he took a moment to steady himself. Jade drew his attention when she mumbled. She suddenly flung one arm out— reaching for him? She had curled onto her side and tucked her knees up. God, she was a heady combination of sex and innocence, making him want to fuck her senseless and protect her from harm to the ends of the earth.

Jake ventured down a short hallway and found a closet, a surprisingly large bathroom, and finally her bedroom. He flipped on a small lamp, pushed a mountain of pillows onto the floor, and turned down the patchwork quilt. The bed looked like an antique, high off of the floor, with one of those little steps next to it. It was small, and he could picture himself sleeping next to her, spoon fashion, with his arms wrapped around her and her round bottom nestled next to his. . . . *God!* Jake looked down at his dick, which suddenly stood at attention and shook his head sadly.

Next thing on the agenda: cold shower.

After tucking Jade into bed, Jake headed back to the living room to check on his clothes. He cringed. Sopping wet. He placed them by the fire to dry and went over to the window to check on the weather.

A full moon shed fingers of bright light glittering on the results of the storm. Tree branches hung heavy with a thick coating of ice. Beautiful . . . and treacherous. He wasn't going anywhere until it melted. *What a pity,* he thought with a grin.

A raging thirst had him heading to the galley-style kitchen cut off from the main room by an open counter flanked by three barstools. He opened the fridge, hoping for a beer.

"Yes!" He found one tucked all the way in the back. He gave the cold bottle a kiss and unscrewed the cap. Jake drained half of it with a long guzzle, and then shivered. He needed some clothes or a blanket or something. He prowled around the main room and then noticed narrow steps near the far wall.

At the top of the steps was a loft. He flicked on an overhead light and raised his eyebrows in surprise. The area was fairly big, with two twin beds, a dresser, and a chest of drawers. Jake pulled open a small closet and his heart started to thud. He found jeans, a few T-shirts, and a pair of drawstring flannel lounging pants.

Jealousy, a foreign emotion to Jake, had him clenching his fists. *You're not Michael,* he suddenly remembered her saying, and slammed the door shut. He was going to get the hell out of here.

Jake stomped over to the steps, but pattering on the roof and pinging against the small window drew his attention. More ice. Shit. He reluctantly opened the closet and yanked a T-shirt and the flannel pants out of the closet. He pulled the shirt over his head and jammed his feet through the pants.

Jake drained the rest of the beer and headed down the stairs in search of another, but came up empty-handed. Restless now, he paced around the small cabin and tried to gather his wits about him. The hum of the computer perched on a desk by a big window might give him some unanswered questions about Jade.

Rachel Manning suddenly popped into his mind, and he wondered how close he was to her cabin. He could have sworn he was on the right road. The directions that he had gotten from her mother were pretty simple.

Jake shrugged his shoulders and touched the mouse

while trying not to feel guilty about poking around in Jade's business. The screen saver faded and text came up on the monitor. Jake read the first paragraph.

Holy shit.

He sat down at the desk, read the entire page, and then backed up to the beginning of the document. "Man Eater," an erotic novella by Jade Johnson. He looked down at the tent in the flannel caused by another erection. He ran a hand over his face, shook his head, and had to laugh. His dick had been hard ever since he had entered this cabin, and was likely to stay that way.

So she was a writer. He chuckled again and wondered if she needed an agent. He was about to push away from the desk, but something made him reread the first paragraph. Something was familiar about the writing. Not the content, but the voice . . .

It couldn't be.

Jake slid open the drawers on the desk and found what he was looking for. The familiar cover of Rachel Manning's latest inspirational romance and several others were stacked in the bottom drawer. Frowning, he opened the back of the book and stared at the picture of the woman smiling serenely with her chin in her hand.

The black-and-white photo didn't begin to do her beauty justice. With her mane of curls tamed in some severe, pulled-back style, she appeared prim and proper, unlike the sexy siren who had pulled him in out of the cold just a couple of hours ago.

Jake held the book closer to the light and angled his head at the photo. Those eyes . . . that mouth. Jake shifted in the chair. God, he was painfully aroused. He thought about her lying in bed at the end of the hallway and wondered if he could wake her up.

He noticed the bottle of wine and groaned. Not a chance. Then another thought hit him. She had been intoxicated not only from the wine, but from the sensual story she was writing. Jake read a few more pages, captivated not only by the content, but also by her unmistakable style.

Jake's clients wrote mostly mystery or suspense and some nonfiction, but basically commercial fiction that he knew he could sell. Against his better business judgment, he had taken Rachel on as a client simply because of the depth and beauty of her writing.

Her latest inspirational romance had been emotionally intense and spiritually moving, making him go for a three-book deal that he thought she more than deserved. He could have handled the whole thing via mail and phone calls, but recent e-mails and pleasant phone conversations had compelled him to deal with her in person.

Attending the writing convention had been a convenient excuse to meet the woman behind the beautiful novels. From reading her bio, he knew quite a bit about her conservative background, small-town life. She was everything he wasn't. He glanced back at the computer screen and frowned. Or so he thought. Nothing could have prepared him for *this*.

Jake broke out in a sweat as he wondered who would emerge from the bedroom in the morning. Rachel Manning or Jade Johnson? Or perhaps a compelling combination of sweet innocence and pure heat.

Chapter Four

Rachel woke up the next morning much later than usual. When she sat up in bed, her head pounded and her mouth felt like it was stuffed with cotton. She threw back the covers and then gasped. Why was she wearing only her pajama top?

She tried to swallow, but her tongue stuck to the roof of her mouth. Rachel closed her eyes and tried to concentrate, but the rhythmic throbbing in her temples made thinking impossible. She slid down from the bed and stumbled to the bathroom. She turned on the faucet, cupped her hands under the cool water, splashed her face, and drank her fill.

She blinked at her reflection in the mirror and had a weird feeling that something was wrong. She frowned. No, not *wrong* exactly, but different.

Her heart thudded, her head pounded. She grabbed the edges of the cold sink while blurred snippets of memory skirted the edges of her brain. Heated skin, deep kisses . . . intense desire. What in the world happened to her last night? Was she just remembering a scene in her novel?

Coffee. She needed hot black coffee to stimulate her fuzzy brain cells. Rachel inhaled a deep gulp of air and frowned. She *smelled* coffee. Or was it just wishful thinking?

She tossed on a white fluffy robe and shuffled toward the kitchen, wondering again why her muscles protested. Her stomach rumbled. Not only did she smell coffee, but also the smoky aroma of bacon wafted through the hallway.

Rachel peeked into the kitchen and smiled. Michael stood with his back to her, bent over while reaching for something in the refrigerator. He wore the flannel lounging pants that he kept at the cabin.

"Michael, when did you arrive?" Rachel wrapped her arms around his waist and pressed her cheek against his back in a swift hug. When she backed up, he straightened and turned toward her with a carton of orange juice in his hand.

Her hand flew to her mouth. "You're not Michael!"

"I thought we covered that last night."

Rachel felt the room tilt and she grabbed the counter for support. Her breath came in short gasps. She stared up at him and remembered—*Wait a minute.* Oh God. His hands caressing her bare body. His mouth on hers. Heat. Passion. She felt the world slipping away . . .

And then she was in his arms.

"Whoa, I've got you," he said as he carried her over to the couch. He hovered above her with a worried frown. "Jade, are you okay?"

Jade? She swallowed. Oh boy. "W-who are you?" she asked, even though something about him somehow seemed familiar.

"Not Michael, I'm afraid. By the way, is he going to show up here and kick my ass?"

"What?" Rachel's head was spinning.

"Your boyfriend."

His harsh statement made her eyes widen. "Michael? He's my brother."

"Oh," he said, and the scowl on his face softened. Ah yes, he seemed to remember that she had a brother—a pro athlete of some sort. "Do you want a cup of coffee?"

"Um, yes," she said, and watched him take long strides to her kitchen like he wasn't a stranger in her house. She felt as if she somehow *knew* him. She closed her eyes and strained for a few moments to remember exactly what happened last night.

"Here."

Her eyes flew open at the deep timbre of his voice. She *knew* that voice. He thrust a steaming cup of coffee toward her. She cradled the welcome warmth in her hands and took a sip.

"It's black. I didn't find any creamer, so I assumed you drank it that way."

Rachel nodded. He sat down across from her in an antique rocking chair and sipped his own cup of coffee. A moment of uneasy silence stretched between them while Rachel tried to collect her scattered and fuzzy thoughts. She eyed him over the rim of her mug and felt a jolt of heat that had nothing to do with the coffee.

"Rachel—"

"Oh God." She sat up quickly, spilling coffee on her robe. Hadn't he just called her Jade? "Who *are* you?"

"Jake Nichols, your agent."

She swallowed. *Oh dear lord.* "B-but how did you know where to find me? And w-why did you come out here in the middle of nowhere in the middle of that horrible storm?" Coffee sloshed again because of fingers that trembled. What exactly had she done with this man? She closed her eyes for a moment, remembering skin, heat . . . passion. Good lord, her *agent,* of all people. Rachel gripped the edge of the couch and had to put the mug down or spill the rest of the hot liquid. "Who told you about my cabin?"

"Your mother told me."

"She's not supposed to tell anyone where this cabin is."

He grinned. "I do have a certain charm. Plus, she was worried. The phone lines were down and when I told her who I was and why I needed to see you, she was more than willing to give me directions." He shrugged again. "I was in Cincinnati for a convention, but the storm closed some major airports, so it was cancelled."

"But why did you need to see me? We've always dealt over the phone and through e-mail before."

"I just secured a three-book contract for you. Since my weekend was shot, I decided to give you the good news in person . . . maybe over dinner." He shook his head. "I had no idea the storm was going to be this bad."

There was a spark of joy over the contract, quickly squelched by her situation. "You can't tell *anyone,*" she said fiercely.

Jake frowned at her. "Tell anyone what?" How much of last night did she remember?

She blushed and pinched her lips together. Clearing her throat, she said, "When you burst in here—uninvited, I might add—I was in the middle of . . . something . . . and had consumed a little bit of wine."

Her sudden prim and proper attitude was rather amusing, considering the circumstances. Jake decided to set her straight. "Listen, about last night—"

"You took advantage of me—"

What? He felt a flash of anger. "Now wait a minute, lady. You were all too willing. It's a good thing for you that I realized you were—"

"Tipsy?"

"Trashed!"

She gasped and put a hand to her throat. "A little tipsy and engrossed in . . . something. And after you . . . you . . . *took advantage*, you snooped around, reading private things!"

Jake laughed. This was too much. His laughter died and his eyes widened at the sudden anger blazing in her green eyes. "Let's get this straight. You're blaming last night on me?"

"Yes!"

Jake pushed up from the chair and in two long strides he towered above her. She came up to her knees and then stood on the cushions with her hands clenched in tight fists. This put her a good head and shoulders above him and she jutted her chin out. Jake wondered if she was going to take a swing at him. The thought amused him and he chuckled.

She swung at him with a little squeal. Her fist connected with his jaw.

"Ouch!"

They both said it at the same time. She clutched her hand and he rubbed his chin. He laughed again. She squealed again and swung at him with the other fist.

"Oh, no you don't." This time he was ready and caught her hand before it connected. The force of her swing stopped by his grip forced her off balance. Jake realized she was going to fall over the back of the couch and lunged for her—sending them both tumbling sideways. *Shit!* He twisted to cushion her from the blow of the fall, landing hard on the back of the couch. It tipped and fell back. Jake landed on the floor with a grunt, taking her with him. She fell on top of him and the air left his lungs in a whoosh.

For a moment, he lay there, stunned, and wondered how many bones were broken. While he fought for air, she pushed with her hands on his chest. He looked up at the surprised expression on her face and attempted to laugh. Although his laughter came out as a wheeze, she must have recognized it for what it was.

And it pissed her off.

"Why you . . . you . . ." she sputtered and he realized she was trying to come up with a name vile enough to call him.

"Bastard?" he wheezed.

"Yes!" Her eyes were closed and her jaw clenched.

He laughed, but the laughter suddenly died in his throat when it dawned on him that she straddled him. The white robe had parted, revealing the red silk from last night.

And she wore *nothing* underneath.

He could feel her moist heat through his flannel pants. Her knees rested on the floor, making him realize that she was parted and open and sat directly on his cock. He hardened faster than he thought possible, and her eyes flew open.

"Oh!" *Yeah . . . oh.* When she leaned to the side to roll off of him, he reached up and held her in place.

"Let . . . go." Her voice was breathless and low, and she caught her bottom lip between her teeth.

Instead, he gripped her waist tighter and moved his hips beneath her, rubbing his penis against her. "Not yet." He rocked gently and she surprised him by moving ever so slightly . . .

With him.

Her eyelids fluttered shut and he watched her features soften as she gave in to the motion. The robe slipped from her shoulders, revealing the jiggle of her breasts against the red silk. Her nipples hardened and he wanted his mouth there, but didn't dare break the spell of anger turned to passion.

With a little gasp, she tilted her head back and rocked harder. Jake slipped his hands from her waist up under the folds of terry cloth and silk until he found her bare skin. He cupped her smooth ass and urged her on until she was almost there. But then she clutched at his shoulders, eyes open and wide. "My God, what am I doing?"

Chapter Five

She pushed at his shoulders and fell over into a trembling heap, flinging an arm over her eyes. "What have you done to me?"

"Ah, blaming *me* again, Miss Manning?"

Rachel opened her eyes to find him propped up on one elbow, looking down at her. His blue eyes twinkled with amusement and his mouth twitched at the corners. "Yes! And I want you to stop."

One dark eyebrow went up. "You do?" he asked, and ran a hand up her leg, stopping just short of where she ached for his touch.

She swallowed, and whispered, "Yes."

"So, you don't want my fingers here?" He oh so lightly grazed her mound, making her quiver.

Rachel squeezed her eyes shut and barely managed a throaty, "No."

"Well, then, how about my mouth?"

Rachel gasped when she felt the moist heat of his breath, the pressure of his mouth—and then his tongue slipped inside. She tried to protest, but the words were trapped in her throat when her whole body seemed to melt. My God, she couldn't let him do *this*! She tried to sit up, but she felt too weak. Her heart raced and she gulped for air, not realizing that she had been holding her breath.

His tongue moved slowly in and out and then up and down. With a strangled cry, she pushed up to her elbows. She had to make him *stop*. But the sight of his dark head moving between her pale thighs made her arms tremble and she sank back to the floor.

For a mere second, he paused. "Rachel, baby, relax." And then—God, and *then*—he slid his palms under her, cupped her buttocks, and tilted her up, easing her open wider. His mouth moved and his tongue dipped deep. The slight nip of his teeth was sweet agony. She whimpered, wanting him to stop, needing him to go on.

"Jake!" She clutched at his head, delving her fingers into his hair.

She was trembling, fighting it, wanting release but afraid to give in. Jake knew she was on the brink and wanted to plunge his dick inside her and let her orgasm milk him dry, but he wasn't wearing a condom. Plus, he wanted to finish her off like this—the most intimate of acts that would somehow make her his.

He eased her limp legs over his shoulders, lifted her ass higher, plunged his tongue as deep as it would go, in and out, in and out, while she moved with him. The muscles in his shoulders bunched and quivered and his arms ached, but he would give no quarter until she came in his mouth.

Jake knew that because she had resisted for so long, her orgasm was going to be explosive, and he knew just how to push her over the edge. He shoved his tongue in one last time and then brought it out flat over her lips and sucked sharply on her clitoris.

She cried out, a hoarse, husky sound of intense pleasure, and blossomed beneath his mouth. Her back arched and she clutched at his head. He slipped his tongue in to feel her clench and pulse, and held her while she rode it out. His tense muscles gave out and he fell against her, panting and sweating. He rested his head on her belly, then rolled over, taking her with him. He held her shaking body in his embrace while she recovered, and wondered if she was going to kiss him or swing another fist at his face.

He wasn't sure which one he deserved.

Or which one he wanted.

The fist would be much easier to deal with. A kiss or even a tender word from her, his name on her lips, would be more than he could handle. This wild encounter was more than just extraordinary sex, and it scared the living shit out of him. This . . . this was a whole new level of something he wasn't quite prepared for.

Jake searched his brain for some asshole comment to piss her off, but nothing came to him. That, in of itself, was a scary thing.

He didn't want the punch. He wanted the kiss. He inhaled deeply, trying to clear his brain, but encountered her sweet scent and it clouded his thinking even more. The taste of her clung to his lips, and it didn't help that he was as hard as a rock. He wondered if there was a chance in hell that she would return the favor. Perhaps he should ask.

"Rachel?"

She heard the sound of his voice against her belly where he rested his head. She was glad not to have to look him in the face after what she had just let him do. She couldn't blame a bottle of wine this time.

She wasn't sure how to react. Part of her wanted to jump up, run and hide.

Oh . . . but the other part wanted to ease her body down to the erection poking her thigh and give him the magic he had just given her. Her heart thudded and she shifted down ever so slightly. After all, she didn't want to . . . *owe* him. She could do this one last thing and then they would be even. Then she would send him on his way.

Her stomach rumbled under his ear and he laughed softly as he nuzzled her there. The sound of his laughter brought her back to reality. To sanity. Hadn't she been swinging her fists at his arrogant face just a few minutes ago? Hadn't her editor once commented that Jake Nichols was a womanizer? She narrowed her eyes, pursed her lips, but then smiled slowly.

She was going to do what Sasha would do. Drive him wild and them push him away. She wiggled and then slid down the length of his body. He lifted his head and propped up on his elbows, but Rachel refused to look at him.

"What are you doing?" His voice was strained and he inhaled sharply when she eased the loose flannel pants over his lean hips.

"Roll over," Rachel demanded. When he remained poised above her, she gave him a little shove and he fell over to his back with a surprised grunt. Rachel scooted between his legs and pulled his pants down to his thighs. Wow. He was hugely erect.

Now what? Rachel just remembered that she had never really *done* this before—unless she had last night and didn't remember. She had written about oral sex like she was an expert, but actually doing it was another story. God, he was so big. How was she going to get the whole thing in her mouth?

Rachel decided to stall while she gathered the nerve to . . . *suck* him. She leaned over and placed kisses on his thighs. With one hand, she pushed his T-shirt up and rained more hot kisses on his lower abs. His penis, velvety smooth, steely hard, brushed against her cheek, and he moaned softly.

His obvious pleasure gave her the courage to lightly run the tip of her tongue in a circle over the engorged head and down the length of him. She inhaled the scent of his freshly showered skin and the underlying hint of sex.

And suddenly, she wanted—no, *had*—to taste all of him. With her hands splayed over the hard planes of his chest, she leaned up and took him into her mouth. She loved the sound of his gasp as he came up to his elbows, giving her better access to move her mouth up and down the length of his shaft.

He was hot, hard, throbbing, as she licked and sucked with a frenzied rhythm. His penis grew slick from her saliva, sliding faster and faster . . .

"God, Rachel . . . stop. I'm going to—"

Rachel looked up in surprise, afraid that she had somehow hurt him, done something wrong. His chest was heaving and sweat trickled down his face.

"Finish me with your hand!"

"What?"

Jake placed her hand on his cock. She moved up and down, once, twice—and he shot like a hot geyser into her hand. With a ragged cry, he fell flat on his back and threw an arm over his head.

Rachel pushed up to a sitting position and gazed down at him. Half of his face was covered with his bent arm. His gray shirt was dark with sweat and pushed up to reveal most of his chest, nicely defined ab muscles, and his thick swollen penis.

Rachel wanted to touch, explore, and play with all of him, especially his penis, wet and shiny from her mouth and his own semen. She swallowed, and the thought ran through her mind that he could slip so easily inside her, he was still hard and so slick.

And so was she. Damp and ready. All she had to do was hop on top and go for a ride. She shyly ran her hand lightly over his penis. He shivered violently, and grabbed her hand and pulled her down on top of him.

He kissed her with a deep, hot possession and held her close. They tasted of each other, of heat and sex. He held her tightly in a full-body embrace, and Rachel never knew a kiss could be so intimate, so totally consuming. She melted into him, the hardness of his body and the softness of his mouth.

When the kiss ended, she laid her cheek against his chest. The strong beat of his heart filled her with a sense of wonder and contentment. This was the man who had encouraged her as a writer. He had believed in her talent, her ability, when she had doubted herself. And now he had made her come alive as a woman. Thoughts of sex became secondary to simply being held in his arms. At that moment she could have told him she loved him and meant it. *Sorry, Sasha,* Rachel thought with a grin. At this point, kicking him out the door wasn't an option.

The deep timbre of his voice vibrated against her ear. "Why don't you go soak in a hot bubble bath and I'll bring you some breakfast?"

Rachel pushed up with shaky arms and smiled, knowing that she was blushing furiously. "That sounds like heaven."

And it was. The hot water soothed her sore spots and aching muscles. She was almost asleep when Jake entered the steamy bathroom with a plate full of food. Her half closed eyes opened wide at the sight of him.

He was shirtless and shoeless with the plaid pants riding low on his hips. She grinned. "No shirt, no shoes, no service" would *not* be a house rule. She watched his blue eyes darken when he gazed down at her in the tub, and she scooted beneath the mounds of bubbles.

Jake knelt down beside the big whirlpool tub under the guise of feeding her a forkful of eggs, but he was glad for the cover to hide his once again raging erection. Chestnut curls piled high on her head revealed the slender column of her neck and framed her face, rosy from the steamy heat.

"You're a good cook," she offered after swallowing another bite of eggs.

Jake shrugged. "Breakfast is about all I'm good at."

"I can think of a few other things."

Jake chuckled, and then laughed harder when she blushed a deeper red. "Yes, you said that out loud." He fed her another bite and then set the plate aside. "Wet your hair and I'll wash it for you."

"No, really, I—"

"Please?" He kissed her softly on the back of her neck and reached for the shampoo bottle.

"Okay," she said uncertainly, and dipped her head under the water.

Jake squirted a dollop of coconut-scented liquid into the palm of his hand and began massaging it into a rich lather on her head. "Close your eyes. Relax."

Jake smiled when her eyelids fluttered shut. He moved his fingers firmly over her scalp, delving his hands into the fragrant soap. Leaning close, he let the lather ooze over his hands and forearms. She leaned back, eyes closed, bottom lip caught between her teeth.

"I've wanted to meet you for a long time, Jake."

"You have?" He continued to massage her scalp.

"Mmm-hmm." Her eyes remained shut, and the bubbles teased him with glimpses of her breasts bobbing just beneath the water. "I had been rejected by so many agents, I was ready to give up when you took me on as a client." Her eyes opened a slit and she gazed at him. "What made you take me on?"

Jake paused, letting his fingers sink into the warm lather. "Something about your writing moved me, Rachel. I was drawn in by your voice. You have the extraordinary ability to write with simplicity and bring depth to the story at the same time. I thought about sending your material to someone I know who represents more inspirational women's fiction, but quite frankly, I couldn't give you up."

Her gaze met his. "What about my . . . other . . ."

He grinned. "You mean your steamy stuff?"

She blushed and nodded up at him.

"It rocks. By the way I know a really good agent who could sell your . . . *steamy stuff*." He wiggled his eyebrows at her.

"I wouldn't want anyone to find out." Her blush deepened. "My parents would have a fit."

"That's why authors have pen names . . . *Jade*," he teased. "Don't be ashamed of something you do so well. Now, rinse," he said gruffly next to her ear, "before your head swells too big to fit into the tub." Her head wasn't the only thing swelling, he thought, and shifted uncomfortably. When she went under, he helped her remove the shampoo and then patted her face with a fluffy towel.

And then he kissed her. She was warm and pliant, wet and willing. His hands slipped under the water and cupped her breasts . . . full, sleek. He ran his thumbs over her nipples and she sighed into his mouth. Water splashed over his chest and lapped over the tub onto his pants.

She wrapped her arms around his neck until he was halfway in the tub with her. He continued to kiss her with his hands braced on the side of the tub.

And then he slipped, falling with a splash. Water slopped everywhere, and when he groped for balance, he found soft wet flesh. Rachel squealed and laughed while he slipped and slid and became thoroughly drenched.

With a growl, he reached into the water and scooped her out of the tub. She shrieked and clung to him, giggling at the same time.

"I'm cold!" she complained between giggles. He set her down, but she clung to him for support while he reached for a towel and wrapped her in it. Her eyes grew big when he peeled the wet flannel off and dried himself with another towel.

"Still cold?"

"A little."

"I can fix that."

Chapter Six

He rubbed her briskly with the towel until her skin glowed and she tingled—everywhere. His own towel had pooled to the tile floor, leaving him once again gloriously naked.

"Warm now?"

She nodded as he swaddled her in the towel and pulled her against him. He gave her a lingering kiss, and she was sure steam would rise from her head.

"You're beautiful."

Rachel shook her head. "No . . . I'm not."

Her heart pounded when he wiped the fog from the wide mirror and then turned her around to face her reflection. He stood behind her and eased the white towel from her shoulders. Rachel clutched the edges of the towel and leaned weakly against him while he kissed the back of her neck.

The towel slipped lower when her fingers went limp. Her eyes, half closed, opened wide when Jake pushed the towel to the floor. She watched, mesmerized, when his hands, dark in contrast to her pale skin, slipped slowly up her torso and cupped her breasts. He moved the pads of his thumbs over her rosy, erect nipples in small circles while they both watched through swirls of steam.

"You *are* beautiful, Rachel," he whispered into her ear

while he continued to stroke her breasts and tease her nipples until her breath came in short gasps. She could feel his erection against her back. Rachel arched against him while moving up and down to stroke him with her skin.

She could feel the rapid rise and fall of his chest and the quick beat of his heart while she moved against him. Moisture pooled between her thighs while her eyes met his in the mirror.

"Watch," he told her, and moved one hand over her belly to the triangle of dark, moist curls. Her knees buckled when he eased one long finger between her swollen lips to stroke her. He supported her with one strong arm wrapped around her waist, pressing her body against him.

And they both watched.

"Wrap your arms up around my neck, Rachel. I want . . . to see all of you in the mirror."

"O-kay," she barely managed to say. Rachel reached up behind him and clasped her hands around his neck. She was totally open, exposed, all the way to where the edge of the cool sink met her midthigh.

Jake held her still for a moment, his hands spanning her waist, to enjoy the view of her body and to slow down the throbbing of his cock. They were going too fast and this little scenario was too good to rush.

"Keep your hands hooked around my neck. Watch. Listen. And hold on." When she nodded, he began slowly. First, he held her face in his hands. "This is a lovely face, Rachel, don't ever doubt it."

Jake ran his hands down the length of her up-stretched arms and reached under to cup her breasts in a firm grip. "And these . . . these are exquisite. Firm, full." He tweaked her nipples between his finger and thumb, and smiled when she gasped. "Perfection."

When he moved his hands from her breasts to graze over her belly, she quivered and arched against him, and her eyelids fluttered shut.

"Open your eyes and watch."

She did, but only half-lidded. He moved his hand between her thighs and thrust his finger into her soft folds, slick heat, while caressing her breast with his other hand. "Move with me," he growled into her ear, and clenched his jaw in an effort not to come until she did.

She began to move with the rhythm of his hand while her arms remained up and clasped around his neck. Jake watched, thinking it was the most beautifully erotic sight he had ever seen. Her whole body was flushed a deep rose, her eyes heavy-lidded, her mouth moist and lips parted.

His penis moved against her back while her ass nestled snuggly against his thighs. Jake moved with her, faster now, watching, feeling. God, she was heat and silk against his hand. She was incredibly wet, pulsing. Her breasts jiggled up and down while his hand moved, his finger slid, circled—plunged.

While they watched.

She suddenly arched up, while her hands pulled his neck forward. "Jake!" Her cry was a throaty half-sob that sent him over the edge as he climaxed against the smoothness of her back. Her hands slipped from around his neck and he had to catch her. With his arms holding her tightly, Jake fought to catch his breath. *And his heart.*

Although his own legs were more than a little shaky, he scooped her up in his arms and carried her to her bedroom. With one hand, he pulled back the quilt and lowered her gently to the mattress. When her head hit the pillow, she gave a weary sigh and held out an unsteady hand for him to join her.

He did. He scooted in under the covers and snuggled next to her spoon-fashion in the small bed, just like he had imagined. Within minutes, they were both asleep.

When Rachel woke up, the sun was sinking low in the sky. She glanced at the red digital numbers of the clock on the nightstand and blinked. It was almost five o'clock. She quietly eased away from Jake's embrace. He mumbled, but remained asleep.

After slipping from the covers and stepping onto the cold wood floor, Rachel shivered, but couldn't resist a glance at him. He was on his side, facing her, eyes closed while breathing softly. In slumber, he seemed younger . . . almost vulnerable. She knew he was a hard-nosed agent, and he had worked hard for her—believed in her when no one else had. His encouragement and comments had gotten her through some tough times of self-doubt. His faith in her talent had made her career take off. Without him, she never would have gotten this far. She gazed over at him and smiled softly.

With a sigh, he rolled to his back, causing the quilt to bunch around his waist, exposing his chest and one long leg.

Rachel almost couldn't resist climbing back into bed with him. One whisper, one touch, and they'd be making love. A protesting growl from her stomach was the *only* thing that kept her from doing just that. With determined steps, she left the room, donned her robe, and headed for the kitchen.

After popping a frozen lasagna entrée into the oven, Rachel headed for her computer, where she had left Sasha in the elevator seducing her football star. This time, Rachel didn't need candles or wine or music to set the mood. All she had to do was think about the naked man sleeping in her bed and her imagination went into overload. She opened up her story and began typing.

Sasha opened the pearl buttons on her blouse to her navel and let the red silk gape just enough to give him a good look without revealing too much. She chuckled low in her throat when he clenched his hands, knowing he wanted to part the blouse and see all of her.

Even in the dimly lit elevator, she could see his blue eyes darken with desire and admired his restraint when he didn't touch her. Ah, the discipline of an athlete, she thought, and decided to test him a bit further.

"You want to see more, Dominick?" Sasha asked, her accent thick, her voice a throaty whisper. She shrugged slightly, but enough for the silk to slip from her shoulders and pool at her waist.

"You know I do."

"Then follow me."

Rachel stopped typing. "Follow me?" she asked out loud. "Sasha, what are you doing? You're supposed to drive him crazy and leave him. He's a womanizer . . . an arrogant jerk! Put him in his place!"

"Put who in his place?"

Rachel turned in her swivel chair and felt heat creep into her cheeks. Jake's dark hair was mussed, stubble shadowed his cheeks, and his eyes were heavy-lidded from sleep. The flannel pants hung low on his hips, and she wondered if he had deliberately left his shirt off to drive her wild.

He walked slowly toward her and her heart pounded harder with each step he took. She reminded herself that he was a rake, a womanizer, a player—and extremely good at it. Falling for him was stupid, dangerous, and she would only end up getting hurt. She would *not* have sex with him again. As soon as the ice melted, she would send him on his way. But when he lifted his arms above his head and stretched, the pants slipped farther south. Muscles flexed and rippled.

"Stop!" She could have kicked herself for saying that out loud.

"Stop what?"

"Looking so . . . so damned sexy!"

"You think I look sexy?"

"You know you're sexy. You ooze sexiness."

"And that seems to piss you off."

He was frowning at her now, and she felt foolish and angry at the same time—out of her league, and out of her element. Writing about this stuff was easy compared to living it. He stopped and kneeled in front of her, placing his big hands on her knees. She tried to swivel away from him, but he held her firmly.

"Okay, what's the problem?"

"There are several."

"Start with the first."

Rachel took a deep breath, closed her eyes for a second to organize her thoughts. His hands slipped up to her thighs and she slapped at them, losing her whole focus in the process. She squeezed her eyes tighter and concentrated on why she didn't want to have sex with him again. It was because . . . because . . . ?

How could she think when he parted her robe and slipped a warm hand inside to cup her breast? Somehow, he untied the knot and gently pushed the fluffy terry cloth from her shoulders, and put his mouth where his hand had been. His mouth was hot, his lips were soft, while his tongue caressed and his teeth teased. His hands were kneading her thighs, working their way up to where she throbbed with need.

"Spread your legs."

"Jake, no."

"Please?"

"Well, okay—no!" She pushed at his shoulders and he fell backward. Off balance, he fell to his butt and then to his elbows, looking stunned, with a huge erection tenting his pants. Rachel wanted to dive on top of him and had to grip the arms of the chair to keep from doing so.

"I'm not having . . . doing . . . *you know*, with you."

"It's a little late for that, Rachel."

She glared at him. "I mean again."

"Too late for that, too."

His grin had her gritting her teeth—or maybe the sustained urge to jump on him had her gritting her teeth—but she held her ground. "I mean not ever *again,* um ... again."

He looked nervous now, and she wondered if he had ever been turned down.

"Why? Because I'm your agent?"

"Yes. And because you'll leave for Chicago and never give this weekend another thought." She felt her cheeks flame but had to continue. "I know that after what has happened between us, you may not think so, but—"

"Let me finish. You're not that kind of girl."

"I'm not!" she shouted with a catch in her voice.

Jake felt his anger rise and hurt slam him in the gut. She regretted giving herself to him. It was written all over her pale face. Now was the time to tell her that they hadn't made love that first night. He couldn't even imagine *never* fully making love to her—being so deep inside her that he didn't know where he ended and she began. He should tell her that the stories about him were exaggerated, and that he'd always wanted a lasting relationship with a woman, but had never found the right partner. Well, okay, someone who could put up with him.

Until now.

But she was looking at him with such regret that it totally pissed him off. Not only that, but she looked like she wanted to throw off that ridiculous robe and jump his bones, but hated herself for her lustful longings. With her frowning, pinched expression, but her robe gaping open, she was a humorous combination of Miss Goody Two Shoes turned total sex kitten. So he laughed.

Chapter Seven

"Whoa!"

She bolted out of the chair and dove toward him, land-ing with a full-body slam that would have made a profes-sional wrestler proud. "Don't you dare laugh at me!" she squealed, then pushed up and pounded on his chest with her fists.

"Ouch! Stop!" Jake tried to capture her wrists, but she moved too fast, plus she straddled him while her robe gaped open, making him focus more on her jiggling breasts than her flying fists. God, she had great breasts. "Ouch!" he grunted when she clipped him in the chin. "That's enough!" He grabbed her wrists and glared up at her.

Shit. She was crying. She put her hands over her face and sobbed. Shit, shit . . . *shit*. Jake pushed from the floor to a sitting position and wrapped his arms around her, trying to ignore the fact that she was half nude and sitting on his lap.

"I'm s-s-sorry that I h-hit you," she murmured against his neck. She pulled back and looked down at his chest where she had pounded, and then placed kisses on the red marks she had caused while tears streamed down her face.

Jake felt the heat of her mouth, the wetness of her tears, and the silky tickle of her hair brush across his chest. He pushed his fingers into her thick chestnut curls, raised her head, and then wiped the tears away with this thumbs. Their eyes locked, held, and then she rocked against him ever so slightly.

Her breath caught and she froze. "Slip on a condom."

"No." Jake forced the word when he wanted nothing more than to plunge inside her. She moved against him again and he barely swallowed the moan in his throat. When she did it again, he placed his hands around her waist to stop her.

"You want me, Rachel?" When she gave him a jerky nod, he continued. "Then you do it. There is a condom in my wallet, but this is your decision. If you want me, I'm all yours. I won't feel guilty if *you* make love to *me*."

She hesitated, and Jake felt his heart plummet. "I see. You want me to do the seducing so you can blame me later—or blame the wine or whatever else you can pin the blame on."

"No. I—"

"Get up."

When she didn't move, he put his hands around her waist and lifted her off of his lap. Pushing up, he stood on shaky legs and turned away from her.

"Jake—"

"I'm leaving, Rachel."

"But the roads aren't safe!"

"I'll chance it." He raked an impatient hand through his hair and stalked out of the room. He heard her scramble to her feet and knew she followed him, but didn't stop when she clutched at his arm as he reached the bottom step of the loft.

"Jake!"

The tears in her voice compelled him to hesitate and he reluctantly turned to face her. He shouldn't have. She looked vulnerable and lost with her wide green eyes and trembling bottom lip.

"I . . . I don't want you to have a wreck on the icy roads. Please don't leave . . . until the roads are safe."

"Wouldn't want that on your conscience, too, now would we? Fine. Just fine." He pointed a finger at her. "Just remember, no more sex with big bad Jake Nichols. We'll keep the rest of our . . . confinement on a strictly business level. And by the way, we never did the deed that first night anyway, so don't feel so damned guilty."

After that parting remark, Jake stomped up the stairs, childishly wishing there was a door to slam. He stepped out of the flannel pants, sadly eyeing his erect penis. "Sorry, old boy. Don't know what got into me. I must be fucking crazy—make that crazy for not fucking." He found his dry boxers, jeans, and sweater, put them on, and sat down on the bed with his head in his hands.

Rachel watched him stomp up the stairs, tilting her head to admire his butt. She wondered how *she* had become the villain in this whole thing. This sudden role reversal was weird. He turned her down? She hurt *his* feelings? Well! She did her own stomping toward the kitchen to check on the lasagna.

The sauce was bubbling around the edges and smelled heavenly. Her stomach growled gleefully in anticipation. After uncorking a bottle of wine, she poured a glass and took a long sip. She was on her second glass and finishing the tossed salad when Jake appeared in the doorway. Her heart gave a little leap, but she lifted her chin.

"Would you like some dinner?" she asked coolly. Her intent was to give him a quick glance and go back to tossing the already tossed salad, but she couldn't take her eyes off of him. With one shoulder, he leaned against the door frame, hands jammed into his faded jeans. He would have pulled off the causal stance, but Rachel detected a slight tick in his jaw that gave him away.

"Well, would you?" she asked again when he didn't answer.

"Would I what?" He frowned and pushed away from the doorway.

"Like some lasagna, salad, and a glass of wine?" She took another sip from her glass and realized she needed food. When he looked like he might refuse, she continued, "Don't worry, Jake. I won't offer dessert." She gestured toward the small kitchen table. "Have a seat, and a glass of wine. I'm going to change out of this robe and then we'll eat."

Rachel turned her back on him without waiting for an answer. She wondered how he would react if she walked back into the kitchen stark naked. Getting rejected stung her newly found sexual pride, and she really wanted him begging for it so she could turn *him* down.

Rachel chewed on her bottom lip while she hung her robe on the bathroom door hook. Naked would be just a little too obvious. Oh no, she would have to slowly but subtly drive him wild. She turned and viewed her naked body in the mirror, and the memory of Jake caressing her, whispering in her ear, moving against her while they watched—

"Oh, stop!" she told her reflection. She yanked on a discarded pair of gray sweatpants and a white T-shirt, but left underwear out of the equation. Pulling her unruly curls into a loose ponytail gave an I-don't-care impression that didn't appear to try for sexiness, yet was. A little dab of clear lip gloss gave her mouth a sheen that looked just licked.

Rachel eyed her outfit and grinned. The pants were just a *little* tight—perfect for bending over. The T-shirt was baggy, but thin enough to show the outline of her breasts. She wiggled her shoulders and was rewarded with a no-bra jiggle as her nipples popped out. "Hah! Eat your heart out, Jake Nichols. You won't be eating *me*." With that last wicked thought, she marched out of the bathroom with her ponytail swinging and boobs bouncing.

Jake twirled his wineglass with his thumb and forefinger, and made a huge effort to not look up when Rachel entered the kitchen, but pretended to read a women's magazine he'd found on the table. Boots were in style again, and he learned that a silver chain belt was a *must* accessory.

When she bent over to retrieve the lasagna from the oven, he sneaked a peek over the top of the page. Jake was momentarily relieved that she wasn't dressed to entice him, so maybe he could pull this no-sex thing off . . . as long as the ice thawed really soon. Sweatpants and a T-shirt. He could handle that.

Jake took a sip of his wine and let his gaze linger a moment too long. When she reached into the oven, her T-shirt scooted up over her butt. The innocent gray pants clung like a second skin and outlined the curve of her cheeks with no evidence of a panty line. The wine went down wrong. Jake sputtered and coughed, drawing her unwanted attention.

"Are you okay?"

Jake continued to cough, but raised a hand and nodded. Then his gaze caught the soft jiggle of her breasts beneath the thin cotton and he started coughing all over again.

She brought him a glass of water. "Here, take a sip. It might help." His fingers brushed hers and he jerked away, splashing water on his sweater as he took a gulp. Rachel came at him with a towel, dabbing at his chin and then his chest, making those damned perky breasts jiggle and sway just inches from his mouth.

Just when he was about to pull her onto his lap, she turned away, leaving his arms empty. After a moment, she placed a steaming plate of lasagna and a bowl of salad in front of him, and then sat down to join him with a smile that made his jaw clench.

Dinner was torture, filling him up and leaving him hungry at the same time. Watching her eat was making him hard enough to raise the table. His eyes kept zeroing in on her mouth . . . chewing, swallowing, licking sauce from her lips. Lowering his gaze meant staring at her breasts, so he finally gave in and concentrated on his plate.

"Is your food okay?"

"Yes." He refused to look up.

"More wine?"

"No." He needed his wits about him.

She outsmarted him by asking him about the book contract, deadlines, and money. He found himself relaxing while answering her questions.

"I've even had a few nibbles for a possible Family Channel movie," he informed her proudly.

"Really?"

God, she had a great smile, he thought, and noticed a cute dimple he hadn't seen before. "Nothing firm, but something to work with. Make sure I give you the contract before I leave." Her smile faded when he mentioned leaving, and he caught a gleam in her eye that made him uneasy.

"Finished?" She nodded toward his plate.

"Ah . . . yes, thank you."

"Would you like some dessert?"

Chapter Eight

Jake wasn't quite sure how to react. He squirmed in his chair. No, he wasn't sure how *not* to react. "I thought you weren't offering dessert."

She shrugged. "After something spicy, I enjoy something sweet. Care to join me?"

Jake struggled to get the words out. "I couldn't eat another thing." *Except maybe you.*

"Suit yourself." She turned, opened the freezer, and pulled out a container of ice cream. "Ooh, it's way too hard. Could you lend me a hand?"

Easy for you to say, he thought. "Put it in the microwave and it will soften up." *Unlike me.*

"But I like it hard, not all soft and mushy." She brought the container of Chunky Monkey over to the table, plopped it down in front of him, and handed him the scoop and a bowl. "Now don't be stingy."

The ice cream *was* as hard as a rock. He had to stand to scoop, and use a considerable amount of muscle. "There," he growled, and plunked a round ball into the bowl.

"You've got to be kidding. Give me that scoop," she grumbled, and bumped him out of the way.

He watched her strain for a moment and grabbed the scoop back from her. She tried to snatch it back and they struggled. He backed up a step and held the scoop up in the air, out of her reach. She jumped for it just as he backed up again, and ended up falling forward and body-slamming into him.

Jake caught her around the waist. With a growl, he lowered his head and crushed his mouth to hers, letting the damned scoop fall to the floor. Jake lifted her to the kitchen counter and she wrapped her arms and legs around him. He tore his mouth from hers and fastened his lips to her breast, making the thin cotton material wet and transparent. When he tugged sharply at her beaded nipple, she gasped and leaned back on her hands to offer him more.

"I thought you didn't want dessert."

Jake pulled back and forced her head up to look at him. His heart was racing and his erection strained painfully against his jeans. "This is a dangerous game you're playing, Rachel. You can only dick-tease so long before you get what you're asking for.

"I'm not asking. I'm demanding." She ran her hands up underneath his sweater, causing him to shiver.

"So, your plan isn't to get me hard as a rock and then shove me out the door?" He arched a dark eyebrow and waited for her answer.

"That *was* the plan," she confessed, to his surprise. "How did you know?" She lowered her gaze, but he tilted her head back up with the tip of his finger.

"I knew I pissed you off before, and besides, you had that little gleam in your eye that gave you away." When she opened her mouth to speak, he silenced her with a fingertip to her lips. "Hear me out." She nodded, and he continued, "I don't want to hurt you, Rachel."

The tip of her tongue licked the finger that still covered her lips. Jake inhaled sharply and tried to pull his hand away, but she grabbed his wrist and sucked his finger into the heat of her mouth. Jake closed his eyes, forcing himself to hold back. "Most of what you've heard about me is true, but not for the reasons you think."

When she paused and gazed up at him, he continued, "I suck with women."

She nibbled on the palm of his hand and he groaned.

"No, Rachel, you don't get it. I suck at the relationship part. I'm moody and arrogant and work too much. After a few weeks, you'd toss me out on my ear."

Rachel paused and swallowed before raising her eyes to meet his. With a start, she realized that he was serious. He was worried that *she* would dump *him*? This role reversal thing was really confusing.

He had just revealed more about himself in that one sentence than he had all weekend, and Rachel was suddenly frightened that she had the power to hurt him. They should end this *now* before they both got hurt.

But she couldn't. The ice was melting and she knew he'd be gone in the morning. She wanted one last night before her life went back to normal and he went back to Chicago. "I'm going to bed, Jake. If you join me, I'll take the lead. I'll seduce you, like you asked, and there will be no guilt, no regrets. If you choose to sleep upstairs, I'll understand." She kissed him softly and slid down from the counter. She paused to put the ice cream away and gave him one last look before leaving the room.

Rachel brushed her teeth and slid into bed naked. Sleeping nude was another first, but paled in comparison to the other firsts she had experienced that weekend. After lighting several candles in anticipation, she watched the clock for half an hour and realized that he wasn't coming. She briefly considered going up after him, but pride kept her from going that far. She closed her eyes and hoped sleep would come easily. She hovered near sleep when she remembered to blow out the candles.

Rising up on all fours, she leaned over to blow one out.

"Leave them lit."

Rachel turned to where Jake stood in the doorway, naked and fully aroused. "Come to me," she offered softly, in a throaty voice she hardly recognized as her own. She moved over and pulled back the covers when he approached. With each step, her heart pounded harder.

"Lie down," she instructed, and reached over to turn on the clock radio. Sultry jazz filled the room. The candles flickered, lightly scenting the room with vanilla while casting a golden glow on bare skin and making shadows on the wall. "Now turn over." He raised his eyebrows, but obeyed.

Rachel straddled him just below his thighs and then reached for a bottle of oil she had placed on her nightstand. After rubbing the oil in her hands to warm them, she began massaging his thighs. He moaned as she rubbed his skin and kneaded his muscles. She moved up to his buttocks, squeezing the taut flesh.

Wild with wanting him, she tortured herself with the deep massage, but loved the feel of his hard muscle and heated skin as her oiled hands moved up to his back and then to his wide shoulders. She was now straddling his waist, and her moist heat moved against his buttocks while she massaged his neck.

"Jesus, Rachel, let me turn over," he protested.

"Not just yet," she answered, and ran her fingers down his spine. He shivered, moaned, and thrashed against the sheets in an effort to turn over. Leaning close, Rachel let the tips of her breasts graze his back while she held him pinned to the bed.

His skin, bronze in the candlelight, took on a wet sheen from the oil. For a heated moment, she was content just to look at him. But then she had to taste him. With a sigh, she ran her tongue down his spine and nipped playfully at his butt. He went tense, causing his muscles to tighten and bulge.

She watched him grip the bedpost while he moaned into the pillow, and a wicked idea came to her. She leaned over, opened the bottom of her nightstand, and found two silk scarves. "You can turn over now," she whispered in his ear, and moved from his back.

When he flipped over, she straddled him once more, then leaned up and grabbed one wrist. With one quick motion, she tied his hand to the bedpost. "What," he began as she tied the other, "are you doing?"

"Having my way with you. I want to enjoy every nook and cranny of that magnificent body of yours. I find that I like being in control."

"Rachel!" He pulled against the silk bonds and lifted his head up off of the pillow. This movement strained his arms and chest. She oiled her hands and ran soothing fingers over his stretched muscles. After a moment, he dropped his head back to the pillow and laughed weakly.

Rachel smothered his laughter with a kiss, hovering on all fours just above his body. He arched up to make contact, straining, moving his penis against her, but she inched up higher on her knees, just out of reach. She knew he was dying to touch her and that knowledge gave her a powerful thrill.

He tugged again at his restraints. "Untie me," he growled.

"No can do. I want to explore a little bit." Since this would be the last time she would experience a gloriously male naked body for God knew how long. Oh no, she was going to make this last.

"You're my dessert, Jake, and I'm going to savor every taste," she whispered, and kissed him lightly. "Every nibble," she continued, and nipped one flat nipple. "And every lick," she finished, and ran her tongue down the salty tang of his skin, the tickle of chest hair. Pausing, she hovered above his engorged penis, letting her warm breath caress him.

"I'm going to devour every inch of you." Rachel raised

her head to look at him. He pulled against the bonds with his head up from the pillow and met her gaze.

"God have mercy, Rachel, untie me!" His voice was hoarse, desperate. Sweat tricked down his chest. "I'm going to explode. There's a condom on the nightstand. Let me put it on."

"I can do that for you."

"No, Rachel . . . please." God, she was driving him fucking insane. If she ran her hands down his dick, he would ejaculate like a sixteen-year-old. He had never, *ever* been this turned on in his life. He was desperate to touch her, to hold her—to fuck her. "If you don't untie me, I swear I'll rip my arms from the sockets and your headboard will snap in two."

She hesitated, catching her bottom lip between her teeth, causing his heart to pound. "Okay," she finally replied, and his held breath came out in a shaky whoosh.

It took her an agonizingly long time to undo the tight knots. Her nude body straddled his chest while she leaned forward, breasts jiggling just inches from his hungry mouth.

By the time he was free, he was wild with desire. With a vicious rip, he opened the condom with his teeth and rolled it onto his impatient penis. In one swift move, he flipped her onto her back and drove inside her. She cried out and clung to him, matching thrust for hard thrust, one, two—and on the third he came with blinding intensity that ripped a cry of her name from his soul.

Jake didn't stop. He couldn't get enough, could never get enough. He tilted her ass to plunge deeper, faster, but then pulled back when he worried that he was being too rough.

"No . . . God . . . don't . . . Jake! Jake, don't . . . stop," she pleaded between breathless pants as she clutched at the sheets.

Jake pumped harder, faster, while her breasts jiggled wildly. He reached up and tweaked one nipple. She arched up and cried out, throwing her head back when he gave one last deep plunge that sent her flying while her slick heat clutched and pulsed, squeezing him dry.

He looked down at her flushed face and smiled. Her invitation to her bed and uninhibited, wild lovemaking spoke volumes. She had given herself to him openly, *gladly*, without a trace of guilt. A warm glow of happiness made him suddenly feel . . . lighthearted. Jake took a deep breath and savored the feeling.

Perhaps this could work, after all, he thought, and opened his mouth to tell her.

Chapter Nine

When Jake started to pull out, Rachel placed her hands firmly on his butt to stop him. She wanted to feel him inside her for a few more precious moments. He was dripping with sweat and slick with oil, positively gleaming in the flicker of the candlelight. He leaned on shaking arms to his elbows and kissed her, replacing wildness with tenderness. When he finally pulled out, she felt incomplete. And at that moment she knew she had fallen in love and would never feel completely whole without him.

Tears welled up in her throat, preventing her from speaking her thoughts. One tear slid down her cheek.

Jake narrowed his blue eyes at her. "Regrets, Rachel? Guilt already?"

She wanted to protest, but he rolled from the bed and stalked from the room before her mouth would work. She heard him stomp up the stairs and slid from the bed to follow, but her weak knees gave out. She stood, holding the bedpost for support before moving. She finally felt steady enough to walk, and hurried on wobbly legs to the bathroom to retrieve her robe.

"Jake!" she called out, but got no answer. She climbed the stairs but he was gone. With a sob, Rachel rushed to the small window and pulled back the lace curtain. The black

SUV spit gravel as he backed out of the driveway and sped away.

For a few moments, Rachel stood at the window, staring out into the dark, moonlit night. She felt shell-shocked, unable to move. One moment he was kissing her tenderly, and the next moment he was gone.

Finally, Rachel moved on wooden legs to the bathroom, where she filled the big tub to the brim with hot water. She soaked her tired, sore body while she relived the weekend. After a while, she dozed off. When she awoke, the water had turned tepid.

If it wasn't for her tender spots, swollen lips, and the whisker burn on her breasts, Rachel would have sworn the whole weekend was a dream, a fantasy conjured up by her vivid imagination.

Wrapped in her robe, Rachel padded on bare feet to the kitchen to make some hot tea. Although it was two in the morning, sleep was the last thing on her mind. When she saw the book contract on her kitchen table, a sob welled up in her throat. So that's how it was to be? Back to a writer-agent relationship?

Rachel settled in at her computer, thinking that writing would take her mind off of Jake. She thought about e-mailing her feelings to him, explaining that her tears were of joy, not of shame or regret. True, she couldn't shake a certain amount of guilt—some things were just too deep-seated—but she refused to feel shame. And regret? How could she ever regret what she shared with Jake, if only for one magical weekend?

Rachel sighed. The only regret was how the weekend ended.

With renewed determination, Rachel placed her fingertips onto the keyboard, but no inspiration would come. She typed a really horrible paragraph and then deleted it. After an hour of struggle, Rachel gave up. "Sorry, Sasha." Rachel closed her file. "You deserve better, but girlfriend, I just don't have it in me today."

Rachel ended up leaving the cabin a day early, thinking that once she was back to her condo, she wouldn't constantly be reminded of Jake.

She was wrong. Even though her condo didn't have a fireplace, a leather couch, or a whirlpool tub, she still couldn't get him off of her mind. The condo, although small, had an open modern feel, with floor-to-ceiling windows in the living room that overlooked a lake. Her office was a small room upstairs that had the same view. As she sat at her computer, Rachel found herself staring at the lake instead of the computer screen.

She had massive writer's block.

By the end of the week, she was ready to pull her hair out. She could barely eat. Each night, sleep was impossible, but she found herself dozing at her computer instead of writing. Deadlines loomed in the near future. Rachel was starting to panic.

Once again she sat at her desk, chin resting in her hand as she gazed out of the window. Shadows fell across the lake as the sun began to set. Rachel closed her gritty eyes and dozed off.

The insistent buzz of her doorbell awoke her with a sudden start. She blinked for a moment, and then, still groggy, headed down the stairs to answer the door. Rachel started to open the door, but a thought popped into her sleep-deprived brain. What if it was *him*? She knew the mystery writer's conference had been rescheduled for this weekend—one of the reasons she hadn't left for the cabin. She had toyed with the idea of attending the conference even though she had never written a mystery. But hey, who knew? She had never written erotica, either.

The doorbell buzzed again and she wished she was wearing something other than her baggy gray sweats. Rachel attempted to smooth her tangled hair, and took a deep breath, making a mental note to install a peephole. She opened the door the length of the chain and peeked through the crack.

"Come on, Rachel, open up. This food is getting cold!"

"Oh." Rachel fumbled with the chain and then opened the door.

"What took you so long to open the door?" asked Michael as he brushed past her to place the Chinese takeout on the table.

"I was . . ."

"Writing?" He shrugged out of his leather jacket and draped it over the back of a chair. Rachel noted with relief that he wasn't using his cane to walk, and she detected only a slight limp.

"Well . . ." She'd opened her mouth to answer, but her face suddenly crumpled, and to her horror, she burst into noisy tears.

"Rachel, what's wrong?" Michael gathered her in his arms and Rachel sobbed against his shoulder. He felt solid and warm, making her realize how much she craved a hug.

Sniffing loudly, she wiped the tears with the heels of her hands and finally stepped back. "I can't"—sniff—"write." She plopped down into a chair, placed her elbows on the table, and cradled her throbbing head in her hands.

Michael sat down beside her, frowning. "You look like hell."

She lifted bleary eyes and attempted a glare. "Gee, thanks. And to think I was glad to see you."

Michael gave her a crooked grin. "I brought your favorite. Pot-stickers, Hong Kong Chicken, and fried rice. Hungry?"

Rachel inhaled the spicy aroma, and to her surprise, her stomach rumbled. She gave him a watery smile. "I think I forgot to eat all day while I was *not* writing." She stood to get plates and forks, but he waved her off.

"I know where everything's at. You sit."

"Wow, you waiting on me? That's a switch."

"You sitting there wrecked instead of me? That's a switch, too. I think I owe ya, sis."

Rachel watched him walk over to the galley kitchen and gather the plates. She smiled. He looked healthy and fit for the first time in almost two years. A car accident had crushed his ankle and blown out his knee. After three operations and gut-wrenching physical therapy, his pro baseball career was over.

A five-time Golden Glove ace pitcher, Michael Manning had been headed for the Hall of Fame. To Michael, baseball was life. When it was taken from him, he went into a downward spiral that almost consumed him. It wasn't until he hit rock bottom that he started to put the broken pieces of his life back together.

"This is wonderful." Rachel swallowed a bite of chicken and scooped up a forkful of rice.

"What? Me waiting on you? Don't get used to it, big sis."

Rachel grinned. "No, Michael. The food." Her grin faded. "And just you being here."

"Spill."

Rachel hesitated, not sure how much she wanted to reveal. She chewed her food thoughtfully and avoided his eyes.

"Come on, Rachel," he quietly encouraged her. "You know my past. Nothing you can tell me can be as bad as the stuff I've told you."

Rachel felt heat creep into her cheeks.

"Well, hallelujah. You've finally had some great sex."

Rachel's mouth dropped open and her cheeks grew hotter.

"Who's the lucky guy?"

Chapter Ten

Having just arrived in town from Chicago for a writer's conference, the lucky guy sat in his hotel room, not more than fifteen minutes from Rachel's condo complex, a fact that was driving him crazy. Earlier in the week, he had convinced himself he just *had* to attend the mystery writer's conference, knowing full well he was only there because it was being held near Rachel.

The past week had been sheer torture. Every damn time he closed his eyes, he relived the final scene at her cabin. Yeah, he might have been pissed at her tears, but he knew the real reason he had split. He was scared shitless. He hadn't lied when he told her that he sucked at the relationship part. The sex he could do, but with Rachel it had gone way beyond sex.

Jake sighed and took a long swallow of beer. He knew that she was home because he had driven by there—twice. Tipping the beer can to his lips, Jake drank the last swallow and crushed the can in his fist.

"To hell with it." He tossed the mangled can into the trash, creating a hollow clank. "I'm heading over there, and this time I'm not going to be a big puss. I'm going in."

Fifteen minutes later, he parked his rental car in her driveway. The lights were on in her condo; she was home. Ten minutes later, he wanted to kick his own ass for being a coward. After five more minutes, and a curious stare from a neighbor, he finally got out of the car and approached the front door.

When a guy answered the door instead of Rachel, Jake wished he had remained a coward. "I, uh, think I have the wrong condo," he began, but something familiar about the guy made him hesitate. He had the same wavy chestnut-colored hair as Rachel, the same intense green eyes—and they were glaring at him.

"You Jake Nichols?"

Jake nodded.

The green eyes narrowed. "You son-of-a-bitch."

Jake barely saw the hand snake out and grab him by the front of his shirt. In a flash, he was yanked into the hallway and thrown up against the wall. At first, Jake was too surprised to be pissed. That quickly changed.

"I oughta kick your ass for fucking with my sister."

"She enjoyed it."

Jake saw the fist coming but didn't care. He took a punch to the gut that took his breath away. When he doubled over, another quick jab caught him under the chin, causing him to stagger backward. Jake ducked; the next swing grazed his cheekbone and he fell to the carpet.

"Get up and defend yourself so I can beat the shit out of you."

Jake pushed up to one knee, tasting blood with his tongue where his lip was busted. "I deserved that, Michael, but I'm not going to let you beat the shit out of me. Just hold on for a minute." Jake held his hands up in a gesture of peace. "I don't want to fight." He pushed painfully to his feet. "Where is your sister?"

"You think I'm going to tell you?"

"I need to talk to her."

"Yeah, right. Talking isn't what you want to do."

"I'm in love with her." Jake watched the green eyes so like Rachel's widen in surprise.

"You're in lust with her, bro. Been there, done that. I'd advise you to fuck her out of your system, but she's my sister. Find somebody else."

Jake ran a shaky hand through his hair. "It goes deeper than that, Michael. I've never felt this damned way before. I never knew I could."

Michael hesitated. "I swear to God. If you hurt her—"

"I'm in love with her, Michael. I'd rather cut off my dick than hurt her."

"Ouch. Okay. You've convinced me. Good luck convincing *her*. She left a while ago for the cabin."

"Thanks. I know the way."

Rachel slammed her fist down so hard that the keyboard jumped into the air and clattered back to the desk. Candles, wine, music, silk pajamas—none of her usual props were working. Poor Sasha was left hanging again. "Damn you, Jake Nichols." She drained the glass of wine and felt like throwing the glass across the room.

The sound of gravel crunching drew her attention. At first she thought Michael might have followed her, but she didn't recognize the car that stopped in front of the cabin. Her heart pounded when she realized that it was Jake walking toward her door.

He knocked. She didn't answer.

"Rachel, open up. I want to talk."

She hesitated. Opening up the door meant opening up her heart.

He knocked harder. "Rachel, please." His voice was low and pleading. "Come on, dammit. I'm freezing my balls off."

Rachel grinned. Now there was the Jake Nichols she knew—and *loved*. When she opened the door, she planned on playing coy and hard to get.

But when he stepped inside, she threw her happy self into his arms. He picked her up and she wrapped her legs around his waist. "My God, Jake, what happened to your face?" She noticed a slight bruise on his chin, a swollen lip, and another bruise on his cheek.

"Your brother wanted to kick my ass."

"You didn't hurt him, did you?" Alarm coiled in her stomach. Michael didn't need any more injuries.

"No. Not that I couldn't have—what are you doing?"

"Kissing your boo-boos to make then better." She softly kissed his chin, his puffy lip, and the bruise on his cheek.

"You're gonna have a shiner."

"Will that make me look big, bad, and sexy?"

"You're already too sexy for your shirt," Rachel murmured, and unbuttoned the top buttons to expose his chest.

"Where?" he asked gruffly.

"In front of the fire."

"I was hoping you would say that," he said against her mouth before sliding in his tongue.

He stopped kissing her long enough to lay her down on the lamb's wool rug and shed his clothes. Rachel watched with pleasure while he pulled his shirt over his head and peeled off his jeans. She came up to her knees and yanked his boxers to his feet.

"You gave me writer's block," she accused as he rolled on a condom. "Cure me."

"You gave me a hard-on," he countered. "Cure *me*."

"Lie down," she ordered, and he obeyed. She unbuttoned her pajama top and let it slide in a pool of red silk to the floor.

"You're making it worse."

Rachel shimmied out of the pajama bottoms, pulled the clasp from her hair, and shook the waves free. She knelt down and straddled him, rubbing her slick heat over his erection. In one swift motion, she angled forward and then back, sliding his penis inside. With a soft whimper, she sat up straight, letting him fill her to the hilt.

She moved slowly at first, letting her body adjust to his size. With her hands splayed across the hard planes of his chest, she moved her hips as she rose to her knees and then sank back down, caressing his steely length all the way to his head and then enveloping him totally.

Jake clasped her hands and pressed up to give her support as she moved, head back, lips parted, breasts thrust forward. Firelight flickered, candles scented the room, and sultry music set the mood. When the music intensified, Rachel moved faster. Her thighs began to quiver. Jake let go of her hands and grasped her hips, moving her faster.

"God, you're tight," he gasped. "Hot." He suddenly gripped her hard around the waist, muscles straining as he arched his back. Rachel watched, fascinated by the ecstasy on his face, the sheen of sweat shining in the firelight. He pushed down with his hands, up with his hips, and hoarsely cried out her name, sending her over the edge she had been clinging to.

Rachel fell forward like a limp rag doll. Her limbs felt like warm liquid as she melted against his solid frame. He held her close, and when she was able, Rachel eased from his body, rolled to the side, and propped her chin up on her hand.

She trailed her fingertips over the hair on his chest, causing him to shiver. He rolled on his side to face her, tucking a strand of her hair gently behind her ear.

"What made you come here tonight?" Rachel asked softly, hoping it wasn't just for sex.

He looked at her, trailed a finger over her lips, but didn't answer. She saw vulnerability in his blue eyes and held her breath while waiting for his response. "I wanted to be with you."

Rachel felt her heart sink. So that was all it was. "Oh."

"No . . . I don't mean for sex. Well, yeah, that too, but . . . shit, Rachel, I suck at this." He put a hand up to his forehead and flopped over onto his back.

Rachel smiled, leaned over and kissed him. "That was beautiful."

"What? You've got to be kidding."

"I needed to hear that you didn't come here just to have sex. We made love. That's what it is, Jake. Not just mindblowing sex. *We made love*. I'm not ashamed." She laid her head down on his chest, listened to the strong beat of his heart while tracing circles in the silky hair.

Suddenly, she felt his chest rise and fall rapidly, and his heart picked up speed. "I love you." The low growl rumbled against her ear and the words sounded like they were being forced through his lips, but hey, he *said* them.

"Geez, Jake, you sound like someone has a gun to your head. You don't have to—"

He pushed up to a sitting position and leaned over her. His blue eyes were serious. "Rachel, I've never said those three little words before. I mean it, dammit. I *love* you," he repeated fiercely.

Rachel sat up, heart beating fast. She was stunned—too stunned to speak. Her eyes searched his face for a sign that he was teasing, but there was no sign of humor, no arrogance, just a trace of fear. "You're sure about this? You've only known me—"

"Hell, yes, I'm sure," he growled.

She frowned and watched him run trembling fingers through his hair, making it stand up in dark spikes.

"I mean . . . I've never been tied in knots like this before, Rachel. You're on my mind fucking constantly!"

"You sound more pissed off at me than in love, Jake, or like, you love me but wish you didn't."

Jake pressed his forehead against hers. "I'm scared shitless."

"Of what?"

"That you don't love me back," he said so softly that she almost didn't hear him.

Rachel slipped onto his lap and wrapped her arms around him. "You're on my mind fucking constantly."

His eyebrows shot up. "Have you ever said *fuck* before?"

"Never." She grinned. "I kinda like saying it. Fuck," she whispered in his ear. "Ooh, that felt naughty." She rocked her bare body against him and locked her legs around his waist. "Fuck me, Jake."

"Not until you say it." He placed his hands around her waist to keep her from moving.

"I just did."

"Rachel, I'm dying here. Say it!"

"I love you, Jake Nichols. Now fuck me!"

"Oh, great. I'm just a wonderful influence. I turn you into a potty-mouthed—"

She stopped his words with a heated kiss and then held his chin in her hand. "Without you, I couldn't write, and writing to me is the same as living. It's what I do . . . it's what I am. I need you, I want you, and I love you. Make love to me, Jake."

"Say it."

Rachel groaned. "I just did!"

"No. I mean the fuck me thing. It turns me on. God, you're such a sweet combination of innocence and sex—"

"Fuck me." She growled the interruption into his ear.

In a nanosecond, he had her flipped over, facedown. She squealed when he nudged his knee between her thighs and lifted her up, bracing one hand under her belly. "Hold on to the edge of the couch," he warned before rolling on another condom and then plunging in from behind.

Rachel desperately held on while he used his position to go deeper than she thought possible—faster than she thought possible. He held on to her slim waist, pumping, slapping against her bottom with enough force to bump her forward with each thrust. "Oh, oh, oh . . ."

And then he stopped. He pulled out to the very tip of his penis, teasing her with slight pressure while she throbbed and waited.

"J-Jake . . . wh-what . . . God, don't stop!" Rachel gripped the edge of the couch and tried to back up onto him, but he held her firmly in front of him. "Jake!" She arched her ass back in open invitation, and moaned when he circled and teased but refused to enter. "Please!"

He gave her an inch. She felt his muscles quiver as he held back. Rachel was throbbing, dripping with anticipation. She was yearning, craving. He gave her another inch and then withdrew.

"Tell me how much you want me," he breathed into her ear.

"No!" She was angry now. Angry and frustrated and half crazy with wanting him. It was insane how much she wanted—how much she needed—*how much she loved him.* "I love you," she said through gritted teeth. "I can't live without you. I can't write without you—aaah!"

She screamed when he plunged hard and deep, filling her, loving her. Her climax was brilliant white light, intense and fulfilling. He joined her with a jagged cry of release and joy, holding her flush against him while she clutched and he pulsed.

Jake collapsed against her. He rested his forehead on the back of her head, heart pounding, chest heaving, muscles like water. "You've been thoroughly fucked."

"Loved," she corrected.

"Loved," he agreed.

Later that night, after a long dual bubble bath, they curled up in bed and talked about their future.

"Come to Chicago with me for a few days." Jake nuzzled her ear and hugged her close. "I want to show you off. We can mix business with pleasure."

"Lots of pleasure?"

He cupped a breast, thumbing her nipple until she squirmed against him. "Lots."

Rachel turned around to face him in the dim light of the moonlit room. "Can we make this work, Jake? Long-distance relationships are doomed."

"We don't have to stay long-distance, Rachel. Chicago is just a city. Home is wherever you are. All I need is my laptop and you . . . or is it *you* on top of my lap?"

Rachel giggled through the tears that ran down her cheeks. "Oh my God!"

He frowned at her. "What?"

"Inspiration. I've got to write." She gave him a quick hard kiss and slipped from the bed, hitting the floor at a run. She sat down at her desk before realizing she was nude, then giggled and stayed that way while her fingers flew over the keyboard.

Sasha unlocked the door of her suite, turned on one light, and invited Dominick inside. She waved her hand toward the sofa before pouring two drinks. Sasha pressed the cold glass into his hand and then sat down on his lap, straddling him, her long legs bent at the knees.

After a swallow of her vodka, she pressed her cold mouth to his heated skin. He shivered and leaned back against the cushions. His suit coat fell open when he braced his long arms over the back of the pillows. Sasha tugged his unbuttoned shirt from his pants and pushed the crisp cotton back to expose his well-defined chest.

And then she paused. Dark purple bruises marred the athletic perfection of his sculpted abs. "What is this? You are hurt?"

Dominick raised a dark eyebrow. "Quarterback sack."

"It hurts?"

"I play pro football, Sasha. I always hurt."

The thought of him in pain bothered her and she felt herself softening toward him. He had a cocky grin, but honest blue eyes and gentle hands for one so big . . . so strong.

"So, when are you throwing me out?"

"What?"

"Come on, Sasha. I saw that gleam in your eye. You were watching me all night. I wondered what game you were playing. 'Fess up. You know I love games."

"You are out of your league in this one, Mr. Football."

"You think this ol' Texas boy don't know that?" He took a swallow of his drink and waited.

Sasha was thrown off balance, not sure if he was on to her game or not. "Arrogant men piss me off," she said with a lift of her chin. "You came on to every woman in the room," she spat. "Men like you use women and toss them away like . . . yesterday's paper."

"Ah, so you're a superhero for sex crimes. Where's your cape? God, but I bet you look good in that tight outfit."

Sasha tried not to smile, tried not to like him. "You are busted, Mr. Football."

He grinned. "I've been waitin' for a woman like you. Someone to take me down a peg or two—ahh, shit!" He lifted her off of his lap and grabbed his thigh.

"What is wrong?" Sasha asked.

"My . . . shit . . . muscle spasm in my thigh."

"What can I do?" She watched in horror as he leaned his head against the cushions and clutched his leg. Finally she pushed his hands away and began massaging the knotted muscles. After a few minutes, he relaxed, and his breathing stopped coming in short hisses.

"I'm sorry." He raised his head and pushed an unsteady hand through his short hair. "Look, I should be going."

"You are not going anywhere. Strip down and get over on the bed."

He paused, took a shaky breath, and pushed to his feet. "Sasha—"

"Do it. You won't be sorry."

She gave him a deep massage that made his muscles pliant and warm—and his cock as hard as a rock. "Your hands are magic," he moaned. "If you ever decide to give up your day job—"

"It is my day job."

He pushed up to his elbows. "You're kiddin'."

"Serious."

He sighed and fell weakly back to the pillows. "Darlin', where you been all my life? You can take me down a peg or two or three . . . just take me."

Sasha laughed deep in her throat, took her big sexy American football player for the ride of his life, and had him begging for more. Sasha had finally met her match.

"Geez, Rachel, you're shivering. What the hell are you doing sitting here buck naked?" Jake wrapped her in a warm blanket. "God, baby, why are you crying?"

"Sasha—Sasha f-fell in love." She wiped away a tear and sniffed.

"The man-eater?"

"Uh-oh, I've got to change that title."

Jake frowned. "Wasn't she supposed to fall in love?"

Rachel shook her head. "No. She was supposed to throw that arrogant ass out on his . . . his—"

"Hard cock?"

Rachel blushed. "Yes. But she found out there was more to him than she thought. Beneath that arrogance and hard muscle was a good guy." Rachel swiveled in her chair. "Like you."

Jake angled his head at her and grinned. "And beneath all your sweet innocence is a hot little sex kitten."

"Jake?"

"Hmm?"

"Make me purr."

"My pleasure." He crooked a finger at her as he backed away. "Here, kitty, kitty."

Please turn the page for a sneak peek at
THE BOOKSELLER'S DAUGHTER
by Pam Rosenthal, a Brava historical romance
coming in January 2004.

They stared at each other, his eyes bright with unspoken questions, hers shining with a new confidence.

The path took a fork. She pressed his hand, guiding him away from the river and toward the empty barn. They stopped and peered in, at the dust motes turned to gold by sunbeams streaming down through a hole in the roof to the straw heaped on the floor.

"You have to get to work," Joseph murmured.

"Not quite yet," she lied, leading him inside.

His kiss was gentle, tentative at first. She put her arms around his waist, and he sighed and pulled her to him.

"I promised myself I wouldn't do this," he whispered. "I've driven myself half mad with my resolve not to touch you. And there's still time to stop. Are you sure it's what you want, Marie-Laure?"

Never surer of anything. But she'd show him. Reaching her hands to his shoulders, she gently moved him backward and onto the pile of straw, dropping to her knees beside him. Lucky she'd worn Gilles's breeches so often, she thought, because if she knew nothing else about this business, she knew the pattern of the buttons, and how to undo them. Just one more little pull, *voilà*, and . . .

"You're sure?" He put his hand on hers to stop her from going any further. "You have to say you're sure."

The words wouldn't come. His hand was tight about her wrist; in another moment he'd pull himself away.

Peasants shouted in the fields. Flies buzzed. Life hurtled on.

"Yes," she whispered.

"Ah." He removed his hand and she pulled open the last button.

"Yes yes yes yes yessss."

Her last *yes* shaded to a gasp of surprise. She hadn't quite expected the length and breadth of flesh suddenly freed from his breeches. Naively, she supposed, she'd pictured something more decorous, less rampant. Less thrilling. On sudden impulse, she leaned over to kiss the dark, purplish head atop the long, erect shaft—like a delicious wild mushroom, she thought, swollen after a rainstorm. She licked a salty drop of moisture from its tip, and traced a slow, adventurous finger along the sort of seam on the shaft's underside, watching awestruck as he continued to grow and harden.

He made a throaty, incomprehensible sound, abruptly pulling away from her and sitting up.

Her boldness disappeared; she froze with embarrassment.

"Oh no," she gasped. "Oh, I'm so sorry. Oh dear, did I do something terrible? Perhaps people don't actually *do* such things with their tongues, but you looked so . . . so lovely, and I just wanted . . ."

He'd taken something out of his waistcoat pocket. It was whitish, translucent. She watched in fascination as he rolled the sheath down over his penis. Ah yes, Gilles had explained that to her. He'd made it sound quite the manly self-sacrifice too.

And it's a sacrifice for me as well. Timidly, longingly, she touched the stretchy stuff that contained his flesh and separated him from her.

"It's important, Marie-Laure . . ."

Though hardly foolproof, Gilles had warned her. Still, it was good of him to think of taking such precautions. She should probably thank him for it.

But there wasn't time to thank him; there wasn't time to say anything, because now it was she who lay on her back on the straw, and he who was rising above her, his hands lifting her skirt and parting her legs. It was happening very quickly now, the pressure of his thighs on hers, his entry into her, his mouth on her mouth, her cheeks, her neck. It was moving so fast, it was taking too long; it was lovely, it was confusing; she felt a marvelous opening and grasping somewhere inside. And then pressure, too much pressure. And too soon, only pain.

He held her tightly, licking the tears from her face.

"Oh, my dear," he said, "I wouldn't planned it that way for you, but you took me rather by surprise, you know."

"*I* . . . took . . . *you?*"

He nodded.

"I've never been seduced quite so expeditiously before. It was all I could do not to make a complete fool of myself."

He sat up, smiling at her astonishment. "Such a determined mouth," he murmured, tracing her lips with his little finger and smiling as her lips parted and the tip of her tongue became visible.

Light as a thistledown, he touched the tip of his own tongue to hers.

"And yes," he added, "people *do* do such things with their tongues. They do it all the time, though not nearly so charmingly as you did."

And please enjoy an excerpt from
DRIVE ME CRAZY,
a sensual contemporary treat
from Nancy Warren,
coming from Brava in February 2004.

Duncan Forbes knew he was going to like Swiftcurrent, Oregon, when he discovered the town librarian looked like the town hooker. Not a streetwalker who hustled tricks on the corner, but a high class "escort" who looked like a million bucks and cost at least that much, ending up with her own Park Avenue co-op.

He loved that kind of woman.

He saw her feet first when she strode into view while he was crouched on the gray-blue industrial carpeting of Swiftcurrent's library scanning the bottom shelf of reference books for a local business directory. He was about to give up in defeat when those long sexy feet appeared, the toes painted crimson, perched on do-me-baby stilettos.

Naturally, the sight of those feet encouraged his gaze to travel north, and he wasn't disappointed.

Her legs were curvy but sleek, her red and black skirt gratifyingly short. The academic in him might register that those shoes were hard on the woman's spine but as she reached up to place a book on a high shelf, the man in him liked the resulting curve of her back, the seductive round ass perched high.

From down here, he had a great view of shapely hips, a

taut belly, and breasts so temptingly displayed they ought to have a for sale sign on them.

He shouldn't stare. He knew that, but he couldn't help himself—torn between the view up her skirt and that of the underside of her chest. He felt like a kid in a candy store, gobbling everything in sight, knowing he'd soon be kicked out and his spree would end.

Sure enough, while he was lost in contemplation of the perfect angle of her thigh, the way it sloped gracefully upward to where paradise lurked, she looked down and caught him ogling. Her face was as sensual and gorgeous as her body—sleek black hair, creamy skin and plump red lips. For that instant when their gazes first connected he felt as though something mystical occurred, though it could be a surge of lust shorting his brain.

Her eyes went from liquid pewter to prison-bar gray in the time it took her to assimilate that he hadn't been down here staring at library books. What the hell was the matter with him, acting like a fourteen-year-old pervert?

"Can I help you with something?"

Since he'd been caught at her feet staring up her skirt, he muttered the first words that came into his head. "Honey, I can't begin to tell you all the ways you could help me."

The prison bars seemed to slam down around him. "Do you need a specific reference volume? A library card? Directions to the exit?"

The woman might look as though her photo ought to hang in auto garages reminding the grease monkeys what month it was, but her words filled him with grim foreboding. He was so screwed.

"*You're* the librarian?"

A ray of winter sunlight stole swiftly across the gray ice of her eyes. "Yes."

"But you're all wrong for a librarian," he spluttered helplessly.

"I'd best return my master's degree then."

"I mean . . ." He gazed at her from delicious top to scrumptious bottom. "Where's your hair bun? And bifocals? And the crepe-soled brogues and . . . and the tweeds."

If anything, her breasts became perkier as she huffed a quick breath in and out. "It's a small mind that thinks in clichés."

"And a big mouth that spouts them," he admitted. God what an idiot. He'd spent enough time with books that he ought to know librarians come in all shapes and sizes, though, in fairness, he'd never seen one like this before. He scrambled to his feet, feeling better once he resumed his full height and he was gazing down at her, where he discovered the view was just as good. He gave her his best shot at a charming grin. "I bet the literacy rate among men in this town is amazingly high."